# THE SECRET JOURNEYS OF JACK LONDON

———————— ✳ ————————

# THE SECRET JOURNEYS OF JACK LONDON

*

## BOOK II:
# THE SEA WOLVES

BY **CHRISTOPHER GOLDEN
& TIM LEBBON**

WITH ILLUSTRATIONS BY
**GREG RUTH**

**HARPER**

*An Imprint of HarperCollinsPublishers*

The Secret Journeys of Jack London: Book 2: The Sea Wolves
Text copyright © 2012 by Christopher Golden & Tim Lebbon
Illustrations copyright © 2012 by Greg Ruth

Library of Congress Cataloging-in-Publication Data
Golden, Christopher.
  The sea wolves / Christopher Golden & Tim Lebbon ; with illustrations by Greg
Ruth. — 1st ed.
    p.  cm. — (The secret journeys of Jack London ; bk. 2)
  Summary: Eighteen-year-old Jack London is captured returning from the
Yukon and taken aboard a pirate ship where the captain, the crew, and their
navigator all have dark secrets.
  ISBN 978-0-06-186320-2 (trade bdg.)
    1. London, Jack, 1876–1916—Juvenile fiction. [1. London, Jack, 1876–
1916—Fiction. 2. Pirates—Fiction. 3. Adventure and adventurers—Fiction.
4. Supernatural—Fiction. 5. Sea stories.] I. Lebbon, Tim. II. Ruth, Greg, ill.
III. Title.
PZ7.G5646Se 2012
[Fic]—dc22

                                                              2011010031
                                                                  CIP
                                                                   AC

Typography by Sarah Hoy
12 13 14 15 16  LP/RRDH  10 9 8 7 6 5 4 3 2 1

First Edition

*For the Booth clan, one and all.*
*You're our Necon family . . .*
*and we can't imagine a kinder or*
*more generous tribe.*

# CONTENTS

*One cannot violate the promptings of one's nature without having that nature recoil upon itself.*
—Jack London

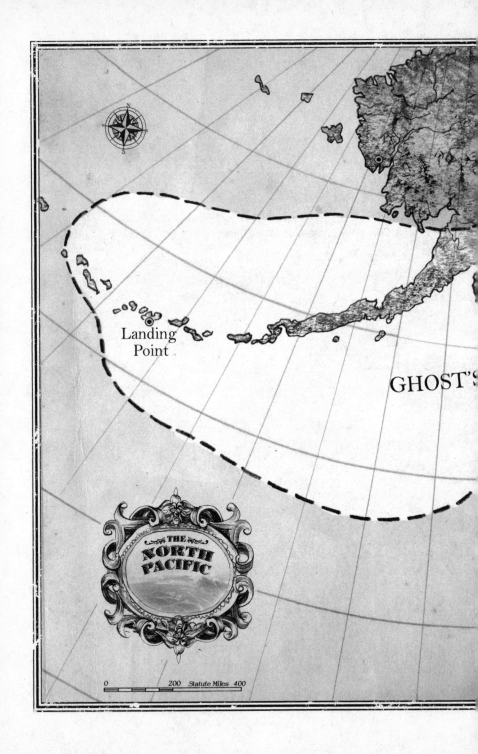

Landing
Point

GHOST'S

THE
NORTH
PACIFIC

0        200   Statute Miles  400

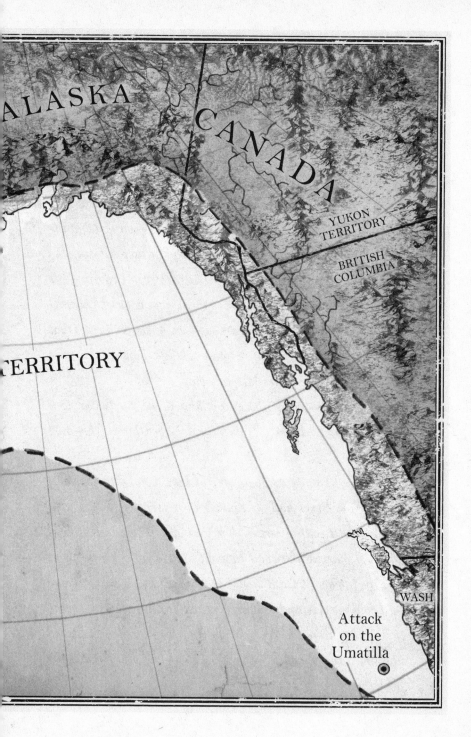

*I've never been much of a writer, but I've always been able to tell a tale. Got Jack London to thank for that. He made me realize that stories are all about heart and soul, not words and spelling, and he had heart and soul aplenty.*

*Jack saved my life many times. Once he did it for real, beating off two evil men who were ready to kidnap me and take me off into slavery. There were other times down through the years, and for most of them he wasn't even there. It was the* thought *of Jack that helped me. The idea of his courage, his outlook, his philosophy that life is for living, not just existing. And his conviction that there are so many unknown things that can never be fully explored in one single life. Some of them are wondrous, some terrible. Jack saw both.*

*I became an explorer because of him, of the spiritual as well as the physical. And I like to think I helped him in his own journeys.*

*It's well known what became of him. One of the greatest writers we've ever had, he could spin a yarn like no one else, and imbue it with a power that was almost . . . well, supernatural. But much as some thought that what he wrote about was the life he'd lived, I knew the truth all those years, because he'd told me: He could never, ever tell of his own real adventures. They were too personal for him to put down on paper, and much too terrible. Some of the things he saw just weren't for human eyes.*

*But he never told me I couldn't tell.*

*Jack died far too young, but in his forty years he lived the lives of many men. And he died knowing there's more here in this world than we can know, or could possibly understand.*

*That's part of the reasoning behind me writing this down at last. I'm an old man now. Who will it hurt to learn the truth? Will anyone even believe? In these modern technological times when the fantastic doesn't seem quite so fantastic anymore, and the wilds aren't quite so wild, I think these stories, terrifying though they are, need telling.*

*They're a warning, and I think we need reminding.*

*These, then, are the true stories of Jack London.*

*His secret journeys.*

*Hal Sawyer*

*San Francisco*

*June 1962*

## CHAPTER ONE

# THE PELICAN

If it hadn't been for the pelican, Jack London would have been murdered by the wolves.

Even lulled by the gentle motion of the ship, he had been unable to sleep or rest, though in truth that was all his body craved. His mind burned with memories of his adventures in the north, and each ache, pain, and wound recalled those experiences as surely as a smell or sound. Confined in a cramped ship's cabin with his friend Merritt Sloper and three weary men whose eyes were flat with defeat, Jack felt his senses sing with yearning. It had been only days since they had departed Alaska. After so long in the wilderness—and with his own wild nature urging him to run, to climb, to *live*—he felt stifled by that room, and it was inevitable that the pressure would drive him up here, onto the deck.

And so it had been for the last three nights. The days were easier, filled with casual conversations and hours spent gazing into the hazy distance, wrapped against the cold and yet buffeted by the sun. But the nights were more difficult. It was as if the darkness called him into its embrace—not just the false shade of a room without light, but the darkness of infinity.

Jack breathed in the fresh air and held on to the railing, legs shifting slightly as the ship dipped and rose through the gentle Pacific swell. His hair was ruffled by the breeze, and it felt like the hand of a loved one soothing his brow. *Perhaps I do need soothing*, he thought, because the memory of all he had been through—the deadly Chilkoot Trail, his near death in the great white silence, Lesya, and the dreadful Wendigo—were enough to drive any ordinary person mad. But one thing Jack had learned during his months in the frozen north: he was *far* from ordinary.

"I'm Jack London," he said, and the name was amazing to him. This was no self-aggrandizement, no hubris; he had begun to learn what a single human being might be capable of, and wanted to explore that potential to its fullest.

There was a light mist settled on the sea, and a heavier bank of it some distance to starboard. He could make out the waxing moon and the stars as vague smudges above and, turning around, he saw the captain and the best of his crew hunkered in the wheelhouse, doing their utmost to ensure that the *Umatilla* sailed true and safe. Two men sat in the crow's nest thirty feet above, their vague shapes and gentle chatter lost to the mist and darkness. Jack walked forward toward the bow, where he knew it was dark and quiet.

He wondered what it would feel like to make a solitary journey across these seas. On his way to Alaska so many months before, he had appreciated the immensity of the ocean, its power, and the respect it required to master it. Now he saw its wildness.

There was movement at the bow. At first he thought it was a clump of impacted snow, or a tangle of material shivering in the breeze. But when he approached, he saw the heavy beak and beady eye, the wings folded in, and the pelican huddled there regarded him with neither trust nor fear.

"Hello, bird," Jack said softly. He glanced back and up, but no one else seemed to have noticed the creature. Swirls of moisture played across the deck, and the rolling bank of mist to starboard seemed to have moved closer. No one else strolled the deck this late at night. He turned back to the bird, and it had raised its head and half spread its wings.

Jack went to his hands and knees, trying to present no threat to this magnificent creature. He looked it over for signs of injury but could see none. The bird had simply seen the ship as a place to rest, and perhaps it had done so many times before, recognizing the bow as one of the quietest places on board come nighttime.

"I'll not harm you," he said softly, and his throat seemed to throb with an unusual vibration. He realized that he had no real idea what sound these birds made, but it bobbed its head, flapped its mighty wings several times, and then hunkered down again. Jack grew still, and found himself staring into the bird's eye. He was reflected in there. He wondered how it viewed him—threat, something interesting, or simply part of the scenery?

He watched the pelican as Lesya, the forest spirit, had taught him to watch, and before long he did not perceive this tableau as man and beast at all. It was simply observer and observed. Though in the end she had proved to be a mad thing, Lesya had given him a gift, opening his mind and senses so that if he focused he could touch the thoughts of other creatures. Reaching out to the pelican, he sensed the same feeling of foreboding that had only just started to settle over him.

In the distance, Jack heard several resounding thuds of waves striking a hull. He frowned. The *Umatilla* rode smooth as ever, and he had not felt even the smallest impact vibration. The pelican lifted and opened its heavy beak.

*When he approached, he saw the heavy beak and beady eye,*
*the wings folded in, and the pelican huddled there regarded*
*him with neither trust nor fear.*

Jack heard that sound again, the *thud-wash*, *thud-wash* of a hull cutting across the waves instead of going with them. Something was out there. He looked up at the two men in the crow's nest, but they were vague shadows behind a gentle haze of mist, and he could not even tell which direction they were looking.

"What's this, then?" he asked the pelican, and the bird spread its wings. But it remained behind the railing, turning on its big feet so that it could look directly back along the deck. *I could call to the lookouts,* Jack thought. But what would he say? Darkness and the mist stirred his senses, and that feeling of things slightly askew might be only in his mind.

He leaned on the railing and looked down, ghostly whitecaps breaking gently away from the ship. They were cutting through the water, not impacting against the waves, and the spray that reached him up here was carried on the gentlest of breezes.

A shadow moved far out across the waves. Jack held on to the railing and scanned the skeins of mist that played like curtains across the ocean's surface. *Something huge,* he thought.

And then he saw the shadow again. A hardening of the mists, a solidifying of shapes that danced where no one normally watched, and a boat emerged. It was cutting a diagonal that would intercept the *Umatilla* within twenty seconds. Three masts, maybe a hundred feet long, the craft was dwarfed by the *Umatilla*. And yet there was something about the way it moved that seemed almost predatory.

The vessel's masts sported dark sails that swallowed the weak moonlight, and it slipped through the water as if it were hardly there at all, a phantom ship. The only sign of its existence was the intermittent thump of waves against its hull, but that lessened as the ship came close to matching the *Umatilla*'s course.

Jack could see shadows busy in the rigging, and more on deck. The booms swung as the schooner drew down alongside the *Umatilla*. And Jack knew then that something was very wrong indeed.

From above, he heard the lookouts' muttering rise in alarm. Then something whistled, the two men groaned, and their speaking ceased.

Behind him the white pelican grumbled like an old man. Jack ducked behind the solid railing and peered over the top. There was a flurry of activity on board the phantom schooner—rigging whispered, shadows moved, and he heard the soft impact of the vessel's buffered hull striking the *Umatilla*.

It was only as the first of several muffled grappling hooks appeared over the railing, thirty feet back along the deck from where he hid, that Jack realized the truth. *We're being boarded!*

He went to shout a warning, but no one would hear. If he moved, he might have time to get belowdecks before the first of the aggressors came on board . . . but he could already see the rope attached to the first grappling hook tensing as it was subjected to weight from below.

Instinct told him to duck down and stay where he was, and the pelican flapped its wings and lifted away from the deck, following its own instinct. It grumbled again as it flew, disappearing quickly across the port side and away into the thickening mist. For a fleeting instant Jack knew its freedom, but then he was back in his cumbersome and heavy flesh again, searching for shadows in which to conceal himself as the first head appeared above the railing.

The man slipped over onto the deck, and Jack felt a tingle of awe. He breathed out a gentle gasp. The man moved like a shadow himself, completely silent, and he stood crouched low while his head turned left and right. His arms were held out from his sides, and he seemed to be holding something in his right hand. There was so much threat in that shape—energy coiled like a wound spring, violence gathering like distant, silent storm clouds.

The man sniffed like an animal, head tilted. Then he

glanced up at the crow's nest, gave a brief hand signal over the railing, and dashed for the first doorway leading belowdecks. His shadow was large—easily half a foot taller than Jack's five feet eight inches, and broad across the chest—and his head was topped with a mane of hair that seemed to writhe its own shadowy pattern as he moved. Jack did not hear a sound, and he breathed the word that his mother had made him fear since childhood.

"Ghost."

But the other five men who appeared on deck over the next few seconds were not ghosts. With a sigh of clothing against metal, the soft exhalation of effort, they boarded the ship and quickly dispersed, full of purpose and oozing menace.

"If only I could fly," Jack whispered. Because he could not remain where he was. Without a plan, and yet also without fear, Jack pulled his knife from his belt and started to follow after the last of the men.

*That first one to board is in charge*, he thought, and there had been something about the man's silhouette that troubled Jack. He slipped across the deck, moving from shadow to shadow, glancing back at the grappling hooks to make sure no one else would overtop the railing in that moment and see him. He ducked quickly through a doorway, into the poorly lit corridor that led to a staircase down toward the cabin deck. Gentle footsteps shuffled on the metal stairs, and he followed, keeping low so that his shadow was not cast ahead of him by the sputtering oil lamps.

Down the stairs, and three treads from the bottom he heard something that changed everything. Until now the boat's appearance from the mist, the boarding, the fleeting shadows, all had been part of some strange dream ghost-witnessed by the pelican. The rush of adventure flushed through Jack's veins.

"You got gold?" a voice asked, low, threatening.

"No . . . no."

*Thunk!*

And Jack knew very well the sound of a knife cleaving flesh.

"Jesus!" he whispered, backing up a step because suddenly this was very real.

That question again, another negative answer, another murder, and then there was a flurry of movement from the cabin as other men came awake. And yet it took only seconds for the intruder to reappear from the cabin.

He turned away from Jack and paused, head cocked. Not the first man Jack had seen board, but still he was big, and strong. He was dressed in loose dark clothing, his hair was long and black, and in his right hand he carried a heavy knife. The blade was wet. The man was not even breathing hard.

*How many men did he just kill?* Jack wondered, letting out a slow, gentle breath, mouth slightly open, conscious all the time that a click of his throat or a whistle from his nose would give him away.

Then there would be knives.

The man walked to the next cabin and opened the door without a sound. He entered, Jack descended to the corridor floor and crouched, and he heard the same question muttered.

"Got gold?"

"Who—?"

"Got gold?"

"No . . . we didn't . . ."

"Who's got gold?"

"I don't—"

*Thunk! Thunk!*

*Merritt!* Jack thought. His friend was sleeping in their cabin on the next deck down, and this man's mates had disappeared into other doors. *Bastards will go for Merritt as well as anyone else.*

There were maybe three hundred people aboard the *Umatilla* on this return journey from the Yukon Territory gold rush, and right now most of them were asleep.

Sleeping men and women were often haunted by shadows, especially people who had been through such hardships, and waking to a nightmare such as this would cause confusion and panic. How someone could do what this man was doing . . .

Jack gripped his blade and faced a decision. He could dash forward and engage this murderer, press a knife to his throat and demand that he submit, and then wake everyone on the corridor and tell them what was happening. In that urgent instant, it felt like the best course of action—it would reduce their enemy by one, and increase those who knew of the attack by a score.

But then the man stepped into the corridor and stood facing away from Jack once again, and his knife hand was so soaked in blood that droplets spattered to the wooden deck. He moved to the next door and opened it, and before Jack could make a decision, the man had disappeared inside.

"Who has gold?" the man's voice came, muffled and low.

"Jack London has gold!" Jack shouted, and his heart galloped, his blood surged, the decision snatched from him by impetuosity. The *Umatilla*'s crew and passengers needed time. Jack might be the only person who could give them that.

He turned and bolted up the narrow, steep stairway,

emerging onto the deck and breathing in the cold, mist-shrouded air. He left the door hanging open and slid to the side, dropping to the deck, grateful for the thickening mist. He pressed himself against the wall across from where the door hung against the bulkhead, the darkened passage below yawning in between. *He'll expect me to be hiding behind the door,* Jack thought. *Or to have run.* But Jack would not run. He felt flushed with fear, but there was also a cold and primal strength rising in him, a wild determination. He was sickened at the bloodshed but ready for a fight.

He heard the man's footsteps, still quiet but no longer so cautious. At the top of the staircase the murderer gave the creaking, swaying door a mighty kick, crashing it back against the bulkhead. Jack moved quickly, grabbing his leg behind the knee and standing, pushing up, lifting and tipping him so that he tumbled hard back down the stairs. The man did not cry out as he fell—made no noise at all, other than the shocking impact of his head against the stairs and the crack of something breaking.

Jack didn't even wait to see if the man would rise. He slammed the door shut, pressed his foot against the bulkhead, and levered the handle off, in the hope that it might jam the latch. He turned and saw that where the grappling hooks had come over the starboard railing, the ropes had been wound about the cleats and tied off, so the killers' vessel must be running alongside.

He'd had the knife for a long time, and it had served him well. But these ropes were wet and his hand was shaking, and Jack found cutting through harder than he'd anticipated. He kept low, remembering the fate that had befallen the lookouts up in the crow's nest. Crossbow, he suspected, or perhaps a small harpoon. He had no wish to present another silhouetted target.

Something crashed against the door behind him, shaking it in its frame. He jumped, and the rope parted. It had been under such tension that it whipped and unwound, strands catching Jack across the face as it fell away to the boat below.

Whoever was down there would now know that something was amiss.

The door shook again, the impact tremendous.

A crack sounded from somewhere; wood breaking close by, perhaps, or maybe a gunshot from farther away.

"Hey, down there!" a voice cried out, and it came from above. Jack spun around and crouched in a fighting stance, knife held out to his right, knees bent, ready to leap aside. "Hey, is that . . . is that a boat?"

"Turn hard to port, Captain!" Jack shouted.

"Who is that? What's happening?"

"We've been boarded by pirates seeking gold. Hard to port, and I'm doing my damned best to—"

The door was struck again, and a long splinter cracked out as the wood around the broken latch changed shape.

"Hard to port!" Jack ran to the next rope and started sawing. Something whistled by his head, lifting his hair and kissing his ear bloody, and he ducked down, heart thumping, eyes wide with dreadful excitement.

*He was just* killing *those men in cold blood,* he thought, and the memory was terrible. He had only once seen such extreme brutality by man upon man, and all but one of those slave drivers was now dead. But the more he dwelled on that, the more it would distract him.

In the pit of his gut, he felt the slight pull that told him the *Umatilla* was starting to turn. *Good on you, Captain,* he thought, and then gunfire erupted from somewhere inside the ship.

The rope parted beneath his knife, and this time he was ready. He ducked down and turned his face away, feeling the frayed ends whip through his hair as he ran at a crouch beside the railing. Two ropes were cut, and there were two more to go. The wind changed, and the ship started to thump through the water as it angled against the swell. Jack heard the two remaining ropes creaking as they were dragged along the railing—as the *Umatilla* pulled to port, so the attackers' smaller vessel was being dragged closer to the hull, even as the ropes tipped it toward the waves.

As Jack approached the third rope, it was under so much tension that water sprang from it and misted in the moonlight. It was almost beautiful.

More gunfire erupted somewhere behind him, and men were shouting. Good. He hoped the returning prospectors had gotten one of the bastards, hoped the pirates hadn't killed many more, and more than anything he hoped that his friend Merritt was alive.

He paused by the rope . . . and then walked on. Because someone was approaching him from behind. They closed on him like his own lost shadow, and though Jack could not hear, see, or smell them, still he *knew* that they were there.

Pausing beyond the straining rope, Jack turned in a crouch, the knife a part of his hand.

The man was less than eight feet away . . . the man who had first boarded the *Umatilla*, but now his dark clothes were wet and there was a splash of blood across his cheek and forehead. He stood casually, as if on an evening stroll rather than a murder spree. He was huge—several inches over six feet tall, broad as a barrel around the chest, and Jack could make out knotted muscles and powerful limbs even beneath his baggy clothing. His crooked nose and the dark circles under his eyes gave him a mortician's austerity.

He regarded Jack as a man might look upon a landed fish about to be gutted.

"Get your gold?" Jack asked.

The man raised one eyebrow. His eyes glimmered, catching the moonlight and reflecting a brutal intelligence. There was no mercy there, but neither was this man vacant. His was a distinct, very decisive sadism.

"So you'll be the cause of my raid being cut so short," the man said. His voice was deep and mannered. Calm.

The ship was turning harder now, and Jack could hear the tumult of the waters below, and see the masts of this man's ship dipping left and right as it was battered against the *Umatilla*.

"I don't like thieves," Jack said. His anger scorched, and he sensed the boiling savagery of his enemy.

"Well then, it's a good thing it's no thief who's going to kill you," the man said, and he flowed forward through the mist.

The last grappling hook, never tied off, creaked and then ruptured. Shards of metal skittered across the deck and whistled through the air. The rope lashed upward like a freed reptile, strands thrashing at the air as it sprang back over the railing. The big man turned his head to protect his eyes, and then Jack was at him, ducking low and driving with his left shoulder. Even after everything, he had no wish to feel his knife sinking into this man's gut. Perhaps if he had simply stabbed him—used that moment of surprise to pierce him through the heart—everything else might have been different.

Striking the man was like hitting a slab of meat hanging in an abattoir. There was no give to his flesh, and no sense that Jack's attack had caused anything other than mild annoyance. Before Jack could gather himself for another assault, he was lifted by two massive hands. And then he was flying.

For a moment he thought of that pelican, and his cry of fear and surprise sounded like the bird's enigmatic grumblings. Then he fell, and his view swirled as he plummeted toward the sea—the pirate's boat being hauled around and bashed by the *Umatilla*, the larger vessel crashing through the waves, and that big man on deck, watching Jack as he fell toward his death.

*No!* Jack's mind roared as he struck the waves and was pulled beneath. The cold took his breath away, and he took in a mouthful of seawater, gagging, forcing it out through pursed lips as he was buffeted at the sea's whim. He recalled those frozen wastelands and his haunted demise, and being brought back by that wolf of the wild. *No, no, I will* not *die again.*

The knife had gone, dropped so that he could use both hands. He pulled for what he thought was the surface, unsure of which way was up, which down. He swam easily, confident, before realizing that he was sinking. There was a weight pulling him down, and it was one weight that he could never part with—the small bag of gold he had acquired in the Yukon, which he always kept in his pocket. Jack kicked off his heavy boots. It was so cold, the depths so shattering. *What's down there?* he thought, and for once he cursed his curiosity.

Checking that the bag of gold nuggets and dust was still with him, Jack took a moment to gather his thoughts. His heart was racing. His eyes blurred, and the cold froze his bones. Above him, he could see the dark hulls of the two vessels passing by.

Jack pulled and kicked as hard as he could, breath leaking from him and desperation driving him up. At last he broke surface close to the pirate schooner's stern, and it pushed him aside as it plowed the waves. He struck the hull so hard that the wind was knocked from him, and he scrabbled for purchase. His fingers closed upon a drooping line, and he clung to the rope for dear life. Coughing, spluttering, fingers clasping the ship's railing, Jack was only vaguely aware of the dark shape that emerged from the water beside him and scrambled up the side of the ship to the deck. *Hardly climbing at all*, he thought, and then that shadow fell across him.

He looked up into the dripping face of the man he'd met on the *Umatilla*. As Jack opened his mouth—to scream or ask questions, or simply in amazement, he was not sure which—the man reached down, grasped Jack's jacket, and pulled him from where he clung to the rope, up onto the deck of the pirate schooner.

"Welcome to the *Larsen*," the big man said, and he turned and walked away.

Shakily, Jack sat against the railing and looked up. Perhaps half a minute ago he had been on the *Umatilla*'s deck. Now he was down on the ship the man had named the *Larsen*, and things were progressing rapidly. Only one rope still secured the *Larsen* to the larger vessel. Gunshots sounded from above, but the bigger ship's deck was almost fifteen feet higher, and it was difficult to see what was happening. The captain's port turn—at Jack's instruction—was causing the smaller ship to buck and crash against the hull, and the sharp reports of cracking wood were clearly audible between gunfire and the crash of waves.

Someone appeared at the railing above, and Jack raised his hand. Shadows struggled, and then a body fell onto the *Larsen*'s deck. A man darted from cover and dragged the fallen person aside.

Jack pulled himself upright, and there was one thing on his mind: getting back onto the *Umatilla*. In moments the ships would part company, and with the pirates' surprise attack compromised, they would make their escape. The fallen man must have been one of them making a panicked return, and once the others were down—

Someone laughed, and three shapes appeared from the shadows. A short black man glanced at Jack and grinned, a gold tooth glimmering in the weak moonlight, and then the three spread out close to where their ship bumped against the *Umatilla*.

Someone shouted, and another shape fell from above. This time it was a woman. She struck the deck with a sickening thud, groaned, rolled over; and then the black man grabbed one leg and dragged her across the deck.

"What?" Jack whispered. "Wait. Hey!"

Several more shapes appeared at the railings above them, one man shouting, another crying. They were thrown down to the schooner just like the others, and the three men let them strike the hardwood deck before taking them away. One man—a prospector Jack had spoken to, but whose name he'd never known—stood immediately and reached for a knife, but one of the pirates waved a hand dismissively, the blow so strong it knocked the prospector's head to one side and sent teeth scattering into the sea. The man fell, and the pirate slung him over his shoulder.

Jack ran for the last rope connecting the ships. Stealth was pointless, because they knew he was here. Panic had taken him. His mind worked quickly and logically, and yet fear was inside him, a darkness that seemed to cloud out the moonlight. *They're taking them below*, he thought, *and they don't care how injured they are.*

Several shadows dropped down, avoiding the rigging, landing along the deck almost as silently as Jack had seen them boarding the *Umatilla*. One man glared at him, hatred in his eyes, and then someone started shooting.

Jack dashed behind a lifeboat fixed amidships. Bullets thudded home, wood splintered. He expected shouting and running, but instead he heard only soft, growl-like laughter.

*I have to get away!* he thought, but deep down he already knew that he was too late. He heard the keen hiss of a blade slashing rope, and the *Larsen*'s movement instantly changed. Rigging rattled, booms swung, and Jack slid from behind the lifeboat as the schooner turned hard to starboard.

In the darkness, in the mist, the *Umatilla* quickly faded away. *Merritt*, Jack thought. He could make out shapes lining the railings, and there were several more reports as they fired more shots after the pirates.

None of whom seemed concerned.

"Sea's washed up a wet rat," the black man said, grinning at Jack.

"Looks more like a dead dog to me," a pale ogre of a man replied.

"He's neither," a voice said, and Jack knew immediately to whom it belonged. A hand closed around the back of his neck and pulled him upright. "He's the one who fought back."

There were six men around Jack. They were all dressed the same—black, loose clothing, knives still clasped in their hands. A couple of them carried small knotted bags that might have held gold. One nursed a wound in his side, and if it was a gunshot, then the man should be down. He should be moaning. But even *he* smiled at Jack, and there was an air of expectation that chilled him more than the sea, and more than his lonely near death in the north.

That had been the wild, at its heart impartial.

This was savagery unfettered by any moral concern. This was evil.

"Shall we, Ghost?" someone asked.

"I think not," the big man said. Jack turned to face him.

"Ghost?" Jack said.

"That's right. And you have me at a disadvantage, sir."

"Not as I view it," Jack said, meaning to sound defiant.

*This was savagery unfettered by any moral concern. This was evil.*

But the man's eyes bored into him, and his mass was a mountain waiting to tumble.

Ghost smiled. He knew Jack's fear and was evidently used to it. "I'll know your name, son," Ghost whispered, and the whole ocean heard.

"I'm Jack London," Jack said. The name gave him strength, defining as it did both the wild part of him and the man he was growing to become, and he felt a rush of delight as Ghost raised one eyebrow.

"Are you, indeed?" Ghost replied. "You fought back, Jack London. That was brave."

"And stupid," another man put in.

"Well," Ghost said, shrugging, then laying a hand on Jack's shoulder. "Truth is, sometimes one is the other."

"I've *never* been stupid," Jack said.

"Why fight us, then?"

"You're murderers and thieves."

A ripple of laughter went among the *Larsen*'s crew. "Oh," someone said, "worse than that."

Ghost raised a hand to silence them, his eyes still challenging Jack.

"And?" Ghost asked, staring expectantly.

When Jack did not reply, he smiled. "Well then, Jack London, time for you to get below."

"With the others?" the ogre asked.

"No. Not with the others," Ghost said thoughtfully. He gestured to a tall, pale man Jack recognized as the pirate he'd shoved down the stairwell. "Finn, make our guest comfortable."

Speaking the word *guest* made the captain grin. Finn, which might have been his name or his heritage, grabbed Jack's arm and escorted him roughly to the forecastle. The man looked unharmed by his tumble down the stairs—nothing broken, nothing bloody.

"I should have stabbed you," Jack said, and his comment provoked another flush of laughter. The sound seemed out of place on the ship, and as Finn pulled at Jack, someone whistled once, sharp.

"There!"

A whisper, a thud, and then a large white shape thumped onto the deck, thrashing for a moment until a sailor stomped his boot down on the thing's exposed neck. The pelican grew still, blood marring its chest, black-tipped wings spread in death.

"Something different for dinner tomorrow, Ghost," the man who had shot the animal said. He came forward, bent down, and plucked the crossbow bolt from the poor creature's body.

"Perhaps," Ghost said. "Perhaps."

Jack felt the man's eyes burning into the back of his

head as he was forced down into the ship, and into the tight, dank quarters of the *Larsen's* bestial crew. And he could still feel that heavy gaze as the door was slammed and he was left alone in the darkness, and the cold.

CHAPTER TWO
———

# AN ANGEL AMONG DEVILS

**J**ack awoke in a stinking bottom bunk in the crew's quarters, startled to find that he had managed to fall asleep in the cold, dank forecastle. They hadn't locked him in, but he knew he had nowhere to run save over the side and into the rolling sea. Though he had struggled not to let his guard down, he had been alone and exhausted. And with his mind a riot of defiant and rebellious plans, his body had surrendered to weariness, silencing his thoughts at last.

Now he blinked awake facing the wall, and stiffened as he realized he was no longer alone.

Something stood behind him. Jack could feel its presence, though he could scarcely hear it breathe. A scent filled the forecastle, the musk of men combined with the stink of filthy animals, and perhaps that aroma belonged to the creature even now stepping lightly toward his bunk. Yet when he inhaled again, he caught that smell on the stained linens beneath him and knew it did not come solely from the intruder.

*Come to kill me*, he thought, and wondered if the thing had seen him stiffen as he woke in the gloom.

Jack waited, listening for the rustle of cloth or the grunt that would presage an attack. But the rustle that came moments later sounded too deliberate, too stealthy, to be the movement of a would-be assassin. He frowned, still facing the wall, as understanding struck him. His jacket had been next to him on the bunk, and it was only now that he noticed its absence. The intruder was not an assassin, but a lowly thief.

Erupting into motion, Jack rolled and twisted and shot out both feet, ramming his kick into the stealthy figure's torso. He gave the kick such force that it drove the intruder across the room, where he crashed into other bunks, slamming his head on the upper and tumbling into the lower. The man grunted in surprise, then hissed as he clawed to pull himself upright.

But Jack was already on his feet. He had no weapons and no time to find one, for he saw now that this was Finn, the sailor he had ambushed on board the *Umatilla* and who had confined him to these quarters some hours ago.

Unshaven, lips peeled back in an instant of hatred, Finn would kill him given the chance. And Jack knew that in such close quarters, the larger, stronger man would have the advantage.

It was greed that saved him. Finn's greed.

The sailor had lost his grip on Jack's coat but must already have discovered the heavy bag in its pocket and realized what it contained. And so instead of attacking Jack directly, he tried to secure his prize, clutching at the jacket that had fallen onto the bunk beneath him. In doing so, he left himself vulnerable.

Jack grabbed the jacket and tugged, raising his right leg and stomping his heel into Finn's groin. The man let out a bellow of pain and released the coat, and Jack was already running for the door. As he climbed three steps and exited the cabin, he heard the furious sailor scrambling in pursuit.

*What's he made of?* Jack thought. He'd dealt him a cruel kick, and Finn should've needed time for such pain to subside. But even as Jack reached the stairs that led up to the deck, he heard the rumble of the man's voice.

"Little bastard," Finn growled. "I'll have your eyes."

On the second step, Jack knew he'd never make it. He turned, saw a flicker of surprise in the scruffy sailor's face, and hurled himself back down. Finn caught him easily, one hand closing around Jack's throat and the other holding his free hand at bay. He squeezed, and Jack felt himself sag, a stringless puppet hanging in that iron grip. Finn smashed him against the bulkhead at the base of the stairs, and smiled as he began to crush Jack's throat.

Jack twisted his fist in the fabric of his coat, felt the weight of the little bag of gold, and swung it with all his strength. It struck Finn on the temple. The man's eyes dilated and his grip loosened only slightly, but that was enough for Jack. He braced his feet against the wall behind him and thrust forward, dropping his shoulder and ramming Finn against the stairs. The sailor tripped and fell back, cracking his skull against a wooden step, and then Jack was clambering over him, swift as could be.

Finn grabbed at his leg, but Jack tore free and launched himself to the top of the stairs, sprawling on the deck. The night sky had cleared and the moon burned bright enough to cast a silver gleam across the ship. As Jack picked himself up, wondering where he could run and what that murderous pirate captain Ghost would make of the concept of justice, Finn crested the forecastle steps and hurled himself at Jack.

In the open, Jack had thought his speed would give him an advantage. Years living rough on the streets of Oakland and San Francisco, and then riding the railways in search of work and enlightenment, had mixed him in hundreds of fights, from the simplest scuffle to the most brutal brawl. At eighteen, he was stronger than most of the older men he'd met, and he knew how to fight dirty.

But Finn treated him like a toy, hoisting him into the air and pummeling his face with a stonelike fist. Twice. Three times. A fourth would have knocked Jack senseless. He grabbed a handful of Finn's hair and yanked, stealing his balance for just a moment. He punched the sailor in the throat, and Finn staggered back. But he did not release Jack.

With a roar, he lifted Jack over his head and hurled him into the foremast. Something cracked inside, and Jack knew he'd fractured at least one rib. The wind knocked out of him, he struggled to drag in a single breath, chest burning for air. He tried to rise, but Finn was upon him.

Voices rose around them. The lookout called some rude observation from the crow's nest. The ogre and the black man from earlier were among those who came to watch, but it was no longer a scuffle. In a moment it had turned from a fight into bloody punishment. Finn seemed to have forgotten all about the gold in the pocket of the coat that Jack still clutched in his hand. Instead, the sailor's entire focus was on inflicting pain.

Jack felt the blows land. Tasted blood. Knew that he

could expect no help, and without it he would surely die.

A shape darted in from the right, a dark silence that blotted out the moonlight, and then Finn flailed as he was yanked backward and flung across the deck. He tumbled end over end, thumping against the deck, and crashed against the railing. So swiftly that he seemed barely to move—appearing in one spot and then the next without passing between—Ghost stood over Finn, glaring down upon him with cold fury.

Finn began to rise, fumbling for words. But even as he opened his mouth, Ghost struck him such a powerful blow that Finn collapsed back against the rail, a boxer on the ropes in some pugilistic nightmare.

"Do not speak," the captain ordered.

Fear filled the sailor's eyes, and he obeyed.

Wiping blood from his nose and mouth, Jack rose unsteadily, maintaining his balance with a hand upon the foremast. Other members of the crew had gathered around, and Jack felt sure that Ghost would command them to return to their duties. But it seemed he wanted an audience. The sailors looked on with hungry fascination, almost licking their chops in the hope of some further violence. Jack prayed they would be disappointed.

The captain turned from Finn and approached Jack, his footfalls on the deck almost silent.

"Young Jack," Ghost began, studying him closely, as though appraising him anew. "An explanation is due, I think."

"Simple enough," Jack said, wincing at the pains in his jaw and face as he spoke. "I woke to find your man trying to rob me. I hoped to keep what was mine and so fought him for it."

"Offered yourself up for a thrashing, more like," Ghost replied, a sly smile lifting the edges of his mouth. *Like the devil's smile*, Jack thought, *it does not reach his eyes.*

"What could you possibly have that would be worth such punishment?" the *Larsen*'s captain continued. "Or worth fighting for at all?"

In the haze of his pain and in the midst of trying to discern the captain's intentions, he had nearly forgotten his jacket, which now lay on the deck a few feet away, as near to Ghost as it was to Jack himself. He racked his brain for a suitable lie to hang on to his hard-won prize, but his eyes gave him away.

Ghost plucked the jacket from the deck, one brow arching curiously as he felt the strange weight in one pocket. He hefted the bag in his hand, dropping the jacket back to the deck.

"Had I caught you with this on board your ship, I'd have killed you for it."

"Finn meant to do just that."

A brief, savage anger flickered in Ghost's eyes as he glanced at the sailor, before he returned his attention to Jack.

"We've boarded half a dozen vessels returning from the Yukon," the captain said. "Yours yielded the smallest amount of gold thus far."

"There's little to be found," Jack said. "The gold rush is more of a trickle. Even what you've got there is just a few small nuggets and some dust."

"Still worth quite a bit, I'd imagine."

"And it's mine," Jack said.

Ghost took three steps until he stood directly before Jack, eyes still more curious than brutal, though Jack had seen the violence in the man.

"We own only what we can keep, Mr. London. It isn't enough to have, nor even enough to take. All things pass into the hands of others, in time." The captain tucked the small bag into his pocket. "If you want this back, you're welcome at any time to attempt to retrieve it. But you'd best be prepared to kill me for it, as I will not hesitate to do the same to you."

Hatred burned in Jack as he recalled the men who had died to acquire that meager bit of gold. Ghost watched to see if he would attack, but Jack London was no fool. Even at his best, without the pain in his ribs and face and the ringing in his head, he would need all of his cunning and a great deal of luck to best Ghost in a fight.

"I'll keep it in mind," he said.

Ghost gave a curt nod and turned back toward Finn.

"My orders were clear, Finn. He was not to be touched. Worse yet, you hoped to rob him and keep the dust for yourself—"

"No, sir," Finn began. "It weren't my intention at all. I only—"

Ghost's cruel smile alone was enough to silence the man.

"And now you've interrupted me," the captain said.

The ship creaked, lines swaying, pulley blocks jangling, but the crew was utterly silent. Jack had seen this before in the packs of sled dogs in the frozen north. He had watched as a member of the pack challenged the leader, as a bloody, snapping, snarling fight ensued, and as the rest of the pack loomed with dark purpose, waiting to savage the loser. These were men, not dogs, but their ominous silence bespoke the same malign intent.

"Do I not give my men a fair share of the spoils, Finn?"

"You do, sir," Finn said, his voice faltering. "My word, you do."

"And yet," Ghost said, almost idly. "And yet."

He turned and paced a bit, tapping his temple as if he were a stage actor performing the part of one deep in thought. Then he glanced at Jack and tipped him a wink, an amused twinkle in his eye.

"Mr. Johansen," Ghost said.

Jack turned to see a sailor step forward, a lanky man with tiny beads for eyes and long, spidery fingers. This, he knew, must be the first mate, for the captain had called him Mister, and to him would be delivered the orders.

"Sir?"

No trace of a smile remained on the captain's face.

"Keelhaul him."

Finn screamed, lunged from his place at the railing, and drew out a wicked-looking knife as he hurled himself at the captain. Ghost slapped the blade from his hand and it stuck in the deck, quivering in the moonlight. So fierce and strong was the captain that he had the man on his back in the space between heartbeats. He raked a single fingernail along Finn's jaw, drawing blood and causing the sailor to cry out in surrender.

"It's the keel or your throat," Ghost growled, his face bent so low that the two men were nose to nose. He almost whispered, but in the loaded silence the whole crew heard. "Pain or death. Those are your only choices."

Finn went slack beneath him, and Ghost stood, turning

his back on the defeated sailor. The captain paused and looked at Jack.

"They are forever our only choices, young Jack. As you will most assuredly learn."

As a boy, Jack London had been something of a pirate himself. Desperate to escape the hellish drudgery of his work at Hickmott's Cannery, he'd borrowed enough money from his foster mother to buy the sloop *Razzle Dazzle*. All his young life, he had been in the company of rough men, and he had been along with some of them as they raided the oyster beds in the mudflats off San Francisco Bay, stealing what they could by night and selling it off in Oakland the next morning. Oyster pirates, they called themselves, and with his new boat, he'd become a pirate captain. At the age of fourteen, it had seemed a glorious adventure.

Now he stood on the deck of the *Larsen*, the sails full of a gentle Pacific breeze as the ship kept a steady course westward, away from the California coast—away from home and safety, and the family who had already waited too long for his return, and the financial salvation they would be praying he had found in the Yukon. In a single night he had seen blood dripping from multiple blades, heard the dying sighs of innocents, witnessed the brutal abduction of fellow passengers, and been savagely assaulted by someone who seemed more beast than man. And he had the feeling that far worse horrors yet awaited him.

Oyster pirate? He had been a laughing boy, an imp, attempting to thwart the Fish Patrol and escape arrest. Here, now . . . *these* were pirates. They lived by the law of blade and club. Bloodletting seemed ordinary and righteous to them, violence the solution to all riddles. And until he could divine some manner of escape, which at this moment seemed impossible, he had to dedicate himself to a single principle: survival. It was a familiar instinct— he had survived a long, hungry winter stranded on the banks of a frozen river, the cruelty of slavers, the obsession of an insane forest spirit, and the wild fury of the dreadful Wendigo. This was a new challenge, but Jack would endure.

Finn, however, might well be dead in the next few minutes.

Jack did nothing to draw attention to himself. The crew was occupied with the punishment being meted out, and no one seemed at all concerned that he might attempt escape. The ship measured perhaps one hundred feet from bow to stern, and its beam couldn't have been wider than twenty-five feet. This was the extent of his world, at least for now. There were four small boats on board—used, he supposed, for hunting and going ashore from deep anchorage—but it wasn't as if he could lower one into the water and paddle away unnoticed.

Ghost, too, seemed almost to have forgotten about Jack's presence.

Johansen barked orders and two men—Vukovich and Kelly—dragged a struggling Finn to the front of the ship and held him still as others tied ropes to his wrists and ankles.

"You bastards!" Finn screamed, trying to shake free as they stripped him. "Stand up to him!"

Vukovich grabbed him by the hair and forced Finn to meet his gaze. "For your greed? We should challenge 'im for that? No, Finn. You'll take what's coming."

Jack stood on the raised foredeck slightly away from the *Larsen*'s crew, his own predicament almost forgotten as he watched the men force Finn toward the bow. He had heard of keelhauling—had read about it as a boy and included it in the pirate tales he shared with his chums— and so he knew what was to come. They would throw Finn overboard and drag him beneath the ship, right along the keel, where the hull would be caked with barnacles that would shred his skin to ribbons. The faster they dragged him, the tighter he would be held against the keel, and the worse his injuries. But if they went slowly, giving him slack to spare him the flaying, he could well drown.

"I don't understand," Jack said, stepping up between the ogre and Louis, the short black man whom he had first seen when Ghost dragged him aboard. "I'd thought a man would be thrown over one side and dragged to the other. If they haul him fore to aft on a ship this size . . ."

He glanced at them for answers. The ogre ignored him, scratching at his huge head. But Louis smiled to reveal an awful mouth: some teeth missing, some jagged as a shark's, and that single upper canine made of gold.

"It'll hurt, *c'est vrai*," Louis said, in an island-lilted French accent. "But if he dies . . . *c'est sa bonne fortune*."

Jack frowned in confusion. "I don't—"

The ogre grunted and cleared his throat, tugging at his filthy beard. "If the captain lets him die, Finn'll be lucky," he said, his voice a deep rumble in his chest. "Fool wants to howl, thinks he can challenge Ghost, but he's no match. If he lives, he'd best fall into line. You challenge Ghost and lose . . . better off in hell."

Then there was shouting and the pounding of feet on the deck, and Jack whipped round to see he had missed the moment when they hurled Finn off the bow. Vukovich and Kelly and two other men were running along beside the railings, ropes held taut, slowing only to feed the ropes around rigging, and Jack tried not to visualize Finn beneath the ship, holding his breath as barnacles ripped his skin. Sickened, he watched the men run as the rest of the small crew followed.

A hand like an iron vise grabbed his arm and propelled him forward, slowly but far from gently.

"Come along, young Jack," Ghost growled in his ear. "This is for all to see."

*Not quite all*, Jack thought, remembering the others abducted from the *Umatilla* who must still be locked below. But he thought it best to hold his tongue for now. That was a question for another time.

With Ghost as his escort, he walked aft, watching as the crew gathered along the stern railing. Together, the four men who'd done the hauling pulled at the ropes, hoisting Finn from the water. Jack watched with dreadful anticipation, because he knew that what he was about to see would be awful.

What they dragged aboard was not at first recognizable as human. The skin had been flayed open on Finn's back, arms and legs, flesh ripped way, so that he resembled little more than a pile of bloody meat. Only when he vomited seawater onto the blood-smeared deck, and tried to rise to his knees, could Jack be certain the creature before him was a man.

Then Finn collapsed, blood running freely from his wounds and flowing across the deck.

The first mate, Johansen, turned expectantly to the captain, and the crew watched impatiently. For a moment, Jack felt sure they weren't done with him. Their captain had inflicted punishment, but the crew seemed to want their own pound of flesh. Jack imagined that attempting to keep a secret stash of one's own must be the worst of sins among pirates. Ghost's own words had suggested that he divided up their ill-gotten gains by some formula they all agreed was fair. For Finn to keep even so small a bit of treasure as Jack's bag of gold for himself was for him to steal from all of them.

Yet though violence remained in the air, the crew glaring menacingly at Finn, none of them attacked. It was as if they awaited some word from their captain, but the word had not come.

"Take him below," Ghost commanded at last. "Louis, doctor him as best you can. Then leave him. Everyone else, back to work. Mr. Johansen, check our course. If we lag, we'll miss our chance."

"Aye, sir!" Johansen snapped, and hurried off to obey.

Denied further retribution, the crew might have balked, but it was plain to see that none would challenge the commands of their captain. After the example Ghost had set with Finn, Jack could see why. They were loyal to Ghost, perhaps, but they feared him as well.

The crew busied themselves about the ship, though it seemed to Jack that in fair weather the *Larsen* practically sailed herself. Vukovich clambered into the rigging, and the others rushed about, and soon the only man standing with Jack by the aft railing was the captain.

Ghost did not look at him.

"Young Jack," the captain said, the diminutive name a purposeful needling. "Can you cook?"

Jack stared at him, but his thoughts were racing. *Survival.*

"I'm a damn fine cook," he replied.

Ghost nodded grimly. "A lad who thinks on his feet and isn't afraid of a fight, bound from the Yukon to San Francisco? Aye, I had a feeling you might've learned to feed yourself. We lost our cook, Mr. Mugridge, in a scrape a few months back. We've been making do with Finn, but he'll be in no condition to man the galley for a time."

*For a time?* Jack thought that once they chucked him below, Finn would be lucky to survive till morning.

"You'll do his job," Ghost went on. "I'm less inclined to kill those who are useful to me. Go and acquaint yourself with what's in our stores. It'll be morning soon and we'll want a bit of breakfast. And then, for lunch, we'll be having a special treat."

Jack shuddered at the way Ghost said that, and the

captain bared sharp teeth in a grin that seemed more hunger than smile.

"What's that?" Jack asked.

Ghost gave him a sidelong appraisal, as though reaffirming his decision. Then he grunted and strode forward, leaving Jack standing on the aft deck without an answer.

The first thing Jack did was clean the galley. In the months since the previous cook had been "lost," Finn had made little attempt to fight the accumulating grease and filth. Every surface bore a layer of grime that required scraping and then washing, and Jack set to work long before dawn. By the time the sun had risen over the eastward waves, he was prepared to cook, although the best he could offer was a meal of cinnamon-spiced oatmeal, some eggs, and rashers of fatty bacon. He had inventoried the food available and wanted to conserve the vegetables and meat that were still relatively fresh for dinners.

From a quick conversation with Louis he had learned that there were chickens in the hold to provide eggs, and eventually they, too, would be eaten. What meat and vegetables they had fresh were in the galley already, having been acquired at their last landfall, only two days before. There was reportedly plenty of salted beef and pork, plus dried beans and baskets of sea biscuits, also in the hold.

But Jack wasn't allowed down there to check.

Even so, he reasoned that though their heading was to the southwest, toward Japan, Ghost must not intend traveling that far or he would have put in greater stores of food. They were a small crew, but Jack did not think they had near enough provisions to make the ocean crossing, particularly given the threat of scurvy without much produce. There were few enough vegetables, and half a bushel of apples comprised a meager store of fruit. He reasoned that it must have been kept only for the officers, but he would not serve it without asking the captain first.

In a bucket in a corner, Jack discovered the pelican that had been shot on the deck the previous night. This, then, was the treat the men were to receive for lunch today— fried pelican. He might have turned it into a stew, but the captain's orders were to preserve the flavor of the bird. Jack would fry potatoes and onions in the pan with a liberal dash of spices, and it would make for an excellent lunch. But he himself would not partake of the meal, fixing something apart from the crew's special treat. He could not eat the creature whose portentous arrival last night had saved his life. He wished that he had the gift of life, so that with the touch of a hand he might restore it, but such a thing was not to be. Instead, the bird would end up in the bellies of the monsters who crewed the *Larsen*.

Ghost's remark about lunch had seemed ominous in the darkness before dawn, but now it only confused Jack. Could the captain have had an inkling that the pelican had some significance for Jack? Surely not. Which meant that despite his grim expression, Ghost had spoken in jest. He seemed an unlikely jokester, but Jack could not read the comment any other way. It brought into sharp relief the observations he had been accumulating about the rough men who were now his crewmates, and their captain.

Ghost had been hewn from different stuff than his crew. They were ignorant brutes, and though he might be the most savage of them all, and certainly seemed the most dangerous, he brimmed with intelligence. Jack could see the mind working behind Ghost's eyes, the dark and voracious intellect, yet the captain had no manners and no fundamental morality, and Jack could only think the man must be self-educated. It would make escaping from this devil ship far more problematic.

"How ye farin', Cooky?" came a voice, and then the Irishman, Kelly, came into the galley.

Jack tried not to flinch at the nickname. "Cooky" was worse even than "young Jack." *I have a name*, he thought. But he held his tongue. He wanted to live long enough to get off this godforsaken craft.

"Tell the men their breakfast is ready," he said. "They

can eat in shifts at the table there. Since no one's popped up and announced themselves as the cabin boy, I take it I've gotta feed the captain and Mr. Johansen myself."

"Nothing slips by ye, eh, Cooky?" Kelly jibed.

He walked through the mess and went up the steps to the deck, shouting profanities at his fellow sailors as a way of summoning them to the table. The man seemed amiable enough for one of the brutish pirates, but still Jack chafed at the invisible bonds of his shipboard captivity. He ran through the faces of the crew in his head. Aside from Ghost and Johansen, there were Kelly and Louis, Vukovich and Finn, and the huge, ugly man he thought of as Ogre. Of the five remaining men, he knew the dark, rangy-looking man was Maurilio and the giant African, his skin black as pitch, was called Tree. The fat man was Demetrius, but he had forgotten to ask Louis the names of the silent, bearded Scandinavian twins.

Any one of them seemed willing to kill him. Which made the question of accommodations a troubling one. How could he sleep among them, knowing they might murder him as he dreamed?

*Simple, Jack,* he thought. *They don't need to wait until you're asleep. And none of them is brave enough to kill you unless their captain orders it.* These points were true, but the former troubled him considerably. As he prepared breakfast, he had been wondering about the strength and agility of Ghost and his crew. Finn could have torn him apart if he'd gotten the upper hand, and such strength was beyond the power of ordinary men. So if the men aboard the *Larsen* were not ordinary, which Jack's own experiences made easy to believe, then what *were* they?

"Something smells good! How the hell can that be?" Ogre rumbled as he came into the mess beyond the galley.

Other men gathered behind him, and Jack took that as his cue. He had no desire to spend time among them, and he knew that Ghost would not be pleased at the thought of his men eating while he waited to be fed.

Jack picked up a huge tray bearing a tureen of oatmeal and plates of biscuits and bacon. At the last moment he had scrambled a few eggs for the captain and his first mate, and he brought those along as he made his way through the cabin to the captain's quarters.

Jack used the toe of his new boot to knock.

"Come!" Ghost called from within.

It was a tricky matter to balance the tray and unlatch the door as the ship swayed beneath him, but Jack managed it and shouldered the door open. Only once he was a step across the threshold did he realize that he had been mistaken—this was not the captain's quarters after all, but some sort of chart room. On the walls were various ocean maps, but they were hung alongside what seemed to be charts of the heavens themselves, maps of the stars, perhaps to navigate by.

Three people sat around the table. Ghost was there, bent over an enormous, weathered map. Johansen sat to his left, which was to be expected. What startled Jack enough to freeze him in midstep was the person to the captain's right, who peered even more intently at the maps and charts spread across the table. Delicate and lovely, with a tumble of dark hair veiling part of her face, the woman seemed to be stroking her fingers across the table as though sightless and in search of something she'd lost.

Then she blinked as though awakening and glanced up at him, her copper eyes alight with intelligence, her coffee skin gleaming in the sunlight streaming through the porthole. And she gave him a smile so sad that it cracked his heart in two.

"Good morning," she said, her French accent adding exotic emphasis to the words. "You must be Jack."

## CHAPTER THREE

# WRAPPED IN BEAUTY'S GAZE

He served breakfast to the crew, accepted their jibes and barbed comments, barely kept his feet when Tree tripped him, avoided catching their eyes, collected their plates, and mopped up their mess, and all the while he was thinking about that beautiful woman and what she might mean.

Sweating as he cleaned the galley after breakfast, Jack had entertained the idea that he might have imagined her. But he could never have dreamed up those eyes, and such underlying sadness. Then he had scoured his mind for any memory of her having been on the *Umatilla* but drew a blank. It was a waste of time; if she *had* been on the ship and he had seen her, he would have remembered her instantly. She had that sort of face. And just as with that mad forest spirit Lesya, if he never laid eyes on her again, he would still remember her forever.

Was she Ghost's woman? Sailors—even pirates—usually considered a woman on shipboard to be bad luck, but if she was the captain's wife or mistress, that would explain it.

"Cooky, that was almost edible," Louis said.

Jack jumped—he hadn't heard anyone approaching along the short corridor to the galley. *Wrapped in beauty's gaze*, he thought, but then he realized that this might be an opportunity. Louis seemed to be a talker, and Jack was an experienced conversationalist.

"I just threw it together," Jack said. "Give me the proper ingredients, and I'll make something *truly* edible."

"I believe that," Louis said, a hint of laughter in his voice. His French accent held none of the beauty of that woman's. It was a mocking, knowing lilt.

"The crew enjoyed it," Jack said. He dropped the wire brush he was using to clean the scarred wooden surfaces and turned to face Louis. The thin man leaned against the galley bulkhead, eyes flicking this way and that, and as Jack turned, his face broke into a feral smile. His golden tooth seemed to glow with an echo of moonlight.

"Of course," Louis said. "Finn feeds us dog waste, and you gave us something . . ." He shrugged, both hands out as if balancing his thoughts.

"Better?" Jack suggested.

"Something to tide us over." The grin remained.

"Who's the woman?" Jack asked. He tried to sound uninterested, turning back to scrubbing down the surfaces. Louis chuckled behind him.

"Ah, you've met Ghost's guest. Well, Monsieur Cooky, once met, never forgotten. Did she cast her spell over you? Possess your eyes? Does she haunt your memory?"

"She's just a woman," Jack muttered, but all those things were true. He could not recall what Johansen had been doing in that chart room, could not even remember how Ghost had been sitting or the expression on his face. But the woman's words repeated to him again and again, chanted into his ear by a songbird on his shoulder. *Good morning. You must be Jack.*

"That's much like saying Ghost is just a man," Louis whispered.

*He isn't?* Jack almost said, but he bit his tongue. He had no wish to betray his doubts. So he turned to Louis again and tried a different tack.

"Is she his wife?"

Louis frowned. "Wouldn't put it that way. But she's precious to him, all right."

Jack couldn't forestall the flash of jealousy that went through him. It was absurd—he couldn't even claim the woman's acquaintance—but the sight of her had made his breath catch in his throat the same way it had the first time he'd seen a snowbird in the wild during the winter he'd spent trapped in a Yukon River cabin on the verge of starvation.

"You know her," he said.

"Me? *Oui*." Louis's smile faltered for a moment, and his gaze went far away.

"And does she know you?"

Louis laughed, then glanced over his shoulder, perhaps checking to see if anyone else could hear their conversation.

"Only so far."

"Only so far?" Jack repeated. What the hell did that mean? *You must be Jack*, the woman had said, and the sadness in that voice was undisguised.

"I am the one who found her," Louis said. "I knew of her, and I told Ghost. Of course I did. He's my captain! Word of her was widespread in New Orleans, and for every ten people who did not believe, there was one like me." He laughed. "And for every thousand of those who *did* believe . . . again, there was one like me. So perhaps, Monsieur Cooky, I was destined to cross paths with Sabine."

"Sabine," Jack said, and the name felt sensuous in his mouth.

Louis sat on the food preparation surface. He touched one of the stove's still-hot coals, winced slightly, and examined his burned hand. *He* wants *to tell me this,* Jack thought, and though cautious of Louis's motives, he saw no harm in listening.

When it came to Sabine, he wanted to know everything.

"Before I signed on with the *Larsen,* I spent some time in New Orleans. I move around. It isn't in my nature to be still. I heard many stories there—demons and conjurers and magical forces imprinting themselves on the city like . . ." He drew back his sleeve and displayed a riot of tattoos, beautifully wrought and yet faded as if bleached by the sun. "Any city attracts such stories, New Orleans more than most. But the story of Sabine remained with me more than all those others because I saw her, once, in a high window, and I never forgot."

Louis seemed transported, eyes seeing something far away, and Jack dared not breathe lest he break the moment. Then the sailor blinked, looked back at Jack, and grinned again. Yet it was so clearly a mask, hiding parts of his story that he did not wish to share.

"How did she come to be on the *Larsen*?" Jack asked.

"San Francisco," Louis said. "I was there seeking Ghost and his ship. I knew of him by reputation, and I needed to get away from . . ." He waved something away, his gold-glinting grin splitting his face again. "And Sabine was there to visit someone very old, very important."

"A relative?" Jack asked.

"Someone with knowledge," Louis said. "The old woman died before Sabine reached her home. But I saw her there, and I knew what she would mean to Ghost and to the fortunes of this ship. With my natural charm, it was only a matter of time before I talked her into joining our crew."

"She's here willingly," Jack said, though he doubted that. Her eyes suggested otherwise, and the sadness in her voice. She might be with Ghost, but she had a lonely air about her that had touched him.

But Louis laughed.

"Of course, Cooky. We're all here willingly. Are we not?"

"No," Jack said. It was a risk, a small voice of defiance. But Louis did not react, and Jack sensed that he was enjoying his tale. "How can she bring the ship good fortune?" he asked.

"She's a seer," Louis said. "A boon to the ship, and I found her. Me." The pride was almost childlike, and Jack nodded in false admiration. "The ship you were on . . . the day it left port in Alaska, Sabine told us where it would be, and what it carried, and that there was"—he tapped his golden tooth with one long nail—"on board."

"She knew that?" Jack asked, and he remembered Sabine's elegant fingers playing over those charts and maps as if searching for home.

"She knows where things will be," Louis said. "Ships, people, gold. She reads the sea. Ghost calls it finding order in chaos, or"—he waved a hand—"some other strangeness."

"And she's with Ghost?" Jack asked.

Louis blinked, and then smiled again. "Well, not exactly *with*—"

"Telling your tales again, Louis?" Ghost's voice was unmistakable, and for a second Jack saw a flicker of abject fear crossing Louis's face. But then he took a deep breath, masking himself again with that gold-glinting grin, and slipped from the galley counter.

"Just complimenting Cooky here," Louis said.

Ghost stood in the door, an imposing presence. "Time to get back to work."

Louis nodded, but Ghost remained blocking the doorway. He was staring at Jack, his gaze so strange that Jack had to glance away. It was like being examined by a shark. Totally inhuman, and yet with an intelligence that could not be escaped.

Not even by turning away.

"Nobody has any conscience about adding to the

improbabilities of a marvelous tale."

Jack held his breath, then began scrubbing again.

"You've read Hawthorne, young Jack?"

"Some," Jack said. He was trying to gauge Ghost's purpose with him, because he knew it went beyond cooking. And while he was striving to figure out what Ghost sought from this interaction, he was hesitant to commit completely to any reply, even to the most innocuous question. He might deny any knowledge of Hawthorne, and perhaps that would be wrong. Or he could admit to Ghost that he had read some of Hawthorne's novels and many of his short stories, respected his complexity, questioned the moral purity of his vision . . . but perhaps that would also be a mistake. He had no idea what might set off the captain's explosive temper.

"Good," Ghost said. "I should like to discuss him with you someday."

Jack heard the captain move aside and Louis scamper away, and then Ghost's gentle, confident footfalls also led away from the galley toward his stateroom at the stern. Jack let out his held breath and took in another lungful, surprised at the tension within him. *Someday*, Ghost had said, promising a future that Jack feared.

And yet his most pressing concern for the future was not Ghost's savage volatility but the question of how soon he might see Sabine again, and if there would ever be an opportunity for them to converse. If she was Ghost's woman, simply gazing too long at her might get Jack killed. But he knew he had to look upon her again. And if she was not Ghost's woman, that only prompted more questions. Where did she sleep on board this ship of rough men? How did she endure their constant presence?

He wondered, also, about the claims Louis had made about her strange gifts. Jack would have doubted him, or presumed the tale augmented with fantasies, but he had seen the way Sabine gazed upon those maps, Ghost and Johansen watching her with anticipation. In addition to whatever covetous affection Ghost might have for her— whether she reciprocated or not—she provided a service to them. That alone might be enough to explain why she had been untouched by the captain's brutality.

*And what of me?* Jack thought. *What service do I provide? Discussing Hawthorne?*

No, Ghost had to have some other purpose in mind for him. The rest of the passengers abducted from the *Umatilla* were prisoners somewhere aboard the *Larsen*, but Jack had been left free, assigned the duties of cook while Finn recovered. The captain had admired his fighting spirit, and perhaps his cleverness.

*And the wildness in you,* Jack thought.

Perhaps that as well.

But whatever the captain's purpose, Jack knew that he had to make use of his limited freedom to locate the other hostages from the *Umatilla*, to do whatever he could to secure their safety and find his way off this ship. And if in the meantime he should discover more about the mysterious Sabine, all the better.

Jack spent the rest of that day either working in the galley or clearing away plates from the mess and Ghost's stateroom. Ghost and Johansen ate together, but there was no sign of Sabine. Jack watched for her everywhere he went, and listened for quiet footfalls on the deck above that might belong to a woman. The one time he found a few minutes to spare and went on deck, he took deep breaths as he left the galley, passed through the mess, and mounted the steps rising up into the open, hoping all the while that he would find the perfumed scent of a woman. But there was only brine and sweat, and that underlying animal stink—wet fur, musk—that he had come to know so well.

It did not belong here on the ship. The last time he'd smelled that, he had seen a wolf and its pack preparing to battle the dreadful Wendigo.

Several times he considered breaking away from his duties and searching the *Larsen*, but each time he'd find one of the crew in the mess or, closer yet, in the corridor outside the galley. They rarely acknowledged him—he was beginning to think Tree could not speak, and the Scandinavians wore the constant glazed expression of people isolated behind a language barrier. But he knew that to step out of line might bring down another beating like the one he'd received from Finn. And with his jaw and nose aching, and his ribs bound tight with torn blankets, more such treatment might just be the end of him.

So he cooked and cleaned, scrubbed the galley and sorted the ship's limited foodstuffs, and by sunset he was so tired that he could barely stand.

In the corner of the galley, bloody pelican feathers and the proud creature's bones sat ready to be flung overboard. All those meals he'd prepared in the Yukon—shooting an animal, skinning and gutting it, making the most of the carcass—had prepared him for his painful duties here. But still he'd found butchering the bird a difficult task, and the compliments from Ghost after he'd cooked and served the meal did nothing to lessen the impact. If anything, knowing that the dead bird had provided an enjoyable meal to these bastards made Jack despise himself, just a little. He could have spat in the meal, or found a bottle to crush and scattered powdered glass inside—a meager, symbolic revenge for the bird's death. But instead, he did the best that he could. It was all part of his instinctive effort to survive, and he was sure the bird would understand.

By the time he went up on deck again, the sun was bleeding across the western horizon, and the sea had risen into a heavy swell. The sails slapped in the wind, and rigging rattled as the *Larsen* dipped and rose. Maurilio stood silently at the wheel, ignoring Jack and staring up at the moon, smudged behind a veil of high clouds. A few others were on deck, but there was no sign of Ghost nor, to Jack's continuing dismay, Sabine.

But the ship was not large, and he knew that she was somewhere close.

Jack tipped the waste bucket over the side and bade a final farewell to the pelican. Then he descended to the galley, blew out the oil lamp he'd been burning for the past few hours, and settled into the galley's tight sleeping nook, which still smelled of Finn. Ghost had moved Jack from the sailors' cabin in the forecastle, at least.

*Midnight*, he promised himself. *It'll be time for a stroll.* And despite everything, he slipped into an exhausted sleep.

Jack snapped awake and sat up, and something smashed him in the head. He groaned and rolled, bringing his hands up to defend himself, lashing out in the darkness and feeling his bare feet striking wood. He paused, listening and sensing. There was nothing. He was alone, and the night-mare had brought him fighting awake, banging his head in that confined sleeping space.

He gathered his senses, breathing in the foul scents of stale cooking that permeated the galley, however much he cleaned. The ship creaked and rolled, and a metal ladle hanging on a wall hook scraped back and forth across the bulkhead, back and forth, a metronome that had aided his sleep.

*No time for sleep.* Jack stood and leaned on the gal-ley work surface, scooping a mug of water from the large bucket kept there. It tasted gritty and warm but quenched his thirst. He'd need a clear head for what was to come.

Beyond the galley lay the mess, and in the other direc-tion, at the ship's stern, the captain's quarters and several other smaller cabins. Johansen kept one of these, another was the chart room in which Jack had served them break-fast, and he guessed Sabine must be in another. He'd have to navigate the mess in complete silence, then venture up on deck to begin his exploration of the ship.

The way he had it figured, the pirates had snatched at least six people from the *Umatilla*. There couldn't be many places for them to be hidden away, and it was time now to find them. *And then what? Steal a boat, row away across these vicious seas?* But that was a problem for another time.

Discovering where they were must be his first step.

He left behind the old boots Johansen had provided for him to replace the ones he'd lost in the ocean before being dragged on board the pirate ship. As he took his first step out of the galley, an image came to him, so sudden and shocking that it brought him up short: Ghost, lying in his bunk with eyes wide open, hearing and sensing everything that happened on his ship and smiling through it all.

Jack glanced along the short, dark corridor. Ghost's door was out of sight in the shadows, but the weight of his presence was undeniable. Jack moved quickly through the mess, worried that thinking so much about Ghost would bring the captain's attention his way.

A single weak oil lamp lit the mess, casting large, troubling shadows. But Jack heard no breathing or snoring and saw no sign of anyone sleeping behind the benches or beneath the table.

Once through the mess, he paused again at the foot of a staircase. Up the stairs, through a small hatch, he would reach the open air. He could breathe more freely up there, and yet he knew that Ghost would always post a watch, even in the dead of night. Someone was steering the ship, and others would be patrolling the decks or doing other sailors' duties. He could not afford to be caught now. He had not been locked away, yet he suspected the punishment for snooping would be severe.

Jack closed his eyes and gave his senses free rein. That underlying scent of old wet animal was just as prevalent here as elsewhere. The ship rode the sea, dipping and shifting in rhythmic motion. Boards creaked, rigging stretched and hummed with tension, sails slapped at the air. And somewhere above him, casual footsteps trod the decks.

For the moment, he would need to remain belowdecks. That suited him, because the prisoners would not be found topside. He needed to explore the ship's hold.

Jack bypassed the staircase and approached the forbidden door. It was not locked. The hinges creaked and he shoved it quickly, darting inside and closing it behind him. He squatted in the darkness and held his breath, and slowly his vision improved. There were four grilles set in the ceiling along the gangway, casting moonlight down from above, and a small gutter ran along either side to take away any water that came through. It smelled of the sea.

With some areas weakly illuminated, shadows along the gangway seemed darker than ever. He walked slowly, crouched down, listening for any movement that would indicate he had been discovered. There was none . . . but there *was* something down here disturbing the dark air, and he sensed an awareness brought alert by his arrival.

Stepping softly, breathing through his mouth, Jack

advanced toward the first pool of light. He looked up before passing through, expecting one of those pirates to be staring down at him with a blade in his hand. But he was still alone.

He stopped at the first door set into the bulkhead to his left. It was a heavy, wide door, bolted shut and locked with three iron padlocks. The hinges seemed to be embedded in the bulkhead, and Jack was sure he could see, in the cracks between timber boards, the glint of metal lining the door's inside surface. He raised his fist and almost knocked . . . then wondered what a door such as this might be used to imprison. The damp, clinging animal smell he'd caught in the air before lingered here as well, but even more powerfully. It was as if the wood itself stank of it, and for a moment he thought he sensed something looming behind the door. But when he reached out with his senses, searching for some living presence there, he felt nothing but the ominous absence of something, like the quiet of a bear's den when the beast is out hunting and might at any moment return.

He moved on, eager to leave that strange door behind.

The second door in the hold area was smaller and nowhere near as secure, and Jack sniffed at the crack between door and frame. He smelled salted meat and slowly rotting vegetables, sea biscuits and flour, and heard the cackle of chickens startled by his arrival.

Footsteps above. Jack froze and shifted along the corridor, out of the weak splash of moonlight, in case one of the pirates looked down through the grille. The sailor moved on, and it was as Jack approached the third and final door that he began to hear the whispers.

He froze, head tilted to one side, and for a moment he was afraid to hear what they said. There was something so strange about this ship, and he'd already entertained the possibility that the prisoners were dead, and that he alone had been kept on as . . .

As what? A cook? For the moment perhaps, but that had been the result of Finn's punishment, and not part of Ghost's initial decision to separate Jack from the others. Had he been kept aside for some more elaborate torment as the pirates' plaything? No, because there was something more than amusement in Ghost's eyes when he looked at Jack. The captain of any ship was kept apart from his crew by virtue of his position, but Jack had noted almost immediately the intelligence glinting in Ghost's eyes and hinted at in his words. Could it be that he truly did want to discuss Hawthorne, or other subjects about which his crew were doubtless woefully ignorant?

The whispers came again, sibilant arguing, and though Jack could make out no individual words, their desperation was obvious. He pressed his ear to the door and listened, and now he could catch snippets of what was being said inside.

"... get rest ..."

"... do something soon ..."

"... kill us, like they did ..."

"... ransom ..."

"... I'm scared!"

These had to be the prisoners from the *Umatilla*.

Jack scratched at the door and the whispering stopped. *They'll think it's rats*, he thought, but then realized that he had seen no rats aboard this ship. Not one.

"Hey, in there," Jack whispered, pressing his mouth to the space between door and frame. There were two bolts here, but he could tell from the air moving between boards that this door was not lined with metal. He glanced back along the corridor to that first, much more formidable door and wondered again just what might be inside.

"Who's that?" a voice hissed, far too loud.

"Keep it down!" Jack said. They fell silent for a few seconds, Jack looking up at the nearest grille. Faint moonlight flowed in, unhindered by the shadow of anyone watching or listening.

"Who?" the voice asked again, quieter.

"I'm from the *Umatilla*."

"What? You're hiding from them?"

"No," Jack said, but he didn't know quite how to explain what had happened to him. "How many are you?"

"Eight of us in here," the voice said. "What of the *Umatilla*?"

"Long gone, friend."

"Then what—?"

"Sh." Now that he'd found them, Jack had no idea what he would do next. Given time and the right equipment, perhaps he could have pried the padlocks loose, or even pulled the hasp and staples from the wood, and freed the prisoners. But what then? He had no weapons or plan, only a certainty that any conflict between prisoners and pirates would end in a bloodbath. They could expect no mercy. At best, the prisoners would be slaughtered quickly. At worst . . . Jack's imagination, rich and given wide scope by his experiences, painted terrible scenarios, of which keel-hauling was a lesser torment.

He blinked them away.

"You'll have to wait," Jack said. "I let you out now, and we'll all be killed."

"But we can take a boat! Escape!"

"Can you feel the ship's motion? We're in deep sea, friend. We'd drown, or starve, or freeze to death. No. There has to be another way."

"What's your name?"

"Jack London."

"Well, Jack London . . . we're locked in here with our own filth and stink, and given a loaf of stale bread and one bucket of water a day."

"And I'm sorry for that. But believe me, I've seen what these men can do. They killed many aboard the *Umatilla*, and—"

"Killed?"

"Dozens, I'd say." Jack paused, heard the man's heavy breathing and others whispering within. "You didn't know?"

"No," the man said. "We thought it was just . . ."

"Gold," Jack said. The man was silent again, and beyond the door Jack could sense a thickening of the atmosphere. *How terrible it must be for them*, he thought. And he almost changed his mind and vowed there and then to get them out.

But when the gangway door to his right swung open, any decision was taken from him.

Jack instinctively crouched low and went for his knife. But he'd dropped the blade when Ghost had thrown him into the sea, and even with a knife, the fight would be one-sided. A shadow paused in the doorway, silhouetted by weak lamplight from the compartment beyond. It was slight—Kelly or Louis, or perhaps the dark-eyed Maurilio.

But whoever had found him down here would doubtless be ready to mete out rough justice. They hadn't forbidden him to snoop, but the last thing he expected from these pirates was fairness.

When the voice came, it stroked a cool finger through his memories.

"Go back," she said, exotic and husky.

Then the ship rose and jarred sideways, and as Jack reached out for support, the shadow came toward him.

Sabine.

"Go back," she said again. The moonlight paled her skin and shadowed the wavy hair framing her face, and it darkened her full lips. "You must go back."

"Sabine." It was the second time he had uttered her name, the first to her face.

"Jack. Go back to the galley. Sleep. Stay alive."

"But—"

"I'm amazed he hasn't killed you." Her voice was almost wistful, quiet, as though talking to herself.

"I can look after myself," he said, and for a moment the scene was frozen and silent, the ship balanced atop a wave as if waiting to see which way the discussion would fall.

"Not here," she said. Her voice was so old and filled with a startling wisdom, and Jack stepped forward to see her face fully. For an instant he was terrified that he had

*Sabine came forward to meet him, and when she stepped into
a splash of moonlight, her beauty winded him.*

been deceived, and that she was in fact a crone, a sea witch casting spells over whomever she chose even as she scried the waters for the *Larsen*'s next target.

But Sabine came forward to meet him, and when she stepped into a splash of moonlight, her beauty winded him. Her eyes were heavy and sad.

Jack and Sabine reached out for each other but did not quite touch. Could this creature love a man like Ghost? It seemed unimaginable. Yet here she was, roaming freely about the ship. Would she have such liberty if she were not here of her own accord? Though she had a gentle sadness about her that seemed entirely opposite to Ghost's looming brutality, logic suggested there must be some relationship between them.

"Last chance," she whispered, glancing up at the deck. Jack could not hear footsteps, but her dark eyes had gone wide, and her head was cocked to one side, listening to things he could not hear.

"You won't give me away?" Jack asked. He breathed in deeply, and hers was the first clean scent since he'd boarded the *Larsen*. She was fresh air, cool and lightly perfumed like a spring day on Mount Diablo. Dangerous thoughts to be having about a woman who might be the captain's beloved, if one such as Ghost was capable of love.

Jack pushed past her in the narrow corridor, and for

a moment they were both bathed in moonlight from the grille above. It surrounded them, blinding Jack to the shadows beyond, and it was just the two of them, so close that when she exhaled, he inhaled her breath and found it intoxicating.

Then, their first contact—she touched his hip and pushed him past her, surprisingly strong. She glanced at the ceiling again, turned from him, and walked along the gangway toward the small door through which he had originally entered the bowels of the ship.

Whispers rose from the hold, but Jack barely heard them.

Sabine opened the small door and slipped through, then glanced back just as she slammed the door behind her, hard. He saw the first smile meant for him. And then footsteps were running above, coming to investigate the bang.

Jack rushed in the opposite direction and slipped through the door where Sabine had entered and found himself in another gangway, with a steep staircase before him and a shadowy space beyond. He heard the sounds of sleeping men—snoring, groaning, the soft moans of unknown dreams—and he paused for a moment. *She reads the sea,* Louis had said. *Ghost calls it finding order in chaos.* She could find people and ships, predict where they would be at any given time.

He wondered just what Sabine had come down here to find.

Someone cried out in his sleep, in a language that Jack could not understand. He moved cautiously to the foot of the steep staircase. To venture fully into the forecastle would be to put himself in too much danger—Sabine had saved him once, and now he owed it to her to return to his small bunk in the galley.

He'd found out enough for one night. And in truth, Sabine's appearance had distracted him. He scratched a fingernail across a bulkhead, banged his head on the staircase's underside. His stealth and sensitivity had been disturbed.

The man cried out again, a despairing noise.

"He's crying for home," a voice said, and Jack gasped in shock.

Ghost emerged from the shadows to Jack's left, slipping through a doorway he had not even seen. He seemed to fill Jack's whole field of vision, bordered by shadow as Sabine had been framed by moonlight.

"All of them do, on occasion," the captain continued. "I come here and listen. Men might be hard, but they're all babies when they sleep."

"I . . . ," Jack began, but he had nothing to say. He didn't want to offer an excuse for his nighttime excursion, or to beg.

"I thought I smelled you prowling," Ghost said. He glanced behind Jack at the closed doorway to the hold. "Found 'em, then?"

"You must let them go."

"Must?" Ghost's single word made Jack feel like a child again.

"They're not animals."

"Not animals, no. Less important than that."

"You've got to give them something more than bread and water," Jack said.

Ghost pondered for a moment and then gave an uncaring shrug. "You can bring them scraps from the kitchen tomorrow, if it pleases you."

Jack nodded. Perhaps if he had time alone with the other prisoners, they could conceive some plan of escape.

"You're not going to thank me?" Ghost asked curiously, studying Jack as he might some laboratory specimen.

"I'll thank you quite effusively when you've put us all ashore, alive and well."

Ghost smiled thinly. "You're brave, young Jack. I'll give you that."

The menace in his tone, and the malicious implications of his words, were unmistakable.

*What am I to do?* Jack thought, panic descending. If it came to it, he would kill this man in order to survive. He had killed the Wendigo. Surely he could kill a pirate? Yet Ghost was more than just a pirate, that much was clear. And though the Wendigo had a savage, wild hunger and ferocity unlike anything Jack had ever encountered, the captain of the *Larsen* had all that and one thing more— cunning. Ghost exuded power and strength, and out here on the wild ocean, they were all alone.

"Come," Ghost said. "It's the last night we can talk for a while. And I have a question." He climbed the staircase to the deck, not doubting for an instant that Jack would follow.

And Jack, confused and disturbed by the terrible man's presence, could only climb up after him.

## CHAPTER FOUR

# NOBLEST OF ALL

The moon was a sliver away from being full. Pale light washed over the *Larsen*'s deck, casting the ship in shades of silver. The night sky was clear, the stars infinite, lighting their way toward whatever fates and destinations awaited. The sails were full, and the vessel knifed through the Pacific as though it were some creature of myth, born to water instead of beaten together by the hands of men.

"Your anger fascinates me," Ghost said, drawing on his pipe and letting out a plume of smoke.

Jack's heart slammed and his temples throbbed to its pulse. Ghost had known he was down in the hold, knew that he had discovered the other prisoners from the *Umatilla*, and yet he had issued no punishment. Beneath the captain's calm veneer, his savagery waited, dormant, and might erupt at any moment. Jack had seen it happen. But Ghost kept trying to draw him in, urging him to speak his mind.

*So be it*, Jack thought. He had wearied of watching his tongue.

"Is there some reason I should be anything *but* angry?" Jack asked.

Ghost raised an eyebrow, clearly surprised and pleased that Jack had engaged him at last. He pressed the pipe stem between his lips, tobacco flaring orange in the night, and let the smoke curl slowly from his nostrils. Jack could not help but see Satan in this devil's face.

*Careful*, he thought. *You're sparring with Lucifer.*

"You believe you have some right to be treated as more than an animal—"

"I *am* more than an animal," Jack said.

"You have been raised to believe in a morality that is a construct of those who wish to control the bestial nature of mankind, in order to protect themselves and what they own," the captain said. "In your life, young Jack, you will encounter two sorts of people: those who are stronger than you, and those who are weaker. And I do not mean only physical strength and weakness. I am stronger, and if there is something you possess, why should I not take it from you?"

Jack looked him full in the face for the first time, meeting him eye to eye. "Taking what does not belong to you is stealing. If you want something, you ought to earn it for yourself. The effort makes the reward much sweeter, and you will have accomplished something, instead of simply appropriating the accomplishments of others."

"I should not steal from you because it is 'wrong'?" Ghost chuckled. "Surely you can do better than that."

But Jack found that he could not, and it troubled him.

"If I am stronger," Ghost continued, "and I take what you have earned, then have I not also earned it, but in my own fashion? We're animals, young Jack. The strong eat the weak. It has always been that way, and always shall be."

"But you *kill*," Jack said.

Ghost considered this for a moment, the word hanging in the night air around them as he drew on the pipe again. Then he nodded.

"Killing is expedient. Sometimes it's necessary. I have never taken a life purely for amusement's sake, but murder is a tool."

"How can you be so cold-blooded?" Jack asked, his voice rising.

Ghost bristled and glanced around. Apparently it was one thing for Jack to challenge his philosophy privately, but quite another to do so within the crew's earshot. The two Scandinavian sailors were close by, one at the wheel and the other in the crow's nest. They seemed always to be near when Ghost walked the deck. The captain spoke softly, keeping their conversation private—perhaps so that the crew would not overhear his opinions challenged—but the presence of the bearded, blond twins did not seem to trouble him, reinforcing Jack's suspicion that they spoke no English.

"Your precious humanity is an illusion, boy," Ghost growled. "Human nature is animal nature. The rest is nothing but putting on airs, feigning a tenderness that is little more than a mask. You would kill if circumstances forced your hand. You would steal if your belly gnawed at you long enough."

Jack glanced away, but too late to prevent Ghost from seeing the flicker of recognition in his eyes.

The captain laughed softly, almost a snarl. "Ah, well, that's just delicious. You're a thief yourself."

"Not by choice—"

Ghost gripped his arm, forced Jack to meet his gaze again. "It's *all* choice, Jack. Embrace the wildness inside you, or attempt to deny it."

"I *have* seen something of the wild," Jack said. "More than you can know. I've fought for my life against a thing more monster than beast, and its blood stains my hands. I found the wild thing inside myself and embraced it. *Mastered* it."

Ghost regarded him anew, cocking his head to one side before nodding slowly.

"I knew I saw something in you," the captain said. He tapped the pipe out on the railing, and the ash was carried away on the wind. "But you say you've 'mastered' it? Impossible. You may have caged it, but that doesn't make you its master. There's only one way to make peace with your animal nature, and that's to surrender to it."

Jack's earlier observation that Ghost was Lucifer now seemed so apt that he almost spoke it aloud. Lucifer's curse was that he thought more than the other angels and did not understand the way in which heaven had defined morality. He'd had differing views and refused to bow to the beliefs of others.

"Have you read Aristotle, Captain?" Jack asked.

"Would it surprise you to learn that I have?"

"It would not," Jack replied. And now he realized for sure that *this* was why Ghost had kept him alive. Not as crew. Not as cook. The captain lorded over the demons of his hell ship, but they were minions, far beneath him in every way.

He had kept Jack because he desired such conversation; he wanted someone to challenge his philosophy that humans were savage by nature. Jack wondered who, precisely, the captain was attempting to persuade—his prisoner or himself.

"Go on," Ghost urged.

"The great philosopher wrote that 'at his best, man is the noblest of all animals; separated from law and justice he is the worst.'"

Ghost smiled, a cruel glint in his eyes. He prodded Jack with a finger.

"So you admit that you're an animal," the captain said.

"You mistake my meaning—"

"I understand your meaning *perfectly*," Ghost interrupted. "You insist on confining your nature with concepts of justice and civility."

"Both of which are necessary for the survival of the species."

Ghost snorted. "What of Darwin's concept of 'survival of the fittest'?"

Jack knew then that the conversation could never end. It was a circle of dueling philosophies, and perhaps Ghost enjoyed the debate so much that he would never *allow* it to end.

"Stripped of conscience, 'survival of the fittest' will make any man a monster."

"Ah, now we get down to the crux of the matter," Ghost

said, savoring the argument. "Am I a monster? Or am I simply an animal? Let me ask you, Jack, what separates man from the animals?"

"The ability to reason," Jack said instantly. "Self-awareness. Faith."

"Faith," Ghost snarled, dismissing the concept with a shake of his head. He held up his hands and waggled his thumbs. "What of these, Jack? Are these what separate us from animals? They make us far more efficient killers, for sure. But apes have them." He touched his fingers to his lips. "And what of this? The complexity of language? Though perhaps all we need to know we can learn from one another without words. No. We deceive ourselves with the idea that we are anything but beasts."

A lull in the wind caused the sails to sag. The guylines swayed and the blocks clanked, and Ghost stepped away from the railing and barked orders. The Scandinavians moved to obey, even as Maurilio and Tree appeared nearby to lend a hand. Jack studied them, and for the first time he noticed how edgy and skittish they seemed, like dogs sensing an oncoming storm.

*What do they know that I don't?* he wondered.

"You'd best go below and get some sleep, young Jack," Ghost said. "You've only a few hours before you need to begin preparing breakfast. And you don't want to see this crew if they're not fed properly. They're absolutely ravenous."

The captain's eyes lit up with some private amusement and he turned away, watching his crew at work. Jack had given him the intellectual stimulation he wanted, and now he was dismissed. It was frustrating—he'd wanted to reason with Ghost to put the *Umatilla* prisoners ashore the next time the ship made port, him included. But the opportunity had not arisen. Ghost's philosophy made clear that no logic would convince him to release them unless there was some benefit to himself. Jack had to figure out a way to persuade Ghost that it was in his best interests to set them free.

He was beginning to think that escape would never be easy. For now, he needed rest. *There's time yet*, he thought. *Days, at least, before we make port anywhere.*

He would think of something.

The fight broke out shortly after breakfast. The whole crew saw it start—heard shouting as the fat Demetrius dressed someone down for his sloppy reefing of the mizzen sail—and coming up from the galley, Jack turned aft to see what it was about. The sight of Finn brought him up short, and he stared in astonishment at the man.

Finn had been keelhauled less than two days ago; much

of his skin was torn and ragged, some of it stripped away entirely. He'd looked as though he might not survive the night. Now, the marks were still there, an angry pink, but his wounds had closed. He looked as though he'd been on the mend for weeks, not just a day and a half.

Jack stared openmouthed, ignoring the men's raucous shouting. He had compared Ghost to Lucifer, considered the *Larsen* a hell ship, the *devil's* ship. Now he wondered if that might be more true than he could ever have guessed. That Finn should have healed so fully—that he could even be walking on his own two feet—was not possible. But Jack had encountered the impossible before.

The rest of the crew finished reefing the sails to make the most of the diminishing wind, then drew into a circle around the fighting men. Finn had six inches on the fat Greek sailor and much longer arms. But despite his miraculous recovery, Finn had lost a step. As they faced each other across the blood-spattered deck, both men already bleeding freely, Finn feinted with a left and then swung with his right, a punishing blow that might have shattered Demetrius's jaw if it had connected. But the fat man ducked low and rolled inside the punch, delivering a trio of thunderous thumps to Finn's abdomen that doubled the taller man over.

Finn grabbed a fistful of Demetrius's greasy hair and

yanked sideways. The Greek clawed at him, but Finn
tripped him up, driving them both to the deck, where the
fight became more vicious than ever. As the ship gave a
gentle roll, they scrabbled for superior position, and the
sailors began to cheer. Finn punched Demetrius in the
throat. Choking, the fat man gouged at Finn's left eye,
driving his thumb in so hard that Jack expected the eye to
splurt from its socket.

The crew was enjoying the spectacle. Vukovich and
Maurilio were partially crouched, as though they might
leap into the fray at any moment. Louis, Ogre, and Tree
were grinning, Louis's gold tooth glinting in the sun. The
circle tightened around the vicious scrap.

"It's hideous," someone whispered behind him, and he
shivered with pleasure, for he knew that voice.

Jack turned. Sabine had emerged from the aft cabin,
and now her sad eyes came to rest on the bloody melee.
Like a single lily growing in ugly, war-ravaged ground,
she brought an incongruous and unearthly beauty to the
moment. Clad in a bone-white dress, her hair pinned back
in a simple sweep that cast the shadows of secrets on her
eyes, she simply did not belong.

"You shouldn't be seeing this," Jack said, taking her by
the elbow and trying to turn her back toward the cabin.

But Sabine refused to be turned. Lips pressed tight,

she watched the vicious brawl as though it had been her purpose for coming on deck.

"I knew it would come," she said softly. "I'm only surprised it happened so quickly."

"Right," Jack said. "You have the sight, or so Louis tells me."

"I do," she agreed. "And it is an albatross. But this has nothing to do with my sight. Finn has grown restless and put himself in disfavor with the captain. Demetrius is at the bottom of the pack, but with Finn weak, this is a chance for him to rise in the hierarchy."

*The pack*, Jack thought. He had already mentally compared the crew to trail dogs or wolves.

"You talk like they're animals," he said.

Sabine gave him a glance that might have been pity.

A roar of pain drew their attention back to the fight. Demetrius had taken Finn's genitals in his fist and now squeezed and twisted. Finn screamed. His lips drew back from startlingly sharp, jagged teeth, and for a moment he was more animal than man. Then he darted his head forward, jaws snapping down, head shaking . . . and tore off the fat Greek's left ear. Blood spurted, Demetrius cried out, and the tables had turned.

"My God," Jack whispered, turning away.

But he saw that Sabine had *not* looked away. She looked

sickened but continued watching the fight as if she were a great queen and one of the sailors fought for her honor. Jack felt a tremor of jealousy in him, and he looked around to see if any of the crew had even noticed her. Who was she trying to impress? But, of course, he knew the answer: *the captain.*

Jack saw him, then, partially hidden by the mizzen. Ghost, watching the barbaric proceedings with his hands behind his back. His eyes were slitted and his face betrayed no emotion. Had he had robes and a gavel, he could have been there as a judge.

The Scandinavians stood flanking him, and when they began to approach the circle of observers, the rest of the crew scuttled aside. Jack imagined Ghost would call a halt to the fight and punish both men. Instead, the captain only nodded and gave a small wave of his hand, as if giving his permission for the crew to continue. Watching, and waiting for the terrible outcome.

Jack glanced at Sabine. Was she right? Had Demetrius picked a fight while Finn was weak, so that he could move up in the pecking order of Ghost's crew? Observing the crew's expectant faces and the ferocity with which Finn and Demetrius fought, he found it clear that something more than pride was at stake here.

*Where do I fit into the hierarchy?* Jack wondered. *A*

*prisoner, but also a member of the crew, at least for now.* Given the choice, he thought the captives locked down in the hold might be better off. They were hungry, but Jack thought they might be safer down there than he was, up here in the pirates' midst.

Johansen had been watching just as eagerly as the rest. He might be the first mate, but Jack had realized that he was not the member of the crew that Ghost trusted most. That role belonged to the Scandinavians, who seemed always to be with him or at least nearby.

Now Johansen caught sight of Jack and Sabine. He gave them a wicked smile and winked perversely, as if inviting them to enjoy the bloodbath unfolding on deck with him.

Finn staggered to his feet. One of his arms hung limply at his side, broken and misshapen. Jack thought he could see yellow bone jutting from torn flesh. He felt sick, wanted to rage at them all to stop this madness. How could Ghost let it continue, knowing that one or both of the men could be useless to him as sailors for weeks to come, or forever, should one of them be killed? Jack turned to look at Sabine. A tear traced a path down her cheek, but she refused to look away. Johansen kept glancing at them, as if equally entranced by their reaction as by the barbarism before them.

Demetrius rose shakily to his feet. One of his eyes was

swollen shut, seeping blood and viscous fluid. Where his ear had been, only ragged flesh remained. Furrows had been clawed in his face and chest. And yet he grinned, and a low growl began deep in his chest. Despite his injuries, he still seemed stronger than his opponent.

Finn limped to one side and then the other, looking for an opening. But he had only one useful arm and one good eye. Where the scars of his keelhauling had begun to heal, many had now been opened afresh. He seemed disoriented. It might have been exhaustion or some new strategy, but he waited for Demetrius to move, and eventually the fat Greek thundered toward him like a charging bull.

Finn stepped deftly aside and snapped a kick at Demetrius's leg, shattering his knee. The fat sailor screamed as Finn descended upon him, wrapping his good arm around his neck and dragging him toward the railing. Finn freed a rope that had been tied to a cleat and wrapped it around the Greek's throat, then began to hoist him over the railing, meaning to hang him there until dead.

Jack glanced at Sabine, but she had lowered her gaze at last. He could not stand and watch any longer. He touched her arm, a tender brush of fingers on silken skin that sent an electrical charge shuddering through him and reminded him of the courage at his core.

"Captain," he said, hurrying toward Ghost, "you can't

let this go on. Whatever happens, it'll be murder, and you'll be a party to it."

The Scandinavians shifted to block his access to the captain. Jack halted but kept his gaze fixed on Ghost until, at last, the pirate chief turned to look at him.

"This isn't your world, young Jack," Ghost said, his voice low. He bared his teeth, but it was no smile. "You'll come to learn that there is no place for civility or propriety here. The strongest eat first, and the runts go hungry. And some would rather die than be the runt."

Ghost turned away, his attention back on the fight. Jack wanted to appeal again, but the twins' cold blue eyes fixed him in his place, their promise of violence and pain overt. He backed off a few steps, heard the splintering of wood; and when he looked, the tables had turned yet again. Demetrius had broken a post off the railing, and now he hammered at Finn, who warded off the first two impacts before catching a blow to the head. Finn moaned, no longer able to fight back or even lift a hand in defense.

Demetrius roared in victory and grabbed a fistful of Finn's hair. Jack watched in stunned horror as the Greek slammed his victim's skull against the deck, then opened his jaws wide to clamp his teeth on Finn's throat.

"No," Jack whispered. The fight had been savage, but this was inhuman.

Ghost strode past the twins, the circle opening for him. He struck Demetrius a ferocious kick in the ribs, and the fat sailor went over onto his own back, just as submissive as the defeated Finn.

"Enough," Ghost said. "You've proved your point."

When Sabine touched his back, Jack almost shouted in surprise. All eyes were on Ghost now . . . all eyes but hers. She kept her hand on the small of his back, a small, secret intimacy that took his breath away. He knew instinctively that he had to be careful of sharing any intimacy at all with her. Ghost possessed her, just as he did this ship and its crew, and he would guard his possessions jealously.

"They'll come for you tonight," she said, that awful sadness even deeper in her eyes, and an urgent caution as well. "We'll be locked away together. Don't fight them, Jack. Don't argue, not even the slightest. Not tonight, of all nights."

Jack frowned. "What's so special about tonight?"

"I'm sorry," Sabine whispered. Then she turned and hurried away, perhaps to her chart room, where she guided the pirates toward their next unsuspecting target. Jack glanced around and saw Mr. Johansen watching them, eyes narrowed with suspicion.

"Cooky!" Johansen shouted. "Help clear these fools off the deck, and do what you can to treat their wounds."

Jack strode over, gaze shifting from Johansen to Ghost to the injured men struggling to their feet without help from anyone else.

"The rest of you, back to work!" Mr. Johansen shouted.

The crew scattered across the ship, some climbing into the rigging and others going below. Tree and Vukovich helped the fighters stagger back to their quarters in the forecastle, and soon Jack stood alone, save for Ghost and the twins.

"Do they have names?" Jack asked suddenly, nodding toward the Scandinavians.

Ghost arched an eyebrow. "I believe the first mate just gave you an order, young Jack."

"So he did. Though after seeing Finn's condition before the fight and after his keelhauling, I'm not sure what help I can be."

"Set Finn's broken arm and Demetrius's smashed knee," Ghost replied, gazing at where the distant horizon had begun to darken with storm. "Wrap them tightly. That should be enough."

"Enough for what?" Jack asked.

"To last the night."

*To last through what?* Jack thought. But Ghost's tone was curt, and Jack could see his temper rising, the tension in the muscles of his neck and shoulders and the way his fists opened and closed, as if the fight on deck had left him hungry for a little violence of his own. Now was not the time to ask more questions. And Ghost was right; Mr. Johansen had given him an order.

He started toward the forecastle.

"Huginn and Muninn," Ghost said.

Jack paused and turned, frowning until he realized the captain had answered his question. Ghost nodded toward the Scandinavians, who seemed uninterested in the conversation, though they must know it was about them . . . considering Ghost had just spoken their names.

"Are those the names their mother gave them?" Jack asked.

"They were mine to name, Jack. Are you familiar with those names? Huginn and Muninn?"

Jack nodded. "From Norse myth. They were Odin's ravens. His eyes and ears, in all the places Odin couldn't be."

"The names mean 'thought' and 'memory,'" Ghost said. "It's interesting to have an educated man on board. Stimulating." The captain stepped in close so that Jack could smell the musky stink of him. "But don't think for a moment that your life is worth anything to me."

Jack forced a nervous smile, staring at the captain's jagged teeth. "I wouldn't dream of it. The only life you deem precious is your own."

"Just so," Ghost said. "I'm glad we understand each
other. Now go and see to Finn and Demetrius, but take
care, young Jack. An animal is most dangerous when it's
wounded."

With that, he turned and descended the steps into the
cabin where Sabine awaited, leaving Jack with much on his
mind. Despite the brutality simmering within the captain
and his crew, they seemed excited, almost giddy. Maurilio
and Louis were already at work repairing the railing that
Demetrius had broken, and they sang together in dueling
French and Spanish, laughing almost drunkenly.

Seeing them so happy, Jack ought to have been
intrigued by whatever secret awaited revealing. Instead,
he felt nothing but dread.

*They'll come for you tonight*, Sabine had said. *Don't fight
them, Jack. Not tonight, of all nights.* How could he simply
surrender himself, let them lock him up? But if he fought,
it wasn't just his own life he was taking in his hands, but
the lives of the other prisoners. And what of Sabine? She
seemed like the ship's version of the lady of the manor, but
he could feel the sadness and loneliness in her. Did she love
Ghost, or did she also dream of escape? Whenever and
however he managed to escape Ghost and his pirates, Jack
knew that he would try to persuade Sabine to go with him.

But considering what her gifts meant for Ghost, it would take a miracle for him to let her go.

His mind went back to her unsettling words. They would come for him tonight. So be it. He would trust in her. And there had been her other comment, as well. *We'll be locked away together.* That, at least, held promise.

Very little went to waste aboard a ship. Fruit and meat on the verge of rotting—but not quite *rotten*—would still make its way into the crew's diet. Jack had managed to get Ghost's permission to bring scraps from the galley to the handful of prisoners from the *Umatilla* who were locked in that room in the hold, but he had not been thinking properly about what the captain would define as "scraps." In the end, the best he could do for those poor souls was a thin stew made from the snippings off the ends of carrots, a handful of moldy potatoes, two cans of beans he found in what he assumed was some private stock belonging to the former cook, and the bones of the pelican. Some meat remained on those bones, and it sloughed off as he boiled the stew, but it was barely enough to add a bit of texture to the meal. He spiced it as best he was able, giving it a bit of flavor. It wasn't much, but it would have to do.

When the meager meal was ready, he tracked down Louis, who already had his orders from Ghost and the keys to the prisoners' hold. Ogre came along, a knife in a scabbard at his hip.

Riding the swells of the sea, Jack followed Louis through that small door and down the few steps into the gangway belowdecks, carrying the steaming pot. Louis had been at sea much longer, and seemed almost unaffected by the rolling of the ship. Jack could not help reeling a bit, staggering right and left, but he managed not to spill more than a few ounces of stew. The ladle clacked against the rim with every sway of the vessel.

Ogre came behind Jack, perhaps to be sure he didn't try anything rash. But the true purpose of his presence was to menace the prisoners once the door was open, in case they attempted to escape. Jack thought the precaution foolish. These people could not overpower the entire crew, and even if they did, where would they go? He doubted the people Ghost had imprisoned were sailors.

"Don't talk to them," Louis said, keys jangling as he led the way past the padlocked door, then the hold containing the food stores, and approached the prisoners' hold.

"I'd like them to know they're not alone," Jack said.

Key in the first lock, Louis glanced at Ogre, and then at Jack. "You've got your orders from the captain. I am amazed he's indulging you even this far. Don't push him, Jack."

Jack heard the voices beyond the door, sensed the fear and the hope in that room, and decided Louis was right. They would know just from seeing him that they had an ally outside their prison. He had wanted to apologize for not bringing them bowls, for them all having to share the ladle, but he told himself they would see such sympathies in his eyes.

Louis finished unlocking the door. He threw it open and stepped back, hand on the hilt of his knife. Ogre did the same but drew his blade, an eager glint in his eye. It seemed he hoped someone would try to escape, and he would get the chance to draw blood. Jack found his expression chilling.

The pleas began instantly. A thin, balding man wearing broken spectacles begged for his life, while a gray-haired matron demanded to know what the pirates intended to do with them. There were eight people in the hold, including a burly, bearded trapper, two young men, a pale and lovely woman in a torn but expensive dress, and a middle-aged black man who stood at the back of the room, studying the pirates with wary intelligence, obviously contemplating some plan of action. The eighth, and last, was a girl of perhaps fourteen. She still had a bow in her hair.

Jack searched their faces. They had all been on board the *Umatilla* with him, sailing from Alaska to San Francisco, but none of them looked familiar to him. They were strangers, but they were his fellow captives, and he racked his brain for some way he could help them. But on a ship of bloodthirsty pirates, in the middle of the sea—at least for the moment—the stew was the best he could do.

It seemed so little, but as he carried the pot into the room, they moved in eagerly. Some of them seemed to realize that he was not one of the pirates, for they began to question him. Jack felt ashamed that he could not respond.

"Hurry it up, Cooky," Louis said, though not unkindly.

Regretfully, Jack left the pot and retreated to the door. As Louis began to haul it shut, the trapper gave a roar and lunged for him, but Louis was too quick. He clouted the big man across the temple with a small fist. Somehow, though the trapper was twice his size, Louis had knocked him down with a single blow. Disoriented, the trapper tried to scramble to his feet for another attempt, but Ogre stepped in and kicked him in the chest, sending the man crashing into the lady in the torn dress.

Jack found himself locking eyes with the bald man in the broken spectacles. "I'm sorry," he said as the door slammed.

Some of them cried out, but moments later they fell silent, and he knew they must be gathered ravenously around the stewpot.

He felt sure he would see their faces in his dreams tonight.

As Louis fastened all the locks, Jack began to turn away, headed back along the gangway toward the galley, but Ogre blocked his path.

"What?" Jack demanded, his frustration overriding his fear of the quiet sailor.

It was Louis who answered. "You're not done." He gestured toward the middle door in the hold. "Go into the food stores. The captain's got a private stock in there. You'll find it easily enough. Make a plate of fruit and cheese, the best there is, and fetch a bottle of the finest wine."

Louis and Ogre waited in the gangway while Jack did as he was told. Sabine had said the two of them would be locked away together tonight, so he presumed this small repast from Ghost's private reserve must be some celebration for the captain, but he couldn't imagine what the occasion might be. Along with the captain's private stock, he found a stack of china plates and quickly arranged the requested food upon one of them.

A bottle of wine under one arm, he emerged from the stores, but once again Ogre blocked his attempt to leave the hold.

"Wait a moment," Louis said, and he went to the triple-padlocked room that had so piqued Jack's curiosity, unlocked it, and opened the door.

The first thing Jack noticed was that there were locks on the inside as well.

"Put them on the table," Louis instructed him.

Confused, Jack nevertheless complied. He entered that room and was stunned by what he found. He could make no sense of the room. Here in the dingy hold was a chamber more richly appointed than any other on the ship, complete with a cot covered in a thick, woven spread, a love seat, oil lamps, and a shelf of leather-bound books. The wooden planks gleamed as though they had just been cleaned.

"What is this?" he asked, turning to Louis. "It's a cabin? But for whom?"

"No questions," Louis replied. "The captain's given his orders."

Burning with curiosity, but knowing he would get no answers from these pirates, Jack set the wine and the plate of cheese and fruit onto the table. For several long seconds he studied the room, until Ogre grew restless and seemed about to come in after him. Jack retreated from the room, wondering what other secrets the *Larsen* was hiding.

The storm started as a few urgent gusts, as if the wind were testing them, toying with them. The black clouds drifted in from the south, enveloping them in premature darkness, the sun vanishing as though in the hands of some celestial stage magician. The moon would be full tonight, but Jack knew he would not see it. The moon and stars would be swallowed.

As he cleaned the galley after dinner, Jack was troubled by the amount of food the crew had left in their bowls. He had tasted it, as he tasted everything he cooked, and though he had no affection for cabbage, he thought the beef stew had come out quite flavorful. *You don't want to see this crew if they're not fed properly*, Ghost had said. There had been an uneasy silence in the mess; calm before a storm.

It was particularly frustrating that they had left so much uneaten, considering the trouble he had gone to earlier to put together a meal for the prisoners. But perhaps Ghost would allow him to give the seven captives in the hold another meal—after all, the crew had abandoned the scrapings in their bowls.

Jack collected the uneaten stew in a large pot, trying to decide how best to frame the request. The rain began pummeling the deck above him as he cleaned and stored the bowls, and he set about washing the rest of the pots and the cooking surface. Finn seemed to have shown little interest in cleanliness during his time as cook, and Jack felt as though he could scrub the galley three times a day for a month and still not strip all of the filth away. Still, it was good to keep busy. To keep *distracted*. All day Sabine's words had been echoing in his mind. With the storm darkening the sky, it would be impossible for him to know when night had truly arrived, so he tried his best not to think about it. The predictable result was that he could think of nothing else. He didn't like the idea of being locked away, but if Sabine and he were together, it would give him the opportunity to learn more about Ghost and his crew.

Every creak of the planks above his head, or rustle beyond the galley door that might be a footfall, made him go rigid with worried anticipation. The ship rose and fell on the heavy swell, but the roll and pitch did not trouble him. He had other concerns.

When they came, it was without stealth or caution. Boots tromped upon the stairs outside the galley, and Ogre ducked his massive head to step inside, with Louis behind him.

"Evening, Jack," Louis said, smiling his gold-glinting smile.

"Louis," Jack said with a nod. Neither of them acknowledged the hulking, intimidating presence of Ogre in the galley with them.

"You won't be sleeping in here tonight," Louis said, his French accent somehow stronger. He twitched, as though he had a desperate itch he had no wish to scratch where others might see.

"No?" Jack asked lightly, keeping his breathing steady, his heart calm. "Back to the forecastle, then?"

Louis laughed. "Not there either. *Non, non, mon ami.* Finn is a terrible cook, *c'est vrai.* But for this evening, you will have other accommodations."

Ogre glowered at him, but it was Louis's earnest reassurance that got Jack moving, not fear of the giant. He led the way out of the galley and into the mess, and then Louis strode past him, through the mess and directly to the previously forbidden door. A certainty gripped Jack. He knew where they must be taking him. Not to the locked room with the other prisoners, and not to the largest section of the hold where the food was stored.

They would lead him to that first room in the hold, with its iron locks and reinforced frame. Jack was startled by the realization that the food he had left in that padlocked room earlier in the day was for himself. As he followed Louis into the belly of the ship, with Ogre looming behind him, Jack's heart began to race. He breathed evenly to steady himself, glancing around for something to use as a weapon, afraid that if they locked him into that room, he would never get out alive. And what of Sabine?

"What's this about, Louis?" he asked. The little man

glanced back at him, gold tooth gleaming in the gathering shadows of the hold. Ogre carried a lamp, and its light danced in the dark, turning their silhouettes into strangely misshapen things.

"Survival, Jack."

"I don't understand."

Louis's breathing had become ragged, almost labored. Something seemed to be wrong with him.

"No more questions, Jack. Pause for answers, and you'll be dead. It's twilight now."

Louis trailed off with a soft grunt. He drew in a long breath and stood up straighter. Behind Jack, Ogre had also begun to breathe strangely, but now another sound came from him—a soft, guttural laugh.

"It's the locks on the inside that really matter," Louis said. Working quickly, he dragged the door outward, light washing into the corridor from within. Jack winced at its brightness, blinded for a moment. And when his vision adapted to the light, he could only blink in surprise.

Sabine waited inside, seated on a tiny love seat, her hands clasped before her in worry. She looked up sharply, her eyes glistening, and when she saw Jack, she leaped to her feet and rushed toward him.

"Stay there, woman!" Louis barked, and Sabine drew up short, terror in her eyes.

The bottle of wine and the plate of fruit and cheese Jack had retrieved only hours earlier from the captain's personal stock were still arranged on the table where he had left them. He had arranged his own prison cell, elegant though it was.

"Louis?" Jack said, turning toward the man. "I don't underst—"

Ogre clubbed him in the face with one enormous fist, knocking him backward into the room. Shocked and confused, Jack began to rise, but the heavy door slammed shut. He heard the locks rattling as they were secured.

"Sabine," Jack said, staring at her pale face. "What is this? What do they plan to do with us?"

Sabine came toward him and set about locking their door from the inside with bolts, clasps, and padlocks—it was now locked both from within and from without. Then she resumed her perch on the love seat and would not meet his gaze. Long minutes passed without a word from her, though he prompted her several times. It seemed almost as though she had shut him out completely, traveled elsewhere within the infinite realms of her own mind.

Something scratched at the door. Jack stiffened and held his breath. He stared at the door, then moved closer and listened to the sounds of things moving out in the corridor, the snuffling and snarling of beasts. The animal stink he had encountered outside the door when he'd first approached this room grew suddenly stronger, and he knew that whatever beast had left that stench behind had now returned.

"What the hell is this?" Jack whispered.

From farther along the corridor came the sound of a heavy door swinging open, hinges squealing. For a quiet moment, the sounds of the ship—the creaking of boards and the rush of the sea against the hull—seemed impossibly loud, and then Jack heard a growl.

"Not yet," a voice said, deep and inhuman.

He heard terrified voices, and a man crying out in shock. In his mind he could see the faces of the prisoners from the *Umatilla*, and he forced himself not to match those faces to the shouts of dismay and cries for mercy.

Another growl, vibrating through the wall. "Not . . . yet . . . ," the voice said again, separate from the growl, yet so similar. "Go. Run."

A sudden clamor of footsteps rushed past the door, and others faded in the opposite direction. *The prisoners, escaping!* But Jack already knew how wrong that idea was. He heard heavy thumps on the floor, smelled the stink of beasts growing even stronger, and then a low rumble that might have been an animal snarl or quiet, monstrous laughter.

This was not an escape.

The whole ship seemed to hold its breath. Distant, muffled screams shattered the moment, and then different footsteps thumped along the gangway outside the locked door, and these had claws. A howl rose up, so powerful and wild and familiar that Jack's spine seemed to vibrate.

"No!" Jack shouted, the word bursting from him. He hammered the door. "Let them alone, damn you! They've done nothing!" He slammed his fists against the wood several times and then froze, chest rising and falling with ragged breath . . . staring at the locks.

He grabbed the latch of the heavy dead bolt and began to draw it back.

"Jack, stop!" Sabine said, clutching his shoulders and trying to pull him away.

The dead bolt unlocked, he spun on her, searching her eyes for a thousand truths that seemed to have escaped him thus far. Who was this tragic creature and what hold did Ghost have over her? Could it truly be love?

"Give me the keys to the padlocks," he demanded.

Some strange exhilaration lit her eyes, and he thought he caught the glimmer of a smile before terror crashed in to fill her features again. "You can't unlock the door. We're safe in here, with all the locks on, but if you go out there— even if you just open the door—we'll both be fair game."

She gave a quiet, brittle laugh. "Fair game."

"They're killing the other prisoners!"

Sabine faltered and lowered her gaze as if in shame. "You can't stop it, Jack. You can only die with them, if that's your choice. But if you open that door, you'll be killing me as well."

Paralyzed by her words, Jack racked his brain for some alternative, some tactic that would let him rescue the surviving prisoners—whose distant screams reached them even now—but he was at a loss. He could picture every one of their faces—the trapper, the woman in her torn dress, the man in the broken spectacles—but the one that haunted him most powerfully was the girl with the bow in her hair.

The horror was unfolding above and around them with each passing second, the howl of beasts overriding cries of human terror, and he had no time to plan something clever enough to save lives. He could set the ship afire and attempt to get himself, Sabine, and any other survivors to the small boats while the crew put out the flames, but he knew in his heart that there wouldn't be enough time. He could do nothing but stand and listen to innocents die.

Jack screamed his fury and slammed his fists against the inside of the door. After several long moments, shaking with grief and rage, he slid the dead bolt he'd opened back into place.

"Sabine . . . ," he said. From elsewhere on the ship came another scream of terror, a cry of immeasurable agony . . . and then silence. "What are they?"

"You *know* what," she said gently. "You're bright enough, Jack, and the clues were all there. Don't tell me you weren't already thinking of them as *wolves.*"

## CHAPTER FIVE

# OUT OF SIGHT

Jack had read that if a person was deprived of one sense, then some or all of the others would be enhanced to compensate. And sitting there with Sabine in that strange room in the ship's hold—*a safe room, built for just this purpose, constructed to keep people protected from whatever might be outside*—he closed his eyes, trying not to listen to the slaughter.

It seemed to go on forever, but it couldn't have been more than a few minutes. He could easily distinguish between footsteps—the prisoners' were panicked and shuffling, running this way and that through gangways and across a deck they did not know; the wolves' were definite, methodical. And fast. A heavy thumping that he could feel in his bones. He followed both sets of sounds in his mind's eye, and each would stop for a moment when another

*He closed his eyes, trying not to listen to the slaughter.*

prisoner was cornered or caught.

Then would come the cry of terror, the scream of pain, the crunch of breaking bones.

And even in the safe room, Jack could smell the blood.

He and Sabine sat close together in the love seat, but for those few minutes they existed very far apart. Jack felt utterly alone, even though he could hear Sabine's uneven breathing and smell her subtly perfumed scent. He thought of holding her hand, but that would feel wrong. She had known what was to come, and she had done nothing to warn him, nor to help those men and women locked away in the hold like rabbits caged in readiness for the hounds' amusement.

Worst of all, if she truly had some second sight and she had used it to lead the *Larsen* to the *Umatilla*, then she had to share in the blame for the murders Jack bore witness to now—sightless witness, though in some ways they were worse in his imagination.

It was a surreal moment, sitting motionless while all around him were the sounds of pursuit and murder, and the ship swayed in tune with the Pacific swell. He felt like the center of things but not the focus. He was like the unmoving observer in the flow of life, a rock in a river of chaos. Sometime soon, he would have to shift.

When the running and screaming ended, the howling

came again. There was more than one howl, and their tones were triumphant, some distant and some close by. The hair on Jack's arms and neck stood on end. He opened his eyes, preferring the brash light of the room to the darkness behind his eyelids. The ship dipped and rose, and he wondered who was steering, who was watching the sails and ensuring the *Larsen* remained on course.

Of course, the answer was no one. The normal people—the human beings—on board were either in this room or scattered across the decks, torn to pieces, their insides being lapped up by monsters that followed the moon.

"But even *we're* not normal," he whispered.

Sabine's hand touched his arm, a shocking contact. Jack jerked away. "Sh," she said, holding his arm tighter.

"No," Jack said, and he pulled away. "You're not normal."

"I'm not one of them!" she said, pointing at the door.

"No, I didn't mean that. I meant . . ." Jack shook his head, not sure how he could verbalize what he had been thinking.

"They're monsters," Sabine said. "You've talked of the animal with Ghost, yes? He cannot stop talking of the nobility of beasts, the beautiful simplicity of wild things. But those things—those wolves—aren't animals. They are low creatures."

"Ghost doesn't seem to believe that."

Sabine scoffed. "Ghost has delusions of grandeur."

"Why do you help them?" Jack asked. It was a question scorching in his mind and sizzling in his gut, because he so wanted the answer to make sense. Sabine was beautiful, and he had been enchanted by her beauty and sadness. But was she just a different sort of monster? "Is it Ghost? You love him?"

"Jack," she said, and her eyes were sadder than ever. "I do hope you cannot even *begin* to equate me with them?"

"No, I—"

"In your voice, then. An accusation."

"No," he said, pulling his arm away from her and then holding *her* arm. "I just need to understand."

"The others from your ship are dead now," she said softly. "It's just the beginning of the night, and I don't think they've all fed. They don't, usually. Not to their heart's content. The pack is large, the prey usually limited. So we've a long night ahead of us."

"We're safe?" Jack said.

Sabine laughed softly. "As safe as a door can make us, or a few locks." She fell quiet, looking down at her hands.

"What is it?"

"They usually leave me alone," she said. Jack picked up on her meaning right away.

"But now I'm in here with you," he said, finishing for

her. He looked at the door, listened, and the sea surged against the hull, boards creaking.

"I have no choice," Sabine said. "You understand that, don't you? If I were not useful to Ghost, I would be up there, my blood washing the deck."

Jack said nothing, searching inside himself for something. Judgment. Justice. Reason. If it weren't for Sabine's gift, he would still be aboard the *Umatilla* and almost home, and those he'd just heard killed—torn apart by unnatural creatures, consumed by *werewolves*—would still be alive.

"We all have a choice," he said.

"No!" Sabine snapped. "Sometimes choices are made for us, and there's nothing we can do about it."

"But can't you fight back?"

"Fight?" she scoffed. "I have no strength. I find things, and see maps as if they were real—as if I gazed down from the heavens. I'm no fighter." She waved her hand vaguely at the door, at what had happened beyond. "I'm no killer."

"Defy them," Jack said. He was trying to fuel his own anger, but there was something so vulnerable about Sabine that he could not. There was strength in her, but it was kept down, hidden—or perhaps trapped—beneath a heavy secret. He only wished that she would tell him.

"I cannot. I *have* to do Ghost's bidding."

Jack looked away from the woman, glancing around the

room. It had been appointed for comfort as well as safety, with their soft seat, oil lamps, a single cot with clean blankets, and a curtained bathroom area. *It's for one person*, he thought again, smelling Sabine's subtle scent, feeling the heat of her. "How long will we be down here?" he asked.

"Until daybreak."

"They become normal people then?"

"Probably."

Jack glanced at her again, his heart taking a familiar jump at the sight of her. He could not blame or hate her, because her misery was plain. She was even more of a prisoner here than he. And how could he judge her, really? He had seen such violence already, even before this night when he had learned the true nature of these pirates, and he had done nothing. He had checked his own anger, amended his behavior, so that Ghost would continue to show an interest in him . . . and keep him alive. How was he any better than Sabine?

"Probably?" he asked.

"The full moon changes them," she said. "One night only, they have no choice but to reveal the beast within. But other times they can control the transformation."

Jack stared at her. "They can change whenever they wish?"

Sabine nodded. "Day or night, at will. But they rarely

change without reason. Louis tells me that it hurts."

He stood and approached the small food table, thinking back to the pirates' boarding of the *Umatilla*. They had been normal men then, though possessing unnatural strength and agility. Not wolves. Not beasts. He tried to imagine the things out there now, prowling the ship or gnawing on the bones of people he had spoken to and hoped to rescue.

Jack glanced at Sabine. Her eyes were downcast, hands fisted in her lap, fingers white where she squeezed them together.

"And you?" he asked.

Sabine's head snapped up, and he saw the anger there. "I told you, Jack. I am *nothing* like them."

"I'm sorry," he said. He picked at the cheese and fruit, nibbled some, and found it good. He took a plate to Sabine and resumed his seat. Somehow it felt safer beside her.

"When they choose to change, they retain some control. It's still . . . horrible, but they keep their faculties. Senses are heightened, and their brutality increases tenfold."

"I can hardly imagine that."

"You don't want to," she said. "But at full moon their change possesses them entirely and there's very little control. This is when they're true animals, driven by primeval instincts to hunt and feed."

"And that's why they take prisoners from the ships they raid."

"Yes. For food, and sport."

"It's hardly a hunt, chasing someone through a ship this small."

"Sometimes they time arrival on an island with the full moon. If there are people living on the island, they suffer."

"And you tell them where these islands are?"

Sabine looked at Jack, and he suddenly felt like a child beneath her woman's regard. Her smile was surprising but welcome, and she laughed softly, sadly. "No, Jack," she said. "Ghost has charts for that."

Something moved outside—a scrape, a shuffle. *That's no wave against the hull,* Jack thought, and then a rumbling growl sounded, so deep that it was almost inaudible.

"Tree," Sabine breathed into his ear, and Jack jumped. He hadn't felt her draw so close.

The growl continued, and something pressed against the door. Jack couldn't see the door move, but he knew it was being pushed inward—bolts strained, pressure built.

"Can he . . . ?" he asked, turning to Sabine, and they were face-to-face. Her eyes filled his vision, and this close they told whole new stories. He sensed guilt, and a multitude of other emotions he could not interpret.

"No," she whispered. He smelled her breath. "Not alone."

They pulled back from each other and sat in silence until the thing outside moved away. Jack could barely imagine the type of werewolf Tree would make.

Footsteps thumped overhead, and a roar came from up on deck. Elsewhere in the ship—the forecastle, he thought, though direction may have been confused—someone cried out, a shriek of rage.

"Someone survived!" he said, half standing from his chair. He tilted his head, turned slightly left and right, trying to place where the scream had come from.

Several sets of footsteps thundered overhead. A howl rose, loud and chilling and vibrating the wood-paneled walls of their room. And then came another scream, this one of pain.

"No one survives unless the wolves allow it," Sabine said. "We should eat, Jack. And have some wine. It's going to be a long night."

Jack went to the door and stood close, though not close enough to touch. He was afraid that contact would communicate his presence to the other side. Something could be waiting out there. *Maybe they stand guard*, he thought, Sabine's mysterious presence a weight behind him.

After a few quiet moments, broken only by the creak of the ship and the crash of the sea upon the hull, the night filled with a baleful howling. Frowning, Jack turned to Sabine for an explanation.

"They're still hungry," she said quietly, voice breaking with the horror of the words. "They wanted more passengers from your ship, but Ghost hurried them. And then he wouldn't let them have you."

"I still don't understand that," Jack replied.

"I think he sees you as a test," Sabine said. "They're wolves, but they are also men, and Ghost sees men as weak. He wants to scour any trace of humanity from his soul."

"So he's kept me alive as, what, a reminder?"

"I suspect that's a part of it."

"I thought he meant to persuade me of his philosophy," Jack said. "That he looked at me as some kind of challenge."

"It may be that as well. But if he only wanted you to be like him, there are swifter and surer ways he could accomplish that," Sabine said.

Jack felt a trickle of ice along his spine at the suggestion. He would rather die than live as a beast. And if he was going to survive long enough to find a way out of his predicament, he would need to learn all he could of the wolves, and of Ghost.

"You said they were still hungry. We're after another target, aren't we? A ship to ransack and rob."

"Yes."

He turned away from the door, trying to catch her looking at him without her realizing. He wanted to know how she saw him, what she thought of him, and seeing her unguarded might reveal all this and more. But Sabine's mystery remained, and she looked at Jack from beneath hooded eyes. Her sadness could not be feigned; her wretched situation was a terrible weight upon her.

"We have to get off this ship."

"Do you believe I have never tried?"

"I don't know," he said.

"Jack . . . sweet Jack." She shook her head. "Come and drink some wine with me."

"What's the target this time?"

"A ship heading to Japan from San Francisco. There are several rich Americans on board, and a Japanese businessman who has made a fortune in printing and newspapers. He's returning home with his fortune and his most valuable belongings. He has . . ." She frowned. "I saw gold, and diamonds."

"Do they care about such things? They're not just looking for . . . victims?" he asked, thinking about stories of ships like the *Mary Celeste*, found adrift with no one aboard, or island colonies like Roanoke, whose population simply vanished.

"Make no mistake," Sabine said. "They are a wolf pack.

Hunting is of great importance to them. But they are also pirates. It is not some masquerade to hide the wolf beneath the human mask. They are both. Ghost has accumulated his crew—his pack—with care and purpose. From what I have been able to discover, all of them were thieves and hard men even before he marked them with his bite and made them wolves. They *must* hunt, and they lust for it, but gold is their true motive. Their true love."

"To what end?" Jack asked. "What do such creatures need money for?"

Sabine's expression darkened. "Shore leave. They hoard the spoils of their piracy and murder, and when they are in port, they spend it in bouts of utter debauchery, if the stories I've heard them tell are to be believed. Though the split isn't even."

Surprised, Jack glanced up at her. "It isn't? Doesn't that create resentment?"

"Of course. But as in any pack, there is a hierarchy."

Jack thought of the sled dogs he had seen fighting in the Yukon, and he understood what she meant. Every pack had a leader, to whom the rest would offer their throats in subservience, and there was a rank, or order, among them. When they were fed, the least of them would get only scraps. He had a feeling that, after today, Finn had fallen to the bottom of the pack on board the *Larsen*. Apparently, having fallen to the last rung on the ladder, he would also get the smallest share of their current hoard, which was sure to rankle him.

Ghost had made them all, tainted them with the curse of the werewolf. He was captain and the leader of the pack, and Jack had seen with his own eyes how much the men feared him. But he had sensed the fierce loyalty in them as well, to the pack as a whole. All of them seemed dedicated to the hierarchy of the pack, except perhaps for Finn. All the punishment he'd received had not seemed to extinguish his fury and resentment. Jack would have to be wary of him at all times.

"And what about this new ship?" he asked. "How many will they kill?"

Pained, and perhaps ashamed, Sabine glanced away. "Please, Jack."

"Men, women, and children? The terror of those children. Being killed by one of *them.*"

"Jack!" She was desperate now, her voice pleading. "You have no idea what it's like for me, having to do this. But I can't refuse him."

"You love him."

"No!" Sabine cried. "I see the way he looks at me, but no."

"Then why? There's something you're not telling me.

Surely death would be preferable to this life, guiding them to slaughter after slaughter."

"You don't understand," she said, her voice trembling with emotion.

"So *tell* me!"

Sabine stood and moved to the food and wine. She poured a glass for Jack, and when he smelled the fruity aroma, he could only take it from her and drink. It was one of the finest wines he had ever tasted. He wondered where Ghost had stolen it.

They sat together again and ate and drank. *I've got to know what she's hiding,* he thought. The only way off this ship for him was with Sabine; the idea of leaving her to Ghost's brutalities was too awful to bear. She was conflicted and suffocating with guilt, as much a victim of the wolves as he was, if not more. And there was something about her. . . .

He'd felt it the first time he'd set eyes on her, though he had yet to give it a name.

"You'll tell me one day," he said.

"If I do, it may be the death of you."

"I've died before," Jack said. He felt Sabine staring at him but kept his attention on the heavy door, their only protection against the horrors beyond.

The ship's movements were soporific. But footsteps

padded the decks and gangways, and werewolves howled at the bloody moon.

When the door handle creaked down, Jack opened his eyes.

A moment of confusion struck him, so intense that his heart stopped in his chest. That familiar instant of constructing his life upon waking—*I'm on a ship; Ghost taunts me; they're killers, monsters, werewolves; I am Jack London*—was overshadowed by other, less obvious facts.

Someone's hair tickled his face. His arm lay around something that moved, something warm. Oil-lamp light flickered and danced as the door behind him drifted open, and an agitated sea breeze forced its way in.

"Sabine," he whispered, rolling away from her across the cot and falling to the floor. He bumped his head, saw stars. His vision cleared in a second or two, by which time Sabine was sitting on the edge of the cot staring past him across the room.

*What will I see?* he thought, and though there was dread in his heart, he had faced monsters before. Nothing was hopeless, and he would fight to the last drop of—

"Clumsy fool." Ghost's voice grumbled in. He laughed low, wet, as if something was stuck in his throat.

Jack sat up and leaned against the cot, looking at the open door. Daylight shone in, weakened by its journey down through the deck grilles. But even filtered like that, Jack could always discern dawn's light.

He had slept all night. A bottle rolled on the floor, set dancing by the ship's gentle movement. There was a speckled stain of wine on the planks, but he remembered that he and Sabine had drunk most of it, and eaten the cheese and fruit, before tiredness had taken them to the cot. He did not remember hugging her to him, but that might have happened during the night. He wondered if she remembered being held.

Ghost stood just inside the doorway. His glance flickered from Jack to Sabine and back again, and Jack had never seen such a smile on the bastard's face. Usually his humor was at other people's expense, and such humor was honest. This smile was as fake as any Jack had ever seen, tight and sharp, meant to mask his displeasure at finding them in what must have seemed a moment of intimacy. For all of Ghost's philosophizing, and despite the savagery of his monstrous species, it was clear he was not as emotionless as he had portrayed himself.

The captain wore only torn trousers. His chest and shoulders were wide and muscled, hairy, and there was blood spattered across his chest as well as his chin and neck. Jack closed his eyes and turned away.

"The crew'll be wanting breakfast, young Jack."

"Haven't you eaten enough?"

The captain's smile relaxed, becoming more honest. Talk of savagery was more comfortable territory for him than the sting of feelings he pretended—perhaps even to himself—that he did not have.

"Never quite enough," he said. "You and the lady Sabine were comfortable, I take it?"

"Very," Jack said. He heard Sabine's sharp intake of breath, perhaps as she remembered sharing the cot.

The moment the word left his lips, Jack realized it had been a mistake, unintentionally emphasizing the intimacy implied by the position in which Ghost had found them. He would have to be more careful. Whatever feelings Sabine might or might not have for the captain of the *Larsen*—and Jack was still not entirely certain how she felt—it was clear that Ghost coveted her attentions.

Ghost glanced around the room, taking in the empty, rolling bottle and the crumb-strewn plate, and there was something about the way he stood that Jack hated—the casual grace of his stance, the way he did little to hide what had happened to him, what he had become. There was an arrogance to Ghost that contradicted the intelligence he tried to project, an egotistical certainty that he was right.

Sabine stood and walked between them.

"I need to track the *Weyden*," she said. "I had dreams in

*"Jack—there's some meat in the galley*

*that needs salting and curing."*

the night . . . sensations that it might have changed course."

"Then you'd best confirm our route," Ghost said.

"I'll need access to your charts, of course." She stood before Ghost, staring at him. The captain glared over her shoulder at Jack.

Jack pulled himself up onto the cot, trying not to wince at the stiffness in his limbs. *Nothing happened between us,* he thought, and he almost spoke his conviction. But it occurred to him that the displeasure he'd seen in the captain's eyes was a vulnerability he might be able to use to his advantage.

Ghost was jealous.

"Very well," Ghost said. "We'll spend the morning in my cabin. As for you, young Jack . . . breakfast and coffee for the men, then clean up any mess you might find around the ship." He grinned, turned to go, then feigned remembering one final point. "Oh, and Jack—there's some meat in the galley that needs salting and curing. A special store I've put aside."

Ghost backed from the room, bidding Sabine follow him with a grand wave of his hand. Jack could smell the man as he moved: a waft of sweat, and something altogether more animalistic. The dried blood on his chin flaked. And there was something caught between his teeth.

After the woman had passed him by, Ghost's smile

remained but was surrounded by more lines, more creases. Forced.

"Tread lightly today, young Jack," Ghost said. "There are no cages at sea."

Kelly and Vukovich were sitting naked in the mess, carefully wiping their faces and bodies with damp, dirty cloths. They were streaked with blood. Vukovich looked up at Jack and away again, disregarding him without a change in expression. Kelly did not even lift his head. He simply wiped at the drying blood on his neck, left to right, again and again. He seemed almost to be in a trance.

The scent of wet fur was stronger than it had ever been, and Jack almost gagged. Behind him stood the steep staircase that led up to the deck. But the galley was through the mess, and that was where Ghost had told him to go. He thought perhaps he'd pushed his luck enough this morning.

It was a month until the next full moon, and suddenly those four weeks felt so precious. He was certain that in a month's time, he would be on the wrong side of that locked door. It was a countdown toward freedom or defeat, and defeat at the hands of these creatures could mean only one thing.

"Needs cleaning," Vukovich said, the first time Jack had heard him speak. He had a clear, sharp accent, eastern

European or Russian, and he was pointing below the mess table.

Jack nodded and approached, and from the stink he already knew what he was about to face. *Meat, that's all,* he thought. *Just remnants.* Kneeling to look beneath the table, he prayed that there would be nothing recognizable.

"I'll need the bucket and mop," he said, glancing back at Vukovich. The man nodded, then grinned to expose teeth too large for his mouth. Kelly kept cleaning, left to right. At first Jack had thought perhaps he was traumatized by the pain of transformation or the horror of his actions, but from this angle he could see the man's eyes. He seemed almost ecstatic.

Jack went through from the mess into the gangway leading to the galley and, beyond, the cabins. *Is she in there now?* he wondered, looking at Ghost's closed door. But there was no way he could know, and no way to find out. The heavy air in the ship felt like a held breath, the calm following a storm that could so easily erupt again. The best place for him now was where everyone else was not.

He stepped into the galley, knowing what he would see on the wooden surface. After he'd finished salting and storing the meat, he would have to get to work with the scrubbing brush again.

*Only meat,* he thought as he worked, and all morning

he repeated the refrain, mopping slick messes above and below deck, scooping up sodden clothing, throwing bucket after bucket overboard so that there was soon a slick of blood marring the ocean behind them, and sharks broke the surface as they sought the pitiful remnants left behind by the werewolves. *Only meat . . . only meat . . .*

He searched within himself until he found a cold, hollow place in which to hide his horror, and his conscience. Without that cold place, he would surely have broken down. But he could not afford to lose control, not if he wanted to live and to keep Sabine alive as well.

It took most of the morning for the pirates to dress themselves again. Tree lay against a railing on deck until almost midday, naked, his stomach swollen by his meal from the night before. The deck around him was scored with dozens of deep scratches, and his hands were bleeding. Perhaps he had been trying to get to something, or maybe it had been an instinctive action. *Sharpening his claws,* Jack thought. The next time he passed that place, Tree was gone.

Most of the clothes Jack collected from around the ship—scattered, torn, bloodied, and ruined—belonged to the pirates, but not all. There was an expensive jacket, the likes of which he could not imagine any of Ghost's men wearing, a dreadful rip across its back stiff with dried blood. He also found some leather shoes and, tangled in the railing at the ship's stern, two-thirds of a woman's dress. It might once have been white. He entertained the brief, bright hope that she might have jumped overboard and drowned, a much less horrific death than that of her companions. But then he found what the arm of the dress still contained and, holding down his vomit, cast it overboard.

Jack stood at the stern for some time, watching the dress floating in the sea behind them until the swell hid it from view. It would sink into the depths and nobody would ever see it again. Lost to the world, just like its owner.

Louis was steering the ship. Jack passed him on the way belowdecks, then turned back to the pirate, not really sure what he was going to say.

"It's not to be talked about, *mon ami*," Louis said.

"You're monsters."

Louis looked past the bow toward whatever the future might hold.

"All of you," Jack said, his disgust surfacing now, perhaps because he thought Louis might be as close to a friend as he could hope for in this crew, or maybe because he had simply seen too much that day. Even when he closed his eyes, he saw red. "Monsters, beasts. And yet you sail from day to day and—"

"It is not to be talked about," Louis said again, harsher

this time. He glared at Jack, and his eyes were as heartless as those of the other pirates.

Jack went below, all the time keeping at the back of his mind the knowledge that Sabine had imparted to him during their long night together. *Day or night, at will. But they rarely change without reason.* He cooked twice the usual amount of food that day. The last thing he wanted was any of the sailors going hungry.

## CHAPTER SIX

# THE TWO-FACED MAN

Working alone in the galley, cleaning again, Jack started counting the ways in which he could have been more prepared. With a whole night spent alone with Sabine, he should have been quizzing her more about Ghost and the crew, drawing mental maps of their movements, searching for weaknesses, and trying to plan a way to escape this hell ship. Instead, he'd been so overwhelmed by the night's revelations that he had eaten the food and drunk the wine the wolves had left them—as if they were house pets—and fallen asleep, numb with shock.

"I slept," he said, as if vocalizing the truth would make it more acceptable. But it was not. He had found rest while the blood of innocents trickled between deck planks and hardened beneath the moon, and unnatural monsters prowled the darkened ship.

He threw down the heavy wire brush and leaned back against the wall.

"All cleaned away?" Ghost said.

Jack started. It was the first time he'd seen the captain since morning, and it was now past noon. He stood in the doorway, silent as his namesake, yet his presence was as powerful and obvious as ever. Ghost exuded a gravity over all those around him, pulling them into his orbit. Sometimes Jack was drawn by it, but today he was repulsed.

"I've spent the day mopping up blood," Jack said bitterly.

"Meat salted and stored away?"

"Meat." Jack was shaking, anger and terror mingling within him.

Ghost blinked softly as he waited for Jack to continue. *He sees my rage*, Jack thought. *He smells my fear.* So Jack merely looked away and nodded.

"Good enough," Ghost said.

"Where is Sabine?"

"We're heading into a storm," Ghost said, ignoring the question. "Might be a harsh one. But the men will still need feeding."

The captain's jealousy seethed behind a mask of calm, just as the wolf hid behind a human face. "She did nothing wrong," Jack said. "We . . . did nothing. . . ." A coolness settled about his heart. How could he really be asking for understanding from this monster?

Ghost frowned as he examined Jack, then waved a hand as if at a fly.

"So what did you discuss all night?" the captain asked.

"I've been told not to talk about last night."

"By whom?"

"Louis."

Later, Jack would think about that moment before the lunge, before the rage exploded, and whether there had been any signs that he had missed. But no. It was as if Ghost's will was contained deep inside, driving and steering him, and it projected no outward appearance. Perhaps it was afraid of the light.

The captain leaped across the galley, moving from motionless to surging in the blink of an eye. It seemed effortless—he flowed, barely touching the floor, and his hand closed around Jack's throat. Ghost hoisted him up and slammed him against the wall, knocking pans and ladles from their hooks and sending them crashing to the floorboards. Though thin, Jack was wiry and muscled, but the effort Ghost expended did not seem to reach his face. Instead, therein lay a simmering fury.

"This is *my* ship," he snarled, his voice the guttural

grunt of a beast. "Do you understand? I don't give a damn what Louis said. He's a mutt. He belongs to me. And you . . . you *answer* to me. No one else."

Jack could not speak. Ghost's hand closed tighter around his throat, and the pain was excruciating. Black dots speckled his vision, and he struggled to draw breath into his lungs. *I'm going to die*, he thought, but for some reason the idea seemed distant from him, remote. He considered plunging his thumbs into Ghost's eyes, kicking him in the crotch, stabbing stiff fingers at his throat . . . but he knew that none of this would stop the monster. His strength was too great, his brutality too dehumanizing. It could be that he no longer even felt pain at all.

Helpless, Jack hung against the galley wall.

"Do you . . . *understand?*" Ghost said again, leaning in close. Jack managed a tiny gasp of air and instantly regretted it. Ghost's breath smelled of rotten meat and tobacco, and Jack had to force back the urge to vomit. There was nowhere for the stink to go but into his lungs.

Jack nodded, chin pressing against the man's huge hand. Blinked, to communicate understanding.

Ghost let him go, and Jack dropped to the floor, grabbing his throat and trying not to wheeze or gasp as he drew in a breath. He failed, dragging in ragged sips of air as Ghost withdrew to the doorway once again. But he knew, as he felt the captain's glare upon him, that this was not weakness. His pain was exactly what Ghost required: an acknowledgment of his superiority. So Jack gasped *beyond* the receding pain, clutched his chest even after he could breathe again, and did not risk glancing up at Ghost.

"What did you talk about all night in there with my sea witch?"

"The *Weyden*," Jack said. "Your plans to attack it."

"Interesting," Ghost said calmly, as if they were talking philosophy once again. "I thought she'd keep that from you. She'll share responsibility for any blood spilled, after all."

"Will she?" Jack said. "She is yours, like this ship and its crew. Like your pack."

"Like you?"

Jack pulled himself upright, leaning against the counter opposite the doorway. Ghost was three steps away from him and filled his field of vision. He was smiling at Jack as though the attack had never occurred.

"You want to kill me," the captain said. "You hate me. You want to tear me apart for what I do. What I am. The killing. The consuming." He watched Jack carefully. "Keeping her prisoner."

"No," Jack said. "You fascinate me."

Ghost raised one eyebrow, then shrugged. "No matter.

The wild heart of you is set deep, but I can draw it out."

"I'm not an animal. I'm not like you." Jack relished the risk of stating as much.

"Yes, Jack. You are. The beast is there, down inside, just waiting to be set free."

Jack scowled. "You think I'm a wolf-man? The moon was full last night, but I remained who I am. Just Jack London."

Ghost's eyes glinted with merriment and dark purpose. "Bitten by one of us, any man will become the wolf. But most would be nothing but curs, whining in a corner, killed by the pack at the first moon. Some are different. Some are *already* beasts, and wild parts of them howl for freedom."

Ghost left, and for a moment Jack wanted to pursue him, to argue his humanity. But the ship jarred sideways and Jack staggered against the galley counter, almost falling across the hot plate of scorching coals. Pots and cutlery skittered across the floor.

Sailors called out and laughed, and from somewhere more distant he heard a cheerful whistle. *So here comes the storm*, he thought. The *Larsen's* crew sounded almost excited, and for the life of him Jack didn't know what the hell to expect next.

——

Jack London had believed himself something of a sailor. He'd prowled the oyster beds beyond San Francisco Bay, steamed up the western coastlin e of the USA on the *Umatilla*, and built his first boat deep in the wilds of the Yukon. But his first experience of a deep ocean storm blew away all his preconceptions.

For the rest of that day and the following night, the *Larsen* was tossed upon the sea like a cork. It was rocked from side to side, tipped forward and back, and the deck creaked and groaned as it was put under immense pressure. The sea seemed to penetrate the hull and seep between boards, and the air inside the cabin was heavy with damp and stinging with salt. In the early hours of the storm Jack heard the pirates on deck, gathering the sails and preparing the vessel for the punishment it was about to endure. But as the storm progressed, and Jack remained huddled away in his tiny sleeping space at the rear of the galley, the *Larsen* began to feel more and more deserted. Whereas before it had been a ship under control—though the control of monsters, not men—the storm stole that away. Nature's fury denied any pretense of control, and Jack realized that the crew was hiding away as well. It pleased him to know that there was at least one thing the wolves feared.

His stomach rolled in sympathy with the ship. He felt his insides massaged by the storm's fury, pulled this way and that as if grasped in invisible hands. But he retained his composure, did not vomit, and even managed to drift into fitful sleep.

He quickly lost track of time. The storm had been raging for hours—perhaps as much as half a day—when Louis appeared in the galley's doorway. He was soaked to the skin and bleeding from a ragged cut across his forehead.

"Sleeping on the job, Cooky?" Louis asked.

"You're bleeding," Jack said.

"That's because I've been working." A wave struck the ship and tipped it onto its side, forcing it over until the decks felt almost vertical. Louis's fingers clasped the doorframe to prevent himself from falling across the galley, and Jack heard the crinkle of splintering wood, and saw the holes pressed into the frame by the man's nails.

As the ship righted itself with a thunderous boom, Louis nodded at the cold coals.

"Fire it up."

"What? Are you mad? I can't cook anything in this— the coals will scatter and—"

"Well, me and the boys have been working hard, and we're hungry," Louis said. He leaned into the galley, squatting so that he could look directly into Jack's eyes. "Hungry for something warm."

So in the height of the worst storm he had ever

experienced on land or sea, Jack lit the coals and cooked a dry meal of meat and fried potatoes, liberally spiced, and softened with gravy moments before he plated it. Several times he had to pick up spilled coals, fingers protected by a cloth soaked in the brine swilling back and forth along the gangway floor beyond the galley. By the time he'd finished cooking, he was hungry enough to eat something himself. Even though he knew it to be only pork, he stayed away from the meat. After the work he'd done following the slaughter, he wondered if he would ever be able to eat meat again.

Nature raged through the night, and then close to dawn the storm abated, and the silence that fell was haunted.

The ship seemed to be moaning in pain. The sailors swarmed across the deck and up into the rigging, surprisingly quiet as they went about their post-storm activities, and it was Ghost's loud shout that brought Jack up on deck for the first time in more than twenty-four hours.

"Young Jack!" he called from above, voice thundering through the mess and gangways much as the storm's had. "On deck now. Something for you to see."

Jack exited the galley, glancing back at Ghost's closed stateroom door. *Is Sabine still in there?* he wondered, but there was no way he could find out. Not yet. The mess was empty, but in greater disarray than he'd ever seen it, with plates scattered across the floor and remnants of the meal spattered across all surfaces—walls, floor, ceiling, tables, benches. He'd have a busy time with the scrubbing brush later.

On deck, he breathed in deeply, realizing how much he'd missed this fresh air. There was a cool breeze blowing spray across the deck, but the sea was much calmer now, the swell wide and more forgiving. Behind them to the north and east, the sky was dark and angry.

The wolves were busy making sail and repairing damage wrought by the storm. A length of railing had been ripped away, and several lengths of rigging flapped in the breeze, rope ends frayed. One of the small boats—Jack had learned that they were used for boarding other ships, or going ashore, or hunting seals in northern climes— had vanished, smashed from its mooring. Jack caught his breath. One less chance to escape.

Ghost stood at the bow, looking back over his shoulder as he waited for Jack to join him. He was motionless amid this chaos. An island in the storm. Jack went to him, wondering what he would see.

"Did you enjoy the storm?" Ghost asked.

"No," Jack said.

"I did."

"I'm surprised. Confronted by an energy greater than

your own, I thought your ego would take a battering."

"Ego?" Ghost said with obvious surprise. "You truly believe I suffer from that affliction?"

"Perceptive as you are, I'm astonished you don't see it," Jack said. "Except that you're not the one who suffers. That's left to everyone around you."

"Ego is comparative," Ghost said. "I place myself in comparison to no one. I exist for myself and am comfortable with my own thoughts and considerations. That does not give me an ego. It gives me sense and logic. It's only you, Jack, who apply the concerns of society and civility to me."

"Maybe," Jack said. "But if you're so damned immune to anything outside yourself, why do you care what I think of you?"

Ghost leaned on the bow railing and looked down at where the ship sliced through the waves. He seemed contemplative, and for a moment Jack thought that he had reached the captain somehow. Perhaps it was not being ignored that would trouble the man, but being pitied.

"What makes you think I care?" Ghost asked at last, and Jack felt a shiver pass through him. It had nothing to do with the cool breeze, nor the fact that they had survived an incredible storm. But the man before him was cold as ice. At the heart of him must exist a void, the darkest of places, and these conversations were fireflies circling that void, mere distractions that would soon be swallowed by his dense, impenetrable heart.

But could any man truly be so distant? Even a creature like Ghost, who existed balanced somewhere between human and beast?

"You spend a night as a monster, and yet you crave the sort of conversation"—Jack waved a hand behind him at the rest of the ship—"no one else here can give you. You're a man of contradictions."

"I know my own mind."

"As well as you think?"

"Of course. I have my needs, and they are many and varied. The meaning of life is to live, not to exist. Surely you're a young man who will agree with that."

"Yes, but not at the expense of others."

"Others!" Ghost snorted. "I only live the life that most men crave. I'm true to myself, because I know that I am most important. Why live a lie? I'll quote you Hawthorne, and you tell me if this is false: 'No man, for any considerable period, can wear one face to himself, and another to the multitude, without finally getting bewildered as to which may be the true.'"

Jack nodded, wondering how any man, beast or not, could have spent so much time pondering the philosophies of humanity and still remain so inhuman. And even as he wondered, he knew the answer: Ghost worked hard at it. The real question was, why? Why did he want to rid himself of any shred of compassion or empathy? Was it only so that he could live with the horrors he had committed, or was there some deeper purpose?

"You see!" Ghost said. "I'm at peace with who I am, and wear no false mask, however much your precious *civilization* says I should."

"And yet aren't you the ultimate two-faced man?"

"Ah, young Jack," Ghost said, "you're assuming the two faces are dissimilar." He lit his pipe and leaned on the bow rail again, looking forward rather than back. His eyes glittered. He seemed to be focused on something ahead.

Ghost was trying to bend Jack to his philosophy of humanity, to draw out the wild he saw in his young captive. And if Sabine had been correct, he wanted Jack as some kind of mirror, so he could be certain he was everything Jack was not. But if Ghost wanted to draw out the beast in Jack, then Jack thought the opposite might also be possible—some trace of human emotion remained in Ghost.

"I can reach you," Jack said, and Ghost glanced back, perhaps thinking for a moment that his prisoner planned to topple him over the bow. Ghost's slightly startled expression—a quick blink, a falling of his smile—was Jack's greatest victory yet.

"You can continue to try," Ghost said, "but it will have to wait for another day." He took a small telescope from his pocket and extended it, handing it to Jack. "South-southwest."

Jack looked, sweeping the telescope slowly from the south toward the west. He missed it the first time and had to turn back before he saw the faint smudge of smoke on the horizon.

"The *Weyden*," he said.

"Indeed," Ghost said. He stood back from the railing, took a deep breath, and then clapped his hands. "Fresh sport. A good day for it!" He turned and shouted down the length of the *Larsen*, and Jack had no doubt that every crewman heard his voice. "Barely hours away, lads! Make haste."

Jack's heart fell. *Barely hours.*

"Fortuitous that the storm should pass before you found your quarry," Jack said.

"We might've been lost in that storm, but she guided us through," Ghost said, enjoying talking about Sabine. "Stayed in my cabin the whole time, reading the charts, scrying the wind and waves. Kept her starved, because that way she sees clearer. She's quite hungry."

He watched Jack for any reaction, but Jack bit down his anger. Now was not the time.

"I'd best get below," Jack said.

"Aye, young Jack," Ghost said. As Jack walked away, he heard the captain's soft chuckle behind him, and it sounded like claws on wood.


He could set fire to the *Larsen*. It would be easy enough. Spread the cooking coals, encourage the flames with some of the fat stored in the galley. It would send a signal to the *Weyden*. It would cost him his life and possibly Sabine's— either burning or drowning, or at Ghost's hands—but if he could save the hundred or more lives on board the other ship, it would be a worthy sacrifice. But as soon as the idea presented itself, he rejected it. The flames would draw the other ship in, not drive it away. The code of the sea and basic decency would bring the captain of the *Weyden* to the aid of the burning *Larsen*. Ghost's wolves would abandon their sinking vessel and take over the other. His sacrifice would be wasted.

He could steal one of the remaining skiffs, try to sail on ahead of the *Larsen* to warn the others. But that was foolishness, and he knew it. There was no way he could lower the boat overboard without being noticed, and it would be difficult to sail it on his own even if he did. They'd be down on him, and though he'd fight, they'd tear him apart in moments.

Some other signal, then. Some way to warn the *Weyden* that they were about to be attacked. He remembered seeing the *Larsen* appearing from the fog and slipping alongside the *Umatilla*, but this attack would be different, because it would be in broad daylight. And Sabine had said that they could change themselves at will. With such a brazen assault, would they need the added speed and savagery of their monstrous forms? Jack thought they might.

As he worked in the galley, agonizing about how he could warn the innocents aboard the *Weyden* about what was to come, he breathed in and caught her scent.

"You've led them to another day of murder," he said softly.

"I have no choice." Her voice was weak, wretched, and Jack turned around in surprise. Sabine stood in the galley doorway, her skin incredibly pale and her sunken eyes dark with exhaustion. She looked drawn and sick. She clung to the doorframe, so sad that his heart broke for her and belonged to her completely. Her malady was far more than physical.

"There's always a choice," Jack said.

"There are over a hundred people on that ship," Sabine said. "Most, if not all, will die today. But if I refuse Ghost's demands, then he will kill me."

"Then it would be a brave sacrifice," Jack said, though his heart cringed at the thought of Ghost harming this beautiful, damaged creature.

She stared at him for some time, and he could sense the turmoil roiling within her. When she spoke at last, he knew that he would remember her words forever.

"Jack, you have become so dear to me, so quickly," she said, the confession spilling out of her, her eyes full of anguish and honesty. "And it pains me deeply to know how you must see me. Two nights ago you asked me if I loved *him*—"

Jack did not have to ask who she meant. Revulsion flickered across her face.

"Merely to have a man of decency think such a thing of me—especially one in whom I feel such instinctive trust, such . . . intimacy—I can't endure it. No living soul knows my secrets, but something within me cries out to share them with you, Jack. I feel such guilt for your being here. I saw that night that you are a man of honor, and I know now that you deserve the truth."

Jack nodded for her to go on, hope rising in him. If she could be honest with him, believe in him, their chances of survival would grow.

She took a deep breath before continuing. "Whoever kills me will breathe in my magic," she said. "Imagine

*Ghost* with my power, able to find anyone or anything he desires, whenever he likes. And now understand that he has *no idea* of the true extent of my abilities. That I have more powers than he can imagine, and they would be his as well. Think on that, Jack."

"The lesser of two evils," Jack said. "The lives that he takes now are only a fraction of those who would suffer."

"Yes. I have considered suicide, but even then . . ." She shrugged. "I do not know if someone on board would inherit my gifts."

"It's eating you. Consuming you." The dreadful weight of her predicament settled upon him. How had she lived with it?

"My secret is yours, now," Sabine whispered.

Jack pulled her close, ignoring her cry of surprise. She was cool and fragile, and beneath her dress her body felt slight, as if eroding before the sea breeze. He could feel her spine and trace the curves of her ribs. But beauty still resided in her eyes, and Jack pressed his lips to hers, hoping to communicate everything in that kiss—his resolve and strength, his understanding of the wild within himself and determination to restrain it, control it. She kissed him back, and when he pulled away, he thought, *I love you.* But when he spoke, there was something more important to say.

"We're going to save each other."

"How sweet," a voice said. Finn sauntered across the mess, Tree behind him. They seemed to block out the light and fill the space with darkness. "The captain will *love* this."

"Aren't you getting ready to kill?" Jack asked bitterly.

"Always ready for that, Cooky. *Always.* Now come with us. Ghost wants you locked away during the festivities."

In spite of everything, Jack felt a moment of delight at the idea of being shut up with Sabine once again.

Finn's grin stretched his mouth, reddening scars across his face. "Only you, boy," he said. "Ghost needs the lady on deck."

Sabine pulled him close, her lips pressed to his ear, but it was not a kiss she gave him. It was yet another secret.

"I know what to do," she whispered.

Then she parted from him and slipped away. She squeezed Jack's hand as she left, one simple gesture that communicated so much. *We're going to save each other,* he'd told her. And now he knew that she believed that as well. No matter what Ghost might feel for her, the only emotion she had toward him was fear.

Finn came for Jack, manhandling him across the mess, shoving him into the side of the steep staircase, and Jack took the pain and bit back any thought of retribution.

Perhaps he might have given Finn a fight, but not with Tree behind him, immovable and unstoppable. Better to let them believe they had him where they wanted him. But Jack made a vow there and then, as they tumbled him into the small, stinking hold where they'd kept the prisoners from the *Umatilla*: their time would come.

He heard bolts being thrown and padlocks clasped, and he thought of the room he and Sabine had been in that night. That had the most important locks on the inside, meant to keep the wolves out more than captives in. Where he was now was a true prison.

He paced the hold, thinking of those who had been in here so recently. Their scents still hung in the air. It was the smell of desperation. He wondered why Ghost wanted Sabine with him now, how the attack would unfold, and what the results would be. Over a hundred people on that ship, Sabine had said. Soon this room would be full once again.

At last Jack sat down, heart heavy with the knowledge that there was nothing he could do. Fate had brought these two ships together—fate, and Sabine's unnatural skills— and all that was left was for their encounter to play out.

It was several hours until they drew close to the other ship, and then there was shouting, and the thump of hulls nudging against each other. Following that, a strange kind of calm for a while—casual footsteps on the deck above him, the *hush* of the sea forced between hulls, and once or twice Jack was sure he heard laughter. Down in the dark hold, he stood in silence and tried to imagine what might be happening. He knew that the quiet was misleading.

The first time he heard the sound, he wasn't sure it was gunfire. He caught his breath and pressed his ear to the door, feeling the cool draft where door met the uneven frame. Then it came again, and again. *Crack . . . crack crack!* He'd heard enough shooting in his life to recognize the sound, and now he knew for sure that the attack was on.

*Where's Sabine, where's Ghost, what is he having her do, is he keeping her safe?* These ideas tumbled, stirred by confusion and concern. He paced the room, then started slamming into the door. It rattled in its frame but held fast. He kicked at where he knew the bolts to be, but though the wood creaked, they were firm. He knew that the room was built to keep people in, sometimes for many days, but there was little else for him to do.

"Damn you!" he screamed, frustration getting the better of him. Shouting would achieve nothing. "Damn you, Ghost!"

More gunshots, some screaming, and then a low, deep boom that vibrated all through the ship and seemed to knock the breath from his lungs. He staggered against the wall and felt the echo of the noise passing away through the wood.

With a crash, one of the doors leading into the hold gangway was thrown open. *Here they come*, Jack thought, and he pressed himself against the wall beside the door.

A terrible idea settled in him then, and it took his breath away that he had not considered it before: prisoners from the *Weyden* would be thrown inside, and he would be left with them, able to tell them everything that was to come, but powerless to resist . . . because what if Ghost had tired of him already?

Panic gripped him, more from the idea that he might never see Sabine again than from anything else. Preparing to fight and run, he listened for voices outside but heard only two sets of footsteps.

The door opened and a huge arm swung in, grabbing Jack around the throat and pulling him out. It was Ogre. He flung Jack along the gangway without even looking at him, casting him away like a bag of flour. Kelly was there to catch him.

"Fun's almost over, Cooky," Kelly said. "Captain says you can come out now."

Jack blinked in confusion, and then the truth struck him hard. The full moon had just passed. They took prisoners so that they had something to feed upon when the moon forced them to change, when they were so bestial that they could not think clearly and might end up killing one another if they didn't have humans to slaughter. But with nearly a month to go before the next full moon, if they took prisoners now, there would be screaming and crying for an entire month, and those unfortunates would need feeding and watering.

Which meant there would be no survivors from the *Weyden* today.

Jack felt sick. He wanted to kill Ghost there and then. Kelly smiled at him. Ogre saw the look of fury and hatred in Jack's eyes and backhanded him. Blood sprayed from Jack's nose and he crashed against the wall again, hauling himself upright only a foot from Kelly. There was a knife in the pirate's belt. If he was quick, if he moved silently, and if he didn't hesitate for one instant, maybe—

"Don't be stupid," Kelly said. "You think you're faster than me?"

The pirate glanced sidelong at Jack, and there was blood streaking the man's shoulder and chest. His shirt was holed, and he held his arm awkwardly. Jack thought it almost certain that Kelly had been shot.

"I hope it hurt," Jack said, stepping out into the gangway.

"What's pain?" Kelly asked. Then he slammed the door closed and fixed the padlocks again, and he and Ogre walked away without sparing Jack another glance.

Jack fled in the other direction, back toward the mess and galley. He plucked up a knife and tucked it into his belt. He paused for a moment, breathing deeply and gathering his thoughts. There were priorities here, and he had to ensure he kept them straight in his head. Otherwise—

Another boom pounded through the ship, carried on the air and conducted through the *Larsen*'s structure, and Jack's ears ached with its aftermath. He ran back through the mess and up the steep staircase onto the deck, making sure his loose shirt covered the knife's handle.

Sunlight struck him, unexpectedly bright and warm, and he took a moment to absorb what was happening.

The ship was not as large as the *Umatilla*, but its deck rail was still several feet higher than the *Larsen*'s. Smoke billowed from its stern, and he could see that the vessel sat low in the water. One of the twins—he could not tell if it was Huginn or Muninn—appeared for a moment, tilted back his head to scent the air, and then slipped toward a doorway and vanished within. A huge wolf shape dashed across the deck, and more gunfire erupted from somewhere out of sight. Jack ducked down and heard laughter from behind him.

"Scared of catching lead, Cooky?" It was Louis, standing close to the *Larsen*'s locked wheel with a rifle in his hands.

Jack didn't answer. Instead, he walked along the deck toward the forecastle, keeping to starboard, away from where the ship was tied portside to the *Weyden*. He passed the place where the skiff had been ripped away by the storm. On the deck stood a collection of trunks, baggage, and leather bags, one of them ruptured and spilling jewelry and coins. Tree hoisted one of the trunks and went into the forecastle, headed for the hold, and Jack realized that the food store down below must also hold the riches the pirates had stolen from the *Umatilla* and other vessels. Treasure, every piece stained with the blood of its original owners.

Ogre and Kelly emerged from the forecastle—they must have passed Tree—and Jack thought they would carry more of the looted valuables below. Instead, they clambered up ropes to the *Weyden*'s deck, neither of them sparing a glance for Jack. For such a monstrous mass, Ogre climbed with an unexpected grace, dropping onto the slightly higher deck in a crouch. Kelly stood beside him, scratching at his gunshot wound as if it were an insect bite. He clapped Ogre on the shoulder, and they disappeared through a door into the other ship's superstructure.

There was no sign of Sabine or Ghost, and the *Larsen* felt deserted. Everything was happening on the steamship alongside it. Glancing back toward Louis, Jack moved to the railing and waited for the wolf to call him back. But Louis simply stared, rifle resting across his arms. *They don't consider me a threat at all*, Jack thought, and he stored that knowledge away.

He'd show them. In time, he'd show them their mistake.

"Nothing you can do," Louis said. "It's already sinking. Ghost has scuttled it."

Jack moved to the ropes Ogre and Kelly had just climbed, feeling the impact as the hulls scraped together and the heat emanating from the steamer's stern, where the two thudding explosions had originated, hating every moment of his helplessness, wishing for some miracle that would allow him to save even one life.

Gunshots erupted nearby, and he turned left just in time to see the two shapes leaping from the *Weyden* to the *Larsen*. They timed the leap well, moving just as the decks were almost level, and they were shooting again as they landed. Louis stumbled back from the wheel, dark patches stitched across his chest and neck. As he went down, Jack heard the two men hissing to each other, and one of them turned around to look along the deck.

As he saw Jack and raised his revolver, his head snapped forward and he fell. The gun skittered into the sea, and beyond him Jack saw Louis standing with one hand clasping the rail, the other aiming his rifle. His chest and stomach were wet with blood.

The other man turned and ran. He almost tripped over his dead companion, jumping just at the last moment, and his eyes were open in terror.

*He's seen what they really look like,* Jack thought. *Seen the beast.* And the man raised his gun, aiming at Jack's heart.

"Louis!" Jack shouted, wondering how it had come to this, with him staring down the barrel of a revolver and asking a werewolf to save his life. The man would die one way or another, of that he was certain. But Jack had no wish to go with him. Not with Sabine still in this hell ship's grasp. Sweet, tortured Sabine.

But Louis could not help. Dead or not, he had fallen to the deck and lay still, blood pooling on the planks around him.

Jack threw himself aside, rolling across the deck, sliding beneath one of the secured skiffs. The man from the steamship fired, but the shot went wide.

A shape leaped from the *Weyden* and knocked the man aside. He flew into the mainmast, his head connecting with a terrible *thunk*, and then Johansen picked him up and swung him, bashing him against the mast again and again. Jack would never forget the sound that man's body made striking solid wood. He hoped death came quickly.

Another shape dropped down from the *Weyden*. It was Finn. He moved silently, crouched low as he watched Johansen battering the man to death. He glanced right at Louis, who lay still, blood running in rivulets across the deck. Then Finn looked left, and from his hiding place, Jack saw the sailor's eyes. There was murder in them, but murder of a different kind. This was not bloodlust; this was revenge.

*He didn't see me*, Jack thought. The sea roared, hulls bumped and grated, Johansen swung the man against the mast one more time, and another voice screamed somewhere on the steamship. But right then Jack was sure that the loudest noise was his heart.

From beneath the skiff he watched Finn take five quick, silent steps across the deck to Johansen. Just as the first mate dropped the leaking bag of broken bones and ruptured flesh that had once been a man, Finn threw his arm around Johansen's face, pulled his head back, and slit his throat with a knife that glinted silver in the sunlight.

Johansen struggled and thrashed, and Finn slashed again and again. Then he started stabbing the silver blade into the first mate's heart.

Jack closed his eyes, but he could not shut his ears against the terrible sound. There was hissing and gurgling, and then grunting as Finn dragged the bleeding man across the deck. He heaved Johansen over the rail, and the first mate hung on for a few moments. Jack saw him staring up into his murderer's eyes, and then Finn sliced his knife across the rail's upper surface and Johansen's fingers, and he fell between the ships.

The *Weyden* rose, the *Larsen* fell, and hulls ground together as the vessels danced close.

Finn glanced around again, guilt and delight drawing his grin, and there was something else about him . . . something terrible. His face began to distort, his jaw widening and his nose lengthening. His hands turned to claws, teeth growing thick and long, and there was a sheen of fine brown hair sprouting across his face, following the contours of his ugliness. He still stood upright, but his legs changed shape, forcing him to hunch down. He laughed, and it sounded more like an animal than a man.

*Blooded*, Jack thought, and actually seeing what these things might be brought the true terror home.

Finn froze in place, sniffing at the salt air, alert and searching, and Jack realized that the monster had somehow sensed his presence. Was it his scent, or had he made some noise? Jack didn't know—perhaps Finn simply smelled his fear, which grew as he watched the way the monster's head twitched. A low growl issued from Finn's throat.

*No*, Jack thought. If Finn saw him, he would not escape. But there were ways for him to remain unseen. In the frozen north he had learned a subtle sort of magic from the forest spirit Lesya. Now he had to put that knowledge to use. He closed his eyes tightly, clearing his thoughts and exhaling as he reached out with his own spirit. When he sensed the voracious beast at the core of the werewolf, it was all he could do not to recoil. Instead, he touched Finn's essence, bared his own teeth, and let himself feel the bloodlust and the violence that boiled inside the monster. Finn's heart beat wildly, and Jack matched his own pulse to that rhythm, felt the growl building in his own chest.

If Finn sensed anything now, it would be another wolf, another monster, but Jack hoped he would sense only his own wildness. He had merged his presence with Finn's, become a mirror of the beast.

Finn breathed deeply, grunting decisively as his concern abated. He was convinced his crime had no witness.

Someone shouted, and it was a voice of authority. Ghost. Finn darted away, snuffling heavily as he flitted past the small boat and disappeared forward. Jack exhaled, shaking with revulsion as he let the persona of the wolf wash from him. He was grateful for the gift Lesya had given him, that small talent she had taught him, but also disgusted. It might have saved his life, but the idea that he could so easily match his spirit with that of a monster disturbed him deeply.

His heart still racing, he pushed himself out from his hiding place just in time to see Finn leaping ten feet across and up onto the *Weyden's* stern deck. Smoke and flames rose there, and the larger vessel was canted at an unnatural angle away from the *Larsen*.

"Back to the *Larsen*!" Ghost's voice called. "Hole the lifeboats, and leave the rest to their fate."

Finn had returned to the sinking ship just in time to be ordered back to his own—so that no one would ever know he had been apart from the boarding party.

Jack stood and ran to the stern, where Louis was slowly hauling himself upright by the steering wheel. He had been shot at least four times, and his gold tooth glittered in his grimace.

Behind Jack, there were thuds as the pirates started leaping back onto their ship. He closed his eyes, thinking about what he had seen. And dwelling also on how he might turn knowledge of such brutal murder to his advantage.

## CHAPTER SEVEN

# FIRST MATE

Just as he was about to go below, Jack saw Sabine at the aft railing, watching the *Weyden* slide into the sea, a plume of smoke rising from the stricken steamship. Demetrius was at the wheel, but the keg-bellied pirate barely glanced at either of them as Jack approached. With the wind gusting and clouds gathering overhead, there was a stillness to the sea in the aftermath of the wolves' violence, and for a moment Jack could imagine that he and Sabine were alone.

Watching Sabine, he could feel the weight of her guilt, even worse than his own. As the steamship's bow slipped beneath the waves—sea boiling with bubbles and steam— there were people still dying on board. With each step he took, and each breath she took, innocents were drowning or burning, being crushed or suffocated. Jack wanted to scream, to storm across the deck and tear the *Larsen* down around him. They should all be dying now. They deserved nothing less.

Instead, he reached for Sabine, his fingers resting lightly on her arm. They could comfort each other, at least.

She turned to look at him, pain glistening in her eyes, but then her gaze shifted and Jack saw the ice forming inside her. And he knew the only thing that could freeze her heart.

"Where the hell is Johansen?" Ghost roared.

Jack spun and saw the captain gripping Demetrius by the throat, the fat man's feet dangling beneath him, the captain strong enough to hold him aloft despite his weight. Other sailors had gathered round. Maurilio looked down from the crow's nest. Vukovich and Tree had ceased their work with the lines. Finn hung in the rigging, paused halfway up to where the halyards had become tangled.

*How could I have felt we were alone?* Jack thought. *We're in the lair of killers.*

"Damn your eyes, all of you!" Ghost raged, hurling Demetrius aside. "How could this happen? Is he back there now, dying with the cattle?"

Nobody spoke. No one dared.

"I have prowled every godforsaken corner of this ship, and Johansen is not on board!" Ghost continued, turning round and round, glaring at his crew. He looked up at the crow's nest and shouted. "What of you, Maurilio? If you're so blind, perhaps you don't need your eyes, and I ought to have them fried with my bacon in the morning?"

But Maurilio said nothing. Jack thought he must have been a part of the assault on the *Weyden*, not even in the crow's nest at the time of Johansen's murder. But did any of them know what Finn had done? He thought not. And Finn was as silent as the others.

Ghost fumed, his chest spattered with blood he had spilled during the attack. He glanced around in frustration, nostrils flaring, trying to catch a scent—Johansen's? A killer's? A liar's? But Jack knew it was useless. Johansen's corpse had been dropped overboard, and they were all killers, all liars.

"Damn it!" the captain snapped. With a snarl he gestured to the crew to return to work. "Sail on, you dogs."

Demetrius looked at Ghost warily and then retook the wheel. The captain glared at him, then at the others, and finally his gaze came to rest on Jack and Sabine.

"Mr. London!" Ghost snapped.

Jack frowned. *Not "young Jack"?*

Summoned, Jack gave a quiet nod to Sabine and crossed the deck to where the captain stood.

"Louis and Kelly are laid out below. Both have some

lead in them. It won't kill 'em, but they could use some help digging it out. I nominate you ship's doctor, at least for the moment. Go and take care of it."

His tone brooked no argument, but that was all right with Jack. With the ferocity of his rage, and the uncertainty of the violence that seemed to simmer beneath every moment on the ship now, he would be better off below. And yet . . .

"Glad to be of service," Jack said, loud enough for others to hear. But then he narrowed his eyes and, quieter, said, "We need to talk about Johansen."

Ghost seemed almost to grow larger, filling his lungs with a breath of rage, so that Jack thought he would erupt again. But that dark intelligence glittered in his eyes, and the captain nodded once, grabbed his arm, and gave him a shove that sent him stumbling forward.

"Get to it."

As Jack dug the bullet out of Kelly's chest, the wounded pirate mocked him, calling him Ghost's dog, the captain's pet. Kelly grunted in pain several times, his fingers hooking into claws and fur sprouting from his hands and arms. Jack knew he ought to be offended by the insults and afraid of the transformation that threatened any moment, but he could not find either emotion within himself. He had gone

*The bullet clinked into the pan Jack had set aside.*

cold inside. Numbness spread through him, the only way for him to combat the guilt of knowing that he still lived while so many had died.

He had believed himself in hell before, but that had been purely metaphor. Now he had been made to salt and cure human flesh, to be a servant of monsters, and to be a spectator of mass murder. And the beast in him raged for justice.

And yet . . .

If it had been only his own life, he would gladly have given it. But there was Sabine to think of. He would not put her at risk, particularly after the secret she had shared. He shuddered to think how many thousands more might die if Ghost had the witch's gifts in his own hands, his own *blood*. And she had hinted at other, greater powers, abilities of which Ghost was as yet unaware.

Filled with hatred and righteous fury, he nevertheless had to keep his emotions in check long enough to find a way for both of them to escape the *Larsen*. And that meant navigating the tension on board carefully.

The bullet clinked into the pan Jack had set aside. He held a clean cloth against the wound and reached for bandages, but Kelly slapped his hand away.

"You've done your work, Cooky. My kind don't need bandages."

Jack glanced at the wound and saw that, with the bullet removed, it had already begun to heal over. Kelly stood stiffly, grimacing, but forcing a smile as he went into the short corridor and up the steps to the deck.

"You still alive in there?" Jack called into the galley, where Louis was laid out on the floor.

"I would not mind dying so much," Louis replied, his voice a rasp coming as if from nowhere at all. "But, yes. I live."

He'd attempted to excavate the bullets from his own torso and failed. Now he waited in pain and frustration, though he had insisted Jack work on Kelly first because he didn't want to listen to the other pirate grumble about his one bullet wound to Louis's four. Jack had been more than happy to get Kelly out of there.

Jack picked up the tools he'd been using on Kelly— tongs and a sharp, thin knife—and the pan with the bloody bullet rattling inside, and started out of the mess and into the galley to work on Louis. The steps leading up to the deck creaked, and he glanced up to see the massive shadow of the captain descending, silhouetted against the daylight. For a moment Jack expected him to emerge from his own shadow wearing the face of the beast, but as he reached the last step and no longer blocked out the sunlight, it became clear he had not changed. This wolf still wore the face of a man.

"Young Jack," Ghost said. "If you know something, speak now."

"I said as much, didn't I?" Jack said defiantly. "You want to know where your first mate has gone? Over the side. He's been murdered, stabbed to death with a silver blade during your assault on the *Weyden*, and dumped into the ocean."

Ghost scowled. "You saw this with your own eyes?"

"I did."

"Absurd. Why would anyone aboard the *Weyden* have such a blade? They'd have to have known we were coming, and what we were, even before they set sail."

Jack blinked in surprise. "You really can't imagine it, can you? It wasn't one of them, Ghost. It was one of *you*."

In the next room, Louis would be listening, but Jack did not glance toward the galley, unwilling to give away the presence of the wounded sailor. He wondered if Ghost would catch his scent but thought that in the midst of the food smells of the galley, Louis and his blood would be lost.

Ghost frowned deeply, working it over in his mind. Then a dark light glinted in his eyes.

"Finn," he growled.

"You knew?" Jack asked.

Ghost shook his head. "No. But he's at the bottom of the pack now, and a desperate fool." He peered at Jack through doubtful, slitted eyes. "Why tell me? Maybe Finn means to murder me next. Wouldn't that suit you?"

"Not if it means Finn becomes captain," Jack said. "Whatever reason you have for keeping me alive, he doesn't share it. With Finn at the head of the pack, it'd be me salted and stored away for the crew's supper."

The smile that lifted the corners of Ghost's lips was the cruelest Jack had ever seen.

"On deck, Mr. London," Ghost said. "With me."

He went up the steps. Jack glanced toward the galley, knowing that Louis must still be listening but unwilling to give him away. If the pirate's wounds had pained him so much that he could not wait a few minutes, he would have called out then. But Louis remained silent, either fearful of the captain . . . or dead.

Jack followed Ghost up onto the deck.

Maurilio remained in the crow's nest and Louis in the galley, but the rest of the crew gathered on deck at the captain's summons. Ghost had no weapon other than his massive hands and the beast inside him, though Huginn and Muninn stood nearby, apart from the others but watching them warily, fiercely protective of their captain.

They were thinner than Ghost, lacking his raw power, but Jack felt sure they were equally deadly.

Not that Ghost needed them. This was his pack. His ship. His crew.

"Finn," the captain said, the word full of grim threat.

They all looked at Finn, edging away from him. The pirate tried to hide his alarm with a nervous smile. He had been keelhauled already, driven to the bottom of the pack, where he would have to bare his throat in supplication not only to Ghost but to even the lowliest among them. Jack knew that they all expected Finn to be gutted, there on the deck. Their excitement was palpable.

Jack hung back, partially hidden by the mainsail's boom, and watched as Ghost strode up to Finn and stood eye to eye. Hatred and terror warred in Finn's eyes, but Ghost fixed the sailor in his gaze without expression, impassive as a cobra waiting to strike.

"Go on," Ghost said, barely a whisper but audible for all to hear. "Let's see it."

Finn raised his chin, attempting to stand firm under his master's glare. "What's that, Captain?"

"Your knife, Finn. The silver blade you've got on board *my ship.*"

Several of the others began to growl, a low rumble in their chests. Vukovich smiled, eyes bright in anticipation of the bloodshed to come. The pirates began to breathe more deeply and to cast hungry glances at Finn.

The fear in Finn's eyes made any real denial impossible. But he tried.

"Don't know what you mean, Captain."

Ghost tapped Finn's chest with a finger, hard enough to knock him back half a step. "The knife you used to kill Johansen. The knife you used to murder the first mate, because you're too much of a coward to challenge him openly."

"Bastard," Demetrius grunted.

"Captain, I swear—," Finn began.

"You were seen, you fool," Ghost said, his tone full of grim certainty. Jack feared Ghost would glance over and give him away, but the captain kept his gaze locked on Finn.

The mystified expression vanished from Finn's face. He glared back, falling silent.

Ghost glanced at Huginn and Muninn. "Search the forecastle."

The rest of the crew waited. The ship creaked and the ropes swayed, the wind filled the sails, and they knifed through the water. On the southern horizon a fogbank churned as if beckoning them to lose themselves in its white folds. Within a handful of minutes the twins returned. The one Jack thought was Huginn—his eyes a paler, icier blue than his brother's—handed the silver blade to Ghost.

The captain grinned, his canines sharp and glistening in the sun. The pack watched the blade, its silver evidently just as poisonous to their kind as the legends claimed. Jack wished he could get his hands on that blade and secrete it away for the moment he would need it most. But Ghost flung it overboard, and it vanished into the sea.

The crew seemed to exhale, but only for an instant. Then they began to move closer to Finn.

"Go on, then," Finn said.

Ghost shook his head. "Oh, no. I won't make it that easy for you, boy." He leaned toward Finn and bared his throat. "Come for me."

Finn blinked. "What?"

Ghost sneered at him. "You want to climb the ranks of this pack, you'll do it properly. Challenge me. Why slink in shadows or kill in secret? You want to kill me, then kill me. If you've got the guts for it, Finn, then try me."

"Captain," Tree said, his voice so deep, Jack could feel it in the deck planks. So he could speak, after all. "This isn't how it's done."

Ghost ignored him, staring at Finn, who dropped his gaze in shame. He did not have the courage to attack the captain directly. Ghost had called him a coward, and the truth crushed him where he stood.

"Kill him," Vukovich muttered.

"Take his throat, Captain," Kelly said, bloodthirsty as ever.

Even Ogre had begun to look at the captain strangely. Jack saw it happening, the wave of discontent among them. This was not how the pack worked. It was clear they expected immediate punishment. Already down a man thanks to Johansen's murder, nevertheless they wanted Finn dead.

"Captain——," Finn began.

Ghost slapped him across the face so hard that Finn went to his knees on the deck. He stood over Finn, waiting for him to try to rise, but instead the sailor curled into a fetal ball and began to whimper and cringe like a whipped dog, utterly humiliated.

"You'll have to try me eventually," Ghost told him. "Either that, or you have to live with your cowardice eating away at you, gnawing at your guts until it drives you mad. I look forward to the day."

He began to walk away, leaving the sniveling Finn on the deck, but then Ghost paused and glanced around at his pack. Their faces betrayed their disapproval, but none of them dared challenge him.

"I'll need a new first mate," Ghost said, glancing at

Huginn and Muninn, the two he trusted most of all. Then he turned to Jack. "It'll be you, Mr. London."

"What?" Jack said, feeling the pack's hateful, violent eyes upon him. "You can't—"

"You'd put a man—and barely a man at that—above the rest of us?" Kelly asked.

Ghost arched an eyebrow. "Are you about to tell your captain what he can and cannot do?" he asked, turning from Kelly to Jack. "Either of you?"

Jack hesitated. He was not one of them, not a part of the pack. His presence as a member of the crew had only ever been some strange capricious whim of Ghost's, his death a matter of Ghost growing uninterested in their philosophical dialogue. The pack would never accept him. Already they were exchanging glances, and he saw the bitter, resentful, almost mutinous way they were looking at their captain.

And Jack thought . . . *I can use this. If it doesn't cost me my life first.*

"No, sir. Of course not," he said.

"No, Captain," Kelly added.

"Excellent," Ghost said, grinning. "Demetrius has our new course heading, Mr. London. See to it. And then finish your doctoring. I notice Louis never joined us on deck. He'll be needed before long."

"Yes, sir," Jack agreed.

Ghost returned to his cabin, leaving his new first mate to discuss their heading with fat Demetrius, even as the rest of the crew prowled the deck, eyeing him carefully and planning for the moment of his death.

Jack knelt in the galley's gloomy light and dug the bullets out of Louis one by one, letting them clink into the blood-dappled pan. The black man grimaced with each twist of the tongs, and his gold tooth gleamed as the others grew longer and sharper. Something changed in his eyes, too, when he was in pain, and patches of fur sprouted on his dark flesh.

"Talk to me, Jack," Louis said, his voice a snarl. "Best you distract me, 'fore I forget we are friends and let the pain make me do something we'll both regret."

So Jack told him everything that had unfolded up on deck with Finn and his knife and the decisions Ghost had made.

"You're joking with me, Jack," Louis said. "Just be glad I have a sense of humor."

Jack had to probe deeper for the last bullet, widening the wound so he could get to it. He thought Louis might claw at him then, but though the werewolf's eyes changed color and grew larger, he only groaned and clenched his claws into fists.

"It's no joke," Jack replied.

Taking deep breaths to calm himself, flesh returning to normal as the last of his wounds began to heal, Louis looked at him worriedly.

"No, I don't suppose the crew finds it funny one bit," Louis said. He shook his head in bewilderment, eyes searching the shadowed corners for some way to make sense of what he'd been told. "This bodes ill for us all."

Jack glanced at the entrance to the galley, listening for the telltale creak that would give away the footfalls of anyone who might be eavesdropping. Then he turned back to Louis, wondering if this man, this beast, might not be his enemy.

"Their faith in him is shaken," Jack said. "I saw it. Hell, I *felt* it."

"Ghost is toying with Finn," Louis said. "He will never let him leave this ship alive. Finn knows it, and he will have to try to kill Ghost eventually. Surprise is his only chance, and a very thin one. Ghost will tear him apart. But Finn killed Johansen, and the punishment for that is clear. I have only been a *loup-garou*, a wolf, for three years, but the laws of the pack are taught to us in our first days. We kill each other, but face-to-face. A challenge is followed by combat, and the winner takes his place in the ranks above the loser. And if the loser should be killed, there is no retribution. It is the law."

"But murder . . . ," Jack said, letting the word hang there between them, echoing with the clanging of pans and ladles swinging on their hooks.

Louis nodded. "Murder is different. The punishment is swift death. Ghost is playing a game with Finn, but the pack will see it as weakness. Might even wonder if he is getting soft."

"Is he?" Jack asked.

The question troubled Louis—Jack could see it in his eyes—and it was precisely the reaction he had hoped for. The pack had begun to doubt Ghost. His savagery was expected, but they would obey only him as long as they respected his authority, and that had begun to deteriorate. Jack had seen it. Now he needed to push it a little further.

"He has been different since you came on board," Louis admitted, nodding thoughtfully. "We wondered at first why he kept you apart . . . kept you alive. The others have all seen it before, most recently with me."

"Seen what?" Jack asked.

Louis frowned, a twinkle of amusement in his eyes. "You don't understand? Truly? Smart as you are, I am amazed."

Irritated, forgetting that he talked with a monster, Jack leaned back and threw up his hands. "Are you going to spell it out for me or make me guess?"

Louis raised his chin, ears pricking up like a dog's, and Jack froze, waiting to see if he had pushed the pirate too far. But Louis only gave an admonishing shake of his head.

"He's grooming you. Just as he did me. Just as he did all the others, in their time. Making you first mate is an insult to all of us. Ghost has spit in our faces. I like you, Jack. But Ghost has marked you for death. The rest of the crew will want you dead, not only because of the insult but because of what it means for you to be first mate."

Jack felt the ice in his gut spreading out to engulf the rest of him. "Grooming me. You mean—"

"I mean he intends to turn you. He'll make you a wolf. And then you won't be an insult or a joke. You'll be a member of the pack, second only to Ghost himself because you're first mate."

"Never," Jack said, bile rising in the back of his throat. "I'll die first."

"Aye," Louis said, climbing to his feet, hands across the healing wounds on his chest. "That would be best for you. But if you want to live, consider this: you've got a much better chance of staying alive when they come for you if you're one of us."

Jack pushed his fingers through his hair, shaking his

head, staring at Louis. "But you just said they hate Ghost now. They don't trust him anymore. Won't they go for him?"

"They might, if they weren't so afraid of him. He's the worst of us, the most formidable. Finn tried his betrayal in secret because he didn't dare try to sway others to his side. Ghost made us, and he keeps us rich and well fed, but there is always some measure of discontent. It's the nature of the wolf to want to move up in the pack. If Finn had tried to enlist others, it's likely they'd have told the captain in order to curry favor. We trust each other with our lives, and yet not at all; for at any time, one might go for another's throat, just to climb a little higher and have a larger share of the spoils.

"Mark this, Jack: I'll speak for you, if the opportunity arises. But if it comes to it, I won't fight for you. I won't die for you." He grinned. "I don't like you *that* much."

Limping slightly, Louis made his way out of the galley, leaving Jack alone in the gloom with the clanging pots and a bloodstained floor. Jack leaned against the wall, mind awhirl. At the moment, the only thing keeping him alive was Ghost. Their fates were intertwined. Even if he could add fuel to the fire of the pack's resentment toward their captain, and turn them against him enough to mutiny, where would that leave him and Sabine?

Next to die, he suspected.

If they had any chance of survival, he would have to play Ghost and the crew against one another. And when he made his move, he would need to time it perfectly, and Sabine would need to be ready.

It was time to talk to the witch who had stolen his heart.

## CHAPTER EIGHT

# DIAMONDS AND DEATH

**J**ack spent the rest of that day going about his duties, keeping a low profile but attempting to fit himself into the role of first mate. It was a trying time. He had read books set at sea, and he tried to remember the mate's duties from them. But they had been stories about high adventure and low men and had concentrated little on procedure or tradition. Still, he did his best, and when Ghost emerged on deck again and instructed him to issue an order, Jack did so with as much confidence as he could muster. Though he felt the crew's loathing like a cool breeze on a hot day, they went about their own duties without a pause, and with no sign that they would disobey.

He knew that his new post was a sign of Ghost testing his crew, as well as Jack, and that they would take out their frustrations in darker, quieter moments.

When sunset came, he descended to his new cabin and tried to barricade himself inside. The first mate's cabin was past the galley, next to Ghost's cabin and across the gangway from the chart room, and Jack had ventured down only once to glance at it since being given his new rank. Much larger than his previous nook at the rear of the galley, it stank just as badly. The bare walls were scuffed and scratched, the cot was piled with bedding that might once have been white but was now the color of the sea, and the few personal belongings Johansen had left behind were broken, cracked, or torn. Occupying the cabin just made Jack feel more in danger than ever before, and he tried to slide the small chest of drawers across the doorway. But it was screwed to the floor to prevent movement during storms, and he sat on the cot and laughed at his foolishness. Even if he *could* move the furniture, it would not keep them out when they came for him.

For a moment hopelessness washed over him, like a tide of inevitability drowning a prisoner buried neck-deep on some alien shore. He sat on a dead man's stinking cot and felt hatred and resentment darkening the air around him, compressing the walls and dulling his senses with their pressure. He was confident of his abilities and content in himself, but the odds stacking against him were staggering. One monster, perhaps, he could find ways to fight

*For a moment hopelessness washed over him,*
*like a tide of inevitability drowning a prisoner*
*buried neck-deep on some alien shore.*

against. But a whole crew? An array of monsters, each horrible in its own right? What would Tree look like changed into his wolfish state? Or Ogre.

And what of Ghost, the worst of them all?

Jack clenched his fists on his knees, staring into the corner of the cabin. In that darkness he saw Sabine's face, so sad and pure, yet hiding such terrible knowledge. His heart swelled, and his breathing calmed as determination once again sought to overcome the hurdles yet to leap. No one who won tremendous victories could ever let the odds grind them down. And no one who had to save someone he loved could let hopelessness divert him from his course.

"Love," Jack said aloud, and the word seemed so pristine in these dank surroundings. He hadn't known Sabine long enough to love her. And yet . . .

He stood from the cot and waited in the center of the cabin, not touching anything, trying to ignore Johansen's stench, which he thought might be ingrained in the wood of this place. And he waited.

The ship rocked in familiar rhythm, timbers creaked, and soon he started to make out footsteps and tried to imagine to whom they belonged and where they might be heading. Closing his eyes, he sent his senses outward, as he had been taught in the Yukon wilderness. In his mind's eye he built a schematic of that terrible ship, reaching out with the senses he had developed under Lesya's tutelage and placing each of the pirates' locations. Some were in the forecastle, ready to sleep the night through. Finn was tucked away back in the galley, shamed and vengeful where he lay in bedding that now smelled of Jack. Louis was up in the crow's nest. Jack thought it was Demetrius who steered, and there were one or two others on deck, keeping watch and seeing to any rigging adjustments that might be necessary during the night.

Huginn and Muninn he could not place. They were an enigma, silent and oppressive wherever they stood. It was as if Ghost had created two shadows from his dark soul to guard him against attack and ill will.

From outside came footsteps and a door opening and closing. The footsteps paused for a moment outside Jack's door, and rather than holding his breath, he breathed long and deep, as if asleep. The footsteps moved on, and Jack listened to Ghost climbing up on deck.

*Now's the time*, he thought. Everything Louis had told him increased his sense of urgency. Jack had always viewed the passing of time as an expansion of his life and experience, but now each second ticked toward something terrible. He resented that theft of optimism.

He opened the door quickly, pulling it past the squeals set into its hinges by the corrosive sea air. The gangway

beyond was home only to shadows. He stood in the doorway and looked left at Ghost's closed and forbidding door.
Across the gangway was the door to the chart room. This
must be where Ghost kept Sabine, watching greedily as she
expended her amazing abilities on finding vessels he could
raid, treasures he could steal, passengers he could kill,
people he could hunt and eat come full moon. Jack's hatred
burned bright as he closed his cabin door behind him.

Even as he touched the chart room door's handle, he
sensed the movement inside. There was nothing threatening about it—indeed, there was a warmth, an excitement
at what was happening and what might come. *Sabine is
waiting for me*, Jack thought, and he opened the door and
pushed inside, left hand at the small of his back where the
knife handle protruded from his belt.

"Jack," a voice whispered, soft and gentle.

"Sabine." He closed the door behind him, and the sense
of this forbidden place was delicious.

She sat on a cot that hinged down from the far wall,
past the table where charts lay strewn and smoothed
stones held them down, safe from the ship's movements.
Her clothing was loosened, and her hair seemed wilder, as
though released from clips he had not even noticed before.
The room was lit by a single oil lamp, which cast soft shadows across Sabine's sad, lovely features.

"Why are you here?" she asked.

"To see you, of course. To talk."

"He'll kill you if he finds you here."

"Do you really think so?" Jack didn't. He thought Ghost would beat him mercilessly, smash him about the ship like a child bouncing a ball against the walls. But he didn't think he would kill him.

Not yet.

"I . . . ," Sabine said. She stood from the cot, her shirt open to reveal the hollow of her throat. Shadows dwelled there, and Jack yearned to kiss them away.

"We have to talk," Jack said. "My arrival has changed things here, upset the balance of the crew. Ghost will change me when he thinks the time is right. And I can never become one of those things."

"No," she said. "You are strong, but you can never be a monster."

"The choice will not be mine, once bitten," he replied. "And that's what we have to avoid. The clock is ticking, Sabine. I want away from here. And I want you to come with me."

"Jack, I—"

He held a finger to his lips to shush her, and Sabine fell silent. He skirted around the small chart table, hand trailing across paper, never taking his eyes from hers. He moved close to the woman and her fold-out cot, and the intrusion into her personal space was obvious to both of them. Sabine did not blush—she was stronger than that, and less concerned with social niceties—but he did hear her slight intake of breath.

"I mean to save us both," he said. "You're trapped here even more surely than I am, because Ghost values your abilities, and he'll do whatever he can to keep you here forever. Me? He welcomes my intellect, and how my nature is so contrary to his. And I strengthen him. He'll argue with me till we're butting heads, because we both know that neither of us can be swayed, until he is certain that he sees nothing of himself in me, that the last vestiges of his own humanity are gone. And then . . ." Jack shivered, really considering for the first time the practicalities of what Louis had told him.

"And then he will turn you," Sabine said. "You have spoken with Louis."

"Yes," Jack whispered.

"He was a man, like you, when he led Ghost to me in San Francisco. Louis had heard of the man but did not know the monster. And it wasn't long before Ghost started toying with him. He welcomed the stench of fear coming from Louis when he realized the predicament he was in. Relished the moment when Louis begged for his life and then did all he could to seek his own death. And then Ghost tied him to the mainmast and bit him, and the crew gathered around to witness his first transformation. The first is always the worst." She turned away, wiping a tear from her cheek.

"The worst how?" Jack asked.

"Worse than death."

Jack reached for Sabine, holding her arms and turning her to face him. She resisted initially, and then leaned into him, her arms encircling his neck and pulling him closer. They kissed. It consumed Jack, negating his surroundings, erasing pirates and werewolves and sinking ships from his mind, and for a moment he and Sabine were the whole world, and they existed only in that single kiss. His past was as vague as his future, and neither mattered when he had her.

Parting, he saw in her surprised eyes that she had felt the same.

"I'm so sorry, Jack," she said.

"Why?"

"I . . ." She pressed her face to his shoulder, and he held her tight, wanting to soothe the truth from her.

"Sabine, you've nothing to be sorry for."

"Huh!" She uttered a brief laugh and pointed at her cot. "I've *so much* to tell you. Sit here with me."

"I think we should be planning how to—"

"This *is* planning," Sabine said. "Sit down next to me, Jack. We might not have very long." Jack did as she asked, and when she sat beside him on the cot, her arm touching his and her leg pressed close to his own, the terrible things she started to say felt so distant.

"Ghost isn't his name. No one knows his true name, not even me. But he's told me of his origins, and how he was made. And he's revealed the nature of his nemesis, because he requires me to keep watch."

"Ghost has a nemesis?"

Sabine was shaking. Jack felt it where their arms touched, and he thought to put his arm around her. But the conversation was about something unpleasant, and it forbade such contact.

"His brother," Sabine said. "Death Nilsson. The original sea wolf, he was the first to form a pack, pull together the wild men, and work them as a functioning group. Before that, Ghost says, werewolves would meet only when chance drove them across each other's paths, and when two met, only one would survive. Death changed that. He gave them drive and purpose, and he controlled the pack with vicious hand and merciless claw. His pack has been pirating the oceans for . . . many years. Even Ghost doesn't know how long, but he suspects it to be over a century."

"A hundred years!" Jack gasped. "That's monstrous! Living so long as such a thing. How terrible that would be."

"Terrible, indeed." For a moment Jack sensed the direction of the conversation shifting. Then Sabine continued. "Ghost describes his brother with some sense of awe, which, considering what he did to Ghost, means that he must be even more monstrous than the man we know. Even more brutal and merciless, and more certain of his own twisted place in the world. Do you see? No matter how cruel Ghost might be, his brother is worse. Death Nilsson is truly evil."

Jack frowned. "It's hard to imagine a creature more soulless than Ghost."

"Ghost says he was part of Death's crew," Sabine said. "An honored part, as the captain's brother, yet still someone lower down the pack. After Death was turned—and his origin is a mystery—he returned home to take Ghost and force him to sea. They plied their trade around the Pacific rim, performing hit-and-run raids on fishing communities, attacking and sinking small ships, and using desert islands as refuges when the time came to regroup, count their winnings.

"Ghost became disillusioned with Death's direction. He calls his brother a fool and a 'dog,' but I suspect the pack hierarchy soon began to frustrate Ghost. He did not like being beneath his brother's boot, thinking himself an equal or even his brother's superior. Ghost challenged Death and lost. Beaten down, Ghost was humiliated by Death in front of his crew. A quick death was called for—they have some *code*, some sense of right and wrong in the dealings of their pack—but Death wanted him to suffer." She sounded disgusted, as though ascribing even the basest morals to these monsters left a rank taste in her mouth.

"It's the same mistake Ghost has made with Finn," Jack said softly.

"Death tied his brother to a mast and tortured him for a day and a night. He never slept but spent the whole time devising new methods of inflicting pain and humiliation. When Ghost told me of this . . . I have never seen him so troubled. And even now I'm not sure whether it was the pain or the idea that it was his brother inflicting it."

"I can't believe family ties mean anything here," Jack said.

"I think they do," Sabine said. "I think they're important in ways we cannot understand. We should remember that."

"So what happened?"

"Death's crew was becoming restless, and Death announced that it was the end of his brother's suffering. He slit Ghost's throat with a sword, buried a silver blade in his chest, and threw him overboard.

"Ghost watched his brother's ship sailing away, and he could see the wolves gathered at the railing, watching him sinking in their wake. Ghost fell unconscious, and when he woke, he'd been washed onto a beach."

"How long was he out there, in the water?"

"I asked him the same question," Sabine said. "He shrugged and said perhaps five days, perhaps seven. The sun had burned most of the skin from his face and arms, and the salt water had softened his flesh so it was almost sloughing from his bones. The knife was still in his chest, and the first thing he did upon waking was to pull it out. This was the most miraculous aspect of his survival—the days and nights floating in the ocean, the interest of sharks evident in his torn clothing and flesh, the baking sun, drowning, life leaking from his slashed throat. All these were nothing to the silver blade he'd had in his chest all that time."

"It's . . . a story," Jack said. "Fiction. That silver will kill a werewolf."

"And isn't the werewolf a part of that fiction?" She turned to Jack and stared at him, and she was only inches away. He could have leaned forward and kissed her again. But this moment felt loaded, and unsuitable for such displays of affection. *Our love is clean and pure*, he thought, and looked away lest his eyes betray his thoughts.

"So what was the miracle?"

"The knife's tip caught in a knot of threads and stitches in Ghost's leather tunic. The blade itself never touched his flesh or kissed his blood, because it dragged the leather into the wound with it. It was Death's great strength that drove the blade home, not its keenness.

"So Ghost spent a day on that beach believing himself dead. And when he stood and walked inland, he found . . . food." Sabine trailed off, and Jack felt her terror.

"Who were they?" he asked softly. He put his arm around her and pulled her close, taking as much comfort from the contact as he hoped to give.

"He didn't say. Perhaps he did not know or care. But there were a dozen of them, moored at the island with their ship. He told me . . ."

"It's okay." Jack kissed Sabine's temple, and she pulled away, standing from the cot and leaning back against the chart table.

"He told me they fed him for eight weeks. And after he took the last of them and locked them in their ship's hold, he managed to set sail himself. And he has spent the years since then building his crew and planning his revenge upon Death Nilsson."

"It was the *Larsen* moored at that island," Jack said.

"It was. And sometime during his stay on the island, he

named himself Ghost."

"Such a man must relish a name like that."

Sabine actually smiled. "When I asked him why, he told me that after the first full moon, he heard them talking in their camp as he circled them. They were terrified, and one of them said, 'What do we name a man who can best four of our own, and then do *that* to them?' And Ghost whispered his new name in the darkness and spent the time between then and their horrible deaths giving them cause to fear it."

"He believed he should have died," Jack said, thinking about how that might affect even a man like Ghost. Rejected by his pack, tortured by his brother, going through experiences that would have killed a normal man a hundred times over . . .

"It's the only time I've ever seen him looking even remotely vulnerable," Sabine said. "He was quiet and contemplative when he told me this. I know Ghost better than anyone now, and I'm sure he is genuinely tortured by his memories. He said to me, 'I am merely the ghost of what I once was.'"

"He thinks his brother stole something from him."

"And he seeks to steal it back, and more. Because of course Death heard of his brother's survival, and when they next meet on land or sea, one or both will die. One day Ghost will use me to locate his brother's ship, but not until he has pronounced himself ready to face Death again."

"Does the crew know about all this?" Jack asked.

Sabine nodded slowly. "Do they know about Death Nilsson, the wolf of the seas? They could not pirate these waters without knowing his legend. And Ghost has never hidden his past. The pack knows the story of how he and his brother last parted. But if you're asking me whether they know they are all merely pawns, that Ghost is using them to his own ends and cares little for gold or for hunting himself . . . no. I do not imagine so."

Jack pondered that a moment, wondering what the crew would do when they learned their pack had been created as little more than cannon fodder for Ghost's eventual showdown with his brother.

"When will Ghost be ready to meet Death again?" Jack asked.

"Not until he has built a pack he feels can destroy his brother's band of wolves. And, more importantly, not until he knows in his heart that he is a better pirate and a better wolf than Death, and that day will not come until Ghost is certain he has stripped the last remnants of human emotion from his own soul and left only the beast behind. That's why you intrigue him so, why he studies you, and why he has not yet turned you into a wolf.

"I think he sees you as a potential asset in the future,

that he admires you and believes you will be useful as a member of the pack. But for now, he uses your humanity as a measure against himself. Yes, he values your mind, the intellectual discourse you provide, but it is your empathy and humanity he studies."

Jack shook his head. "It will never work. He can never rid himself of the last vestiges of the man he once was. I can't call what he feels for you 'love,' but he feels something. He is prey to jealousy and disappointment and hurt. I've seen it."

"And yet he is closer every day," Sabine said. "In any case, one day he will believe he is ready to exact revenge on his brother and his pack, and regain what was his."

"His pride?" Jack asked, and Sabine shook her head, coming to sit next to him again. She placed her hand on his leg, and he felt the warmth through his clothing.

"I think it's something much deeper than that," she said. "I'm not sure it's something we can ever understand. Ghost really is unique."

"It sounds like he impresses you," Jack said, hating the petulance he could not keep from his voice.

"Oh, Jack," Sabine said softly, "he fascinates me." She leaned in to kiss him, and he was taken away again. They parted reluctantly, and Jack knew instantly that there was still more to tell.

"What is it?"

"Nothing."

"Sabine. There are things about me you can't quite know. I've seen and done things beyond your imagining, and perhaps one day I'll tell you." She looked haunted, and he was sorry for upsetting her. But he also believed she deserved to know that he had encountered the supernatural before, and that he had expanded his own senses to the point where he bore a touch of the supernatural himself. "I know there's something else bothering you right now, because I can sense it."

"Death," she said. For a moment Jack wasn't sure quite what she meant, and then she explained. "Death Nilsson is coming for Ghost. His ship is two days away."

Jack stared at her, his heart thundering into a gallop. "So the confrontation is coming at last. And soon." He ran a hand over his scruff of beard. One ship of monsters was perilous enough, but in a fight between the two brothers and their packs, he and Sabine would surely die. "Ghost is planning his revenge?"

Sabine stood and rifled through the charts on the table, choosing one and placing her hand just above it, fingers splayed.

"He would be, if I'd told him Death was coming. I've decided not to wait until Ghost is ready for their reunion.

I'm going to give him what he wants, but ahead of schedule." She moved her hand slowly left and right, humming so softly that it was barely audible, then moved around the table to do it again from several other angles. She touched the map with the small finger of her left hand. "Here. Death's ship is here."

Jack looked, then asked her where they were now. She passed her hand across that chart and pointed to another spot.

"When will Ghost know?"

"Unless I tell him, not until the ship is spied on the horizon."

Jack understood then. Sabine had sensed Death's ship but had purposefully kept it from Ghost, so that the *Larsen* would be taken by surprise. She might die, but she was willing to risk it so that Ghost might also be destroyed.

"And then?"

"Death's ship is bigger and faster, and his crew is twice the size of the *Larsen*'s."

Jack thought about it, then began to nod.

"All right. This can work. It forces us to move quickly, but all the better, I think. Sometime just before the attack is when we make our escape. There'll be confusion as Ghost and his wolves react. But . . ." Jack frowned, trying to think of how they could flee across the sea without dying in its depths, how they might distract Ghost and his crew for long enough to jump ship.

"This crew is already unsettled," Sabine said. "Your arrival here has upset the balance more than I've ever seen. *Everyone's* balance." She kept her gaze on him, frank and confident.

"A distraction," Jack said.

"Foment unrest in the crew, and when the time comes, they'll be less than prepared. Off their guard."

"They're already upset at Ghost appointing me mate," Jack said.

"Another of his games. But our greatest weapon lies in the hold."

"Their loot."

The chart room was cool and quiet, and all theirs, and the temptation to remain there together was great. Jack looked up at the ceiling and half closed his eyes, and he sensed Sabine watching him with the same expression he'd worn while watching her divining with the charts—fascination, and respect.

"Ghost is still on deck," he said.

"It doesn't matter." Sabine came close, and her presence was everywhere—he could smell her faint perfume, feel the heat of her, hear her soft breathing and the exquisite rustle of her clothing as she moved. She looked Jack in the eye, her pupils dilated in the murky room. "We can't risk anything right now."

"Your powers," Jack said. "What else do you know?" She was so alluring, and there was knowledge in her eyes that threatened to haunt him. Sometimes her expression exuded such age, and yet her skin was smooth and soft, and she couldn't have been more than twenty-five. Jack loved an enigma.

"Other things," Sabine said uncertainly. *Bad things?* Jack wondered. But she clasped his hands in hers and pulled him even closer. "We shouldn't risk staying here any longer."

"You're right," Jack said, and her mystery beguiled him. "The hold. Tell me what we need, and why."

Sabine leaned in to whisper in his ear, told him, and Jack smiled as he began to understand.

Jack returned to his new cabin before making for the hold, pausing five steps away from the galley doorway and listening for Finn. He heard uneven snoring and incoherent, sleepy mumbling, and contented himself that the man was still asleep. *He's dreaming of his imminent death*, Jack thought, and a pang of pity for Finn surprised him. He had been a normal man once. A man like Jack, living and breathing, concerned about his family and contemplating

*"The hold. Tell me what we need, and why."*

what fate the future might bring, good or bad. He'd gone wherever the work was, doing his best to survive, struggling against the obstacles life put in his way as best he could, living as well as life let him. And then he had been brought onto the *Larsen* and made a monster. All hope and aspiration had been ripped away from him, leaving only a need to eat.

Or perhaps he had always been a murderer.

Thinking of family troubled Jack—by now the *Umatilla* would have arrived back in Oakland, and his friend Merritt would have tracked down Jack's mother and sister to tell them of his fate. Everyone beyond this boat now considered him dead, and the *Larsen* had become his whole world. But to consider their grief would form a weakness within him. It was survival that must drive him on.

In the cabin Jack rooted through Johansen's belongings, pocketing a sheathed stiletto, a ring of keys, and a bent eating fork—rare among pirates—that was rusting away beneath the cot. He paused for a moment by the closed door and listened, breathing softly as he tried to probe his senses outward in the way of the wild. But he was being drawn back toward the chart room, where something warm, soft, and loving awaited him with bated breath. *She's still awake*, he thought, and he knew that Sabine was thinking of him, hoping that he might be the chance she had been awaiting for a long time.

How long, she had not told him. Those mysterious aspects of Sabine intrigued him, though they did not unsettle. There was an honesty about her that he had never sensed in that twisted tree spirit Lesya, far to the north in the wastes of the Yukon. She had been a monster in woman's clothing, but Sabine was a woman who had suffered monstrously. Jack was her chance, and he would not let her down.

He closed his door and moved past the galley into the mess. It was filled with shadows, but nothing else. Two sets of footsteps moved on the deck above, casual and calm. Huginn and Muninn, perhaps, which meant that Ghost was also still up there. Through the mess and into the gangway, he paused at the foot of the staircase, finding himself drawn strangely upward. *That's not the way*, he thought, but there was something about Ghost's monstrous presence that lured him. Perhaps it was something to do with pride, because he knew that Ghost valued his conversation and intellect. Or maybe it was fascination, because Jack could not deny that while he found the captain repellent, he, like Sabine, also found him mesmerizing. As a child Jack had picked at scabs on his knees, poked angry cats with sticks, balanced on the dock's edge looking down at the waters below. Danger was alluring, horror compulsive.

He shook the urge and moved on, opening the forbidden door and entering the gangway that ran the length of the hold. He passed the secure room's heavy door and thought of the long night he'd spent in there with Sabine, and how Ghost had tried shielding his anger when he'd opened the door to find them huddled together on the cot. He paused at the middle doorway and peered through the crack between door and frame. It was pitch-black, but he could smell the faint aroma of rotting fruit and vegetables, and hear the few chickens' clucking.

It took him several minutes to open the lock. He'd assumed it would be easy—he'd learned how to pick locks from Flowery Bob, a hoodlum from the Oakland docks who'd made a living preying off other people—but in practice it took a level of calm and subtlety that Jack was rapidly losing as the minutes passed. Each failed attempt set him more on edge, and eventually he had to lean back against the bulkhead and take a breath. He expected one of the doors at either end of the gangway to open at any moment. It would not matter who stood silhouetted there; discovery by anyone would put him in peril. With most of the pirates, he'd expect a good beating at least. A few would probably kill him.

*One more time*, he thought, moving slowly, breathing deeply. He put the bent fork tine into the padlock, then one of the smaller keys from the ring, jiggling and twisting it. The padlock clicked open, and Jack was so surprised that he fumbled it as it fell. It struck the floor with a heavy thump, and he ducked down, trying to reduce the shadow he'd throw when one of the doors opened. He was thirty feet from the forecastle, where most of the pirates slept. If one of them had heard the noise and decided to investigate, he'd be rising from his cot now, climbing the short ladder from the quarters, passing the steep steps leading to the deck, reaching for the door handle, pausing with his head to one side as he listened, and then . . .

The gangway door remained closed. Jack gasped in relief, pushing the hold door open and entering without checking inside. He closed the door behind him and placed the padlock on the floor beside it, then felt around for a lamp. He found one hanging on a hook, and as he lit it, he tried not to imagine things hunkered down in the heavy darkness, watching.

The light fought back the night and showed him that he was alone.

Baskets of hardtack lay piled against one bulkhead. Crates of cured meats were stacked elsewhere, and he tried not to consider that which had been salted and packed by his own hand. Jars of dried fruit sat tied on a rough shelf, tobacco hung from ceiling supports, several large crabs rotted slowly in one corner, and there were other containers whose contents he could not discern. Three crates held the ship's chickens, ragged, thin things that sometimes laid, sometimes did not. When the time came to kill and eat them, their meat would be tough and stringy.

It came as no surprise to see at least five different ships' names on the baskets, crates, and sacks.

But what he sought was not immediately visible. He had no real wish to go rooting through the piles of foodstuffs— he was afraid he might disturb some of the stacks and send them tumbling. If the dropped padlock had not woken anyone, a ruckus from the food store surely would.

*I could poison every part of it*, he thought. But even if he'd carried a vial of poison, he was not sure he could have gone through with it. They were werewolves *and* men, killers and, like Louis, perhaps once unwilling victims. Descending to their murderous level might save lives in the future, but to kill them in secret instead of in combat would damn Jack's own.

He turned in a slow circle, wondering where the true hold might be. What if Sabine was wrong, and all their loot was kept in Ghost's cabin? If that was the case, then their plan could never work, and they'd have to find another way to do what was required.

"Damn it, it's *got* to be here!" he whispered, and then he saw the line in the floor. Jointed boards were generally staggered to give strength, but stretching between a pile of bulging sacks and a stack of crates was a cut directly across the floor, and it could mean only one thing. He moved bags, ignored the clucking chickens as he shifted their crates aside as quietly as he could, and revealed the hatch, just wide enough for a man to lower himself into.

Another padlock, another heart-shaking few minutes to pick it, and then he lifted the hatch and leaned it against the bulkhead. From the darkness below came a deep, constant growl, and the creaking of boards, and the swish of water flowing this way and that. He was deep in the ship here, maybe four feet from the lower hull, and the growl was the sound of water passing over the barnacles clustered on its belly. Finn had had close experience with those barnacles, and if anyone caught Jack here, he'd likely receive the same punishment.

But he was only a man, and imagining those terrible wounds ripped across his own flesh almost made him sick.

Grabbing the oil lamp, he lowered himself into the hole beneath the hold. It was barely four feet high and eight feet square, and piled with boxes, bags, and other containers. He opened a few and saw the glint of precious things.

This was what he had come for. Sabine knew some of what was here, because she had been told. The currents communicated to her, the sound of a ship's hull transmitted through a thousand miles of water, the swirl of schools of fish, the weight of displacement from one hull to the next, the warm flow and cold draft of different depths. She had not been able to tell Jack how she sensed such things—there was no sight or touch, no sense of discrete awareness or mysterious communication—and the closest she had come to defining her knowledge was to call it forgotten memories remembered once again.

She had told him about the diamonds, and how precious they were.

Jack was surprised that such items were all kept together, but however brutal and animalistic the crew were, they had all signed agreements about division of gains, and there was a firm sense of loyalty among pirates. It was a loyalty that kept squabbling on board ship to a minimum and was designed to hold back jealousy and rage to direct at their targets.

It was a loyalty that Jack was about to challenge.

Increasingly aware of the time he had spent breaking in and finding this place, he rooted through the loot, touching treasures that would have set his family up for life a thousand times over. But everything here was stolen, and the glinting gold and shine of precious things all held a taint of red in his eyes. The blood of hundreds of victims smeared every surface of this room.

When he found the diamonds, they took his breath away.

He took a small handful, trying not to think about what they could buy, and then restored everything to its previous condition. The pouch of diamonds he closed, returning it to the leather satchel where he'd found it, and then the satchel to its trunk, among other treasures. He climbed up out of the crawl space and returned the trapdoor to its original position, half covering it with a box of canned vegetables. But he took care not to do too good a job, as that would work against his plan.

Jack stood inside the storage hold, listening for footfalls out in the gangway, trying to use his senses to feel if anyone approached. Holding his breath, he opened the door and stepped out, but the narrow corridor in the hold was empty. He leaned back into the room and scattered a couple of diamonds on the floor, then did the same in the gangway. Greed and suspicion were powerful tools.

He relocked the trapdoor, crept back into the gangway, closed the door, and clasped its lock tightly. But then he paused, troubled. It would not do to have the theft be too clever. The one he wanted to implicate as thief certainly was not. From his pocket he withdrew the stiletto he had found among Johansen's things and dug into the wood around the lock and the latch, so that any fool would see it had been tampered with.

Bent there, intent upon the task, he heard the creak of weight upon the steps at the far end of the gangway, coming down from the forecastle.

Jack spun. Finn stood on the last step, staring at him in uncomprehending suspicion.

"What are you up to, meat?" Finn growled.

Panic thundered in Jack's chest, the moment of discovery precisely what he had dreaded. Another half minute and he'd have been away, with none the wiser. Jack took two steps back, slowly, toward the stairs up to the main deck, and then it hit him.

This was perfect.

Jack smiled, turned, and bolted, boots pounding on timber. With a snarl, Finn gave chase, so much faster and stronger, his weight shaking the floor. Jack only prayed he wouldn't see the diamonds or stop to pick them up.

Really, he couldn't have planned it better.

As long as he didn't die in the next few minutes.

## CHAPTER NINE

# DEATH ON THE WIND

For an instant Jack had second thoughts, but it was far too late for that. If he did nothing, he and Sabine would surely die soon enough. *Better to die trying to save us both than simply wait for death to arrive*, he thought, and he reached the steps up to the deck as Finn exploded from the hold, tearing that small door off its hinges.

"Traitorous little bastard!" Finn barked as he struck the wall, then twisted to pursue. "Sneak thief! What've you stolen?"

Jack didn't slow. If he hesitated, he would be caught, and Finn would tear out his throat before he could even begin the deception. Heart beating like a caged animal inside him, rioting to be free, he hurtled up the steps as Finn lunged for him.

They'd been here before, he and Finn, though on the

other end of the ship. Jack had survived that encounter. This time, he had to do more than survive.

The wind hit him as he reached the deck. The ship creaked beneath his feet, canted to one side with the sails full, but he kept his footing. Several lamps burned, affording a weak illumination. Clouds were heavy tonight, and little starlight found its way through. Demetrius was at the wheel, his girth pressed up against it, and he frowned as he saw the terror on Jack's face. But he did nothing.

Finn reached the deck a moment later. "Cooky!" he snarled, giving chase.

Demetrius scowled in disgust and went back to steering the ship, no longer interested in Jack or Finn, or whatever the two might do to kill each other. The sea wolves didn't like Jack and they no longer trusted Finn, but if they were not going to intervene, his plan might backfire quickly.

"You're a lunatic!" Jack shouted at Finn. "What the hell d'you want?"

Finn bounded after him. In seconds he would catch up. Jack darted beneath the shrouds and around the mizzenmast. Lines hung around them, and Jack set them swinging in the darkness, trying to buy himself precious moments. He carried the stiletto in his hand but knew it would do him no good. So he sheathed it, running for the starboard railing amidships. A pair of gaffs hung there for ready use. He began to lose control of his momentum, almost hurling himself down the canted deck. A shout rose up and he recognized Louis's voice, but then he slammed into the railing and a post cracked. Pain shot through his knee from the impact.

He clasped a gaffing pole and jerked it loose, turning just as Finn bore down upon him. Salt spray stung his eyes, and he squinted in the faint light as the snarling Finn lunged, fingers clawed, eyes reflecting nothing.

Jack braced himself against the railing and thrust the gaff into Finn's chest.

The pirate's eyes went wide with pain and shock as the hook sank deep. The cant of the ship put gravity on Jack's side, and after a moment he twisted out of the way, staving Finn off with the pole. The hook acted as a claw; it snagged on the pirate's rib cage, and he roared in pain and fury as he tried to tear the thing out of his chest.

"Run, Jack!" someone shouted.

He looked up and made out a shadow in the crow's nest that must have been Louis. Jack didn't need urging again—a hook in the chest wouldn't kill a werewolf, no matter how hard he wished it.

A snarl came from behind him, and then a splintering of wood, and Jack knew he'd bought himself mere seconds. He climbed the deck at an angle, rushing for the foremast.

As he reached the rigging, Tree and Ogre emerged from the forecastle, befuddled, rubbing sleep from their faces as they took in the latest madness unfolding on deck. Vukovich and Kelly were close behind them, but they already looked alert and even excited. They watched with keen interest.

"Come on, you bastards!" Jack shouted at them. "He'll kill me!"

"And eat you!" Vukovich cried merrily.

"And save your heart for me, if he knows what's good for 'im!" Kelly added.

It was dark, the swell heavy, but Jack did the only thing he could—he leaped into the rigging and began to climb. The ocean wind scoured his face and blew his hair across his eyes, but he climbed as if the devil nipped at his heels.

A heavy weight tugged at the rigging below, and he glanced down to see Finn climbing . . . but the beast beneath him was not really Finn anymore, and it was close enough for Jack to see. Fur had sprouted from its flesh and the snout belonged to something no longer human, but not entirely wolf—this was a monstrous combination of the two. The weight of the thing shook the lines as Jack climbed, but he kept on. Louis shouted encouragement. Jack felt the wind on his skin just as he did the rise and fall of his chest with every breath, and the thrum of his heart with every beat, more keenly than he had ever felt anything in his life. A copper tang filled his mouth, and he thought he must have bitten his tongue before realizing what he tasted was not blood, but the flavor of death on the wind. It filled the air around him and overwhelmed his senses.

Jack reached the fore-topsail yard and started edging outward. Such a move would have been folly during the day, but at night . . . ? Suicide. He could fall to the deck and split like an overfull sack of fruit, and even if he kept his balance, he had nowhere to run save a leap to the sheets, which would end badly. But a moment later, he grabbed hold of a line to steady himself and knew he had made the right decision. The monster could not follow him. It could not balance well enough, and the yard might not hold its weight.

But Finn or not, the werewolf possessed a bestial cunning, and it caught enough starlight for Jack to see the cruel glint of its eyes. It could shake him loose, but he didn't think Finn would want that death for him. The pirate hated him, and Jack had risked a great deal on a split-second presumption: that Finn would want Jack to die at his hands.

The monster growled in pain as bones shifted and fur receded, and in moments, Finn stood there once again,

*What he tasted was not blood, but the flavor of death on the wind.*

clinging to the rigging. Shouts rose from below, and as Jack glanced down, he saw that Ghost had appeared at last. He stood, watching impassively, his expression grimly curious. Huginn and Muninn stood behind him, but they were not watching Jack and Finn. The twins studied the rest of the crew, alert for any threat to the captain.

"You've given me a great gift, Cooky," Finn growled. "I caught you in the midst of yer thievin'. Might be enough to save my life."

Crouched on the yardarm, ready to leap, Jack knew his life would be forfeit if he made the slightest misstep. But he smiled, just for a moment, then quickly hid his amusement so that Ghost would not see it.

"You've gone rabid, Finn! I'm no thief. Looked more like *you* were up to something, down in the hold. That why you want me dead?"

Ordinary men might not have heard him from down on the deck, but Ghost and the others weren't human. They would hear, and Finn knew it. His eyes narrowed with understanding and hatred as he realized not only that Jack would attempt to turn the accusations back upon him, but that given his current standing in the pack, it might work.

"You little bastard," Finn growled.

Jack glanced down and saw Ghost signal to Huginn,

who dashed for a cargo grille in the middle of the deck, flung it back, and dropped down into the gangway that ran through the hold. Finn snarled and started to inch out along the yard. Jack wrapped his fist in the rope to which he clung for balance, heart hammering, wind gusts threatening to knock him from his perch. Coming up into the rigging had seemed, on the spur of the moment, a stroke of genius—the perfect stage upon which to perform his deception. But if Finn managed to kill him up here, all would be for naught. Already the wound in Finn's chest had begun to heal.

*What were you thinking?* Jack asked himself.

"Kill me if you want!" he shouted suddenly, startling Finn. "Neither one of us is ever getting off this ship alive. But I won't die with you painting me as a thief."

He looked across toward the crow's nest on the mainmast but caught only a glimpse of Louis between topgallant and mainsail. Desperate, he looked down at the rest of the crew gathering below. Ghost and Muninn stood together.

"I went into the hold," Jack shouted, half a truth in his confession. "I wanted to sabotage the outer lock on the room you shut me and Sabine into so I could work it from inside. I thought we might have a chance to escape the next time. But I didn't even get to it! I saw Finn coming out of the food stores, caught him at something, and now he wants me dead before I can tell you."

"Lies!" Finn screamed, and lunged.

Jack put his weight on the rope and pushed off, swinging away from the yardarm and out over the deck. His arc took him around Finn, just out of arm's length. Finn reached farther and lost his balance, windmilling his arms and slipping from the yard even as Jack swung back toward the mast and caught the rigging.

Finn twisted in the air and stretched out—his hands becoming claws—and dug them into the wood of the yard. He flailed, trying to climb back up, claws scoring the wood. Shouts rose from below, some mocking Finn and others urging Jack to knock him off. But Finn moved swiftly.

Arm hooked into the rigging, Jack brought up some slack and looped the rope in his hands.

"Captain's pet or not"—Finn huffed—"I'll feed your innards to the sharks . . . and save the tastiest bits for—"

Jack darted forward, nearly lost his balance, and slipped the loop over Finn's head. Steadying himself on the tautness higher up the rope, he gave a small tug to cinch the makeshift noose tighter, then kicked Finn in the face. The sea wolf clutched at the yard but missed, and he fell backward toward the deck . . . until the slack Jack had gathered played out, and the rope snapped taut around his neck.

Finn bucked and kicked his legs, reaching up to free

himself from the rope. Fur sprouted once more from his flesh, and he became that half-wolf monstrosity again, snarling and spitting, swinging back and forth. Jack watched from the rigging, amazed at what he had done. His heart still slammed against the inside of his chest as though it longed to escape, but it had calmed somewhat. The immediate danger was over, but that did not mean he would survive the next few minutes.

He scanned the deck below for Sabine, but she had not come up from her cabin to watch. Perhaps that was for the best. Her presence would distract Ghost, and his jealousy made him unpredictable. Better for his beautiful slave—for what else could she be to him but that?—to hide herself below until the night's fates were decided.

Huginn emerged from the forecastle and ran to Ghost, whispering in close to the captain's ear. Jack saw the Nordic pirate show Ghost the small handful of diamonds in his open palm before they disappeared quickly into the captain's own pocket.

*Now we'll see*, Jack thought.

He pulled out the stiletto. Designed as a stabbing weapon, it would make for a poor saw, but with Finn's weight drawing the line taut, he thought he could cut the rope. He caught it in his hands, and then Finn reached up over his head and grabbed hold of the rope and started to climb. Jack stared, frozen for a moment with the stiletto in his hand.

"Mr. London!" Ghost called from below. "Don't cut the rope, if you please. It will only mean repairs later."

Jack hesitated but then sheathed Johansen's stiletto again. He had to move quickly. Finn had hauled himself up enough to give the rope slack, and holding himself aloft with one hand, he used the other to tug at the makeshift noose around his neck. Jack had no time to hesitate. He swung into the rigging and descended as fast as he could, hand over hand, until he dropped to the deck.

Finn freed himself and fell thirty feet, landing on all fours ten feet away. Jack could have run toward Ghost, but he had no faith the captain would protect him. Everything now was uncertain. His life would be decided in moments.

Jack spun and drew the stiletto again, and this time when Finn saw it, he paused. It made no sense. Werewolves were incredibly difficult to kill. A single stiletto should not have made Finn hesitate to attack, unless . . .

The blade glinted in the poor lamplight.

"Hold him," Ghost said.

Jack stiffened, afraid that the captain referred to him. Huginn and Muninn grabbed Finn. The murderous sailor thrashed against them, but then Ogre and Tree moved in as well and he stopped fighting. Even if he freed himself from the twins, the rest of the crew would not let him escape the captain's judgment. They might hate Ghost and disapprove of the decisions he'd been making of late, but Finn had murdered one of their own, and they had been awaiting his punishment. Their eyes shone with anger, hunger, and hope that the time had come to fulfill the laws of the pack.

"What the hell is wrong with you, Ghost?" Finn snarled. "You heard me. I know you did. Your ridiculous pet, your 'first mate,' was in the hold, breaking into the stores, trying to get to the loot."

Ghost began to pace, walking in a circle around Jack and the crewmen who held Finn.

"Why would he do that, Finn? Where would he go?"

"He said himself he planned to escape."

"Not tonight, surely. Mr. London may suffer from the weakness inherent in humanity. He may believe in honor and love and dignity and other foolishness. But he is not a fool."

Ghost paused and glanced around at the rest of the crew.

"Kelly!" the captain barked. "You'd like to see our Mr. London dead, I'd wager."

"Wouldn't hurt my feelings, Captain," Kelly said, nodding.

Ghost reached into his pocket and brought out the fist-ful of diamonds, letting them glitter in his open palm.

"Someone broke into the stores, went into our treasury below, and took these diamonds. They were scattered on the floor as if the thief had been surprised in the act. You heard Mr. London and Finn, here, arguing about it just now. Of the two, which is fool enough to try such a thing?"

Tree swore. Vukovich began muttering furiously. Maurilio had come out onto the deck at last—perhaps he'd been sleeping below—and sidled up beside the captain to look greedily upon the precious diamonds.

"Finn killed Johansen," Kelly said. "He hates you, Captain. He's at the bottom of the pack and knows he hasn't got long to live. But I wouldn't have thought even Finn fool enough to try to steal from you."

"Not from me," Ghost said, showing the diamonds around. "From all of us. And perhaps you're right. Maybe Finn walked in on Mr. London in the midst of the crime, caught him red-handed."

"Maybe," Maurilio said.

"Not a chance," Kelly sneered.

Jack kept his breathing steady, but his throat had tightened and his mouth gone dry. He looked back and forth from Ghost to Finn to Kelly, knowing he could not speak out of turn. It had to be played just right, and he had to choose his words carefully.

"Why not?" Ghost asked.

"You heard him," Kelly said, nodding toward Jack. "Might be soft, but he's smart. What good would it do him? He wanted to fix the lock down there so he could escape. If he took the diamonds then, I'd say sure, maybe it's him. But where would he hide 'em now?"

"Damn you, Kelly!" Finn roared, trying to break free of his captors and failing. Huginn and Muninn held him tight. "I'll kill you. I'll kill you all!"

"Sounds like a guilty man to me," Vukovich muttered.

Maurilio, Ogre, and Tree were nodding in agreement.

"You can't let him live, Captain," Kelly said, staring expectantly at Ghost. "First he killed Johansen, and now this. Whatever game you're playing, we can't afford to let it go on."

Ghost ignored him, instead walking over to Jack and staring at him, eye to eye, searching for the truth. Jack felt only hate and loathing inside him and he let it radiate outward, hoping it would mask his fear of discovery. He had lowered the stiletto, letting the blade dangle at his side. Now Ghost took it from him, carefully, and held it up to the light.

"Where the hell did he get that?" Vukovich growled.

"In his cabin," Ghost replied, glancing from the blade

to Jack. "He found it among Johansen's things and took it for himself, which is his right as the new first mate. Or it would be, except for one thing. This blade belongs to me."

Jack stared at him, and for a moment the rest of the crew—the rest of the world—did not exist. "It's yours?"

"You couldn't have known," Ghost said. He smiled grimly. "I never even noticed it missing. Johansen, the sneaky bastard."

"Why would 'e do that?" Tree asked, obviously doubtful. "He'd know you'd kill 'im for it."

Ghost's smile was as haunting and unsettling as ever. "I think maybe he wanted to be captain."

"So I did you a damn favor, killing him!" Finn snarled.

Ghost lashed out, clawing deep, bloody gashes across Finn's cheek and jaw. Then he crouched in front of Finn as the sailor struggled against the hold the twins had on him.

"You tried to do *yourself* a favor, Finn. But it backfired, didn't it? As all of your plans have, because you are a fool."

Ghost held the silver stiletto out to Jack, careful not to touch the blade. The sea wolves stiffened, alert and anxious. They hadn't realized the blade was silver when Jack had first brandished it, but now they stared at it and then at Ghost as though the captain had lost his mind.

"Take it, Jack," Ghost said. "Finn has tried to kill you more than once. If you let him live, he will succeed. You have no choice but to kill him first."

The pack went utterly silent. Jack glanced at Kelly and Vukovich, their faces blank with sheer disbelief, and he watched as their expressions turned to quiet, simmering fury. Ghost might be planning to turn Jack, as Louis had said, but he was not a werewolf yet. He might have been made first mate, but he was not a member of the pack, and the wolves bristled at the sight of their leader surrendering the life of one of their own into the hands of a human. They were already riled up by the fact that Ghost hadn't killed Finn for the murder of Johansen, and Jack suspected they had been bitterly disappointed not to have the chance to eat Finn's remains. They wanted him dead, but not at the hands of an ordinary man.

Jack stared at the stiletto. *I didn't bargain for this.* All his plans began to unravel as the urge to take the blade grew within him. There could be no doubt that Ghost was correct—in fact, the captain did not know *how* correct. Jack had successfully framed Finn as a thief, and the lowest member of the pack would not rest until he had Jack's throat in his jaws. Even now the hatred blazed in Finn's eyes. But if Jack took the stiletto, he would have to choose to use it on Finn or try to kill Ghost.

The temptation hit him so powerfully that he began to reach for the blade.

*All his plans began to unravel*

*as the urge to take the blade grew within him.*

Ghost's eyes narrowed, a trace of smug satisfaction touched his lips, and Jack froze. If it would please Ghost, then it had to be a terrible idea. And there was more. Yes, it would make the pack hate Ghost, fomenting mutinous thoughts. But their hatred would be toward Jack as well.

And it would be cold-blooded slaughter. Finn might be a monster, and killing him might be saving Jack's own life, but if he couldn't fight back, it would still feel like murder. And Jack London was no murderer.

Ghost saw the change in his eyes.

"I will not offer you this blade again," the captain said.

Jack took a long breath, then shook his head. "I'd kill to save myself, or someone I love. But I won't murder a defenseless man. And I'm sure not going to kill for your amusement."

With a scowl, Ghost backhanded Jack, knocking him sprawling at Ogre's feet. He rose to his knees, mouth bleeding, heart pounding. Ghost snatched him up like a rag doll, fumbled with his belt, and tore it off him, removing the small leather scabbard in which he'd discovered the stiletto. Then the captain hurled Jack to the deck again, discarding him. He sheathed the stiletto in its scabbard and turned to go, but paused to look back at Jack and then at Huginn and Muninn, still holding Finn.

In one fluid motion, impossibly swift, Ghost drew the

stiletto and drove it into Finn's heart. Huginn and Muninn
let go of him, and the pirate dropped to the deck. His skull
thunked on the wood, and his dead eyes stared up at the
full sails, unseeing.

"You son of a bitch!" Kelly snarled, rushing toward
Ghost.

It took both Vukovich and Maurilio to stop him, but
they saved his life. Jack knew the look in Ghost's eyes. He
would have killed the entire crew in that moment if they'd
dared to challenge him further.

Ghost loomed over him. "Stay on your knees, Mr.
London. That's where cowards belong."

The captain strode aft and vanished below, and a moment
later Huginn and Muninn took up positions on either side of
the cabin steps, making certain no one dared follow.

Jack staggered to his feet. Maurilio sneered at him.
Vukovich hawked up something from his throat and spit
on Jack's shirt, but otherwise they ignored him. They
mumbled to one another about the captain, their hatred
for him blazing like the inferno, overriding the loyalty that
membership in the pack demanded. At first Jack did not
understand, but then Ogre and Tree picked Finn up by his
hands and feet, careful not to touch his spilled blood, and
carried him to the railing. As they tossed the corpse overboard as unceremoniously as they might have the remains

of their dinner, the truth dawned on him, and he realized the enormity of what the captain had done.

In the eyes of the pack, Finn had deserved to die, killed by Ghost and then savaged by the rest. He ought to have been torn apart and eaten, but instead of killing Finn in combat, Ghost had tainted him with silver. Poisoned him. They wouldn't dare eat the corpse.

Ghost had given them what they wanted, but in a way that only added insult to earlier injury. He must know how they hated him, and that he had only made things worse. But he did not care. He might as well have spit in their faces. It was just another example of his disregard for their loyalty. The rules of the pack seemed to apply less and less to its leader, and the wolves were growing angry.

As Jack watched the crew disperse, the dread fluttering in his chest merged with sick excitement. Ghost had lost respect for him, but as long as the captain still had plans for him, it didn't matter. In two days or less, Death Nilsson would come for his brother, and all hell would break loose.

But Jack wondered if the crew would last two more days. If Ghost continued to treat them with such disrespect, it was only a matter of time before they would be driven to mutiny.

In the aftermath of Finn's death, a strange new dynamic developed on board the *Larsen*. Ghost kept mostly to himself, living behind the closed door of his cabin and emerging only every few hours to inspect the ship and its crew. Once that first night and several times the next day, he went into the chart room that doubled as Sabine's quarters and consulted with her. Each time he visited her, Sabine would wait until the captain had departed and then come up to walk the deck in ghostlike silence. No one troubled her, and she spoke to no one. Jack's only contact with her came while he was preparing meals—a task that was his once again, now that Finn was dead.

As first mate, he could have ordered any member of the crew to take over as cook, but in truth he did not like the idea of inviting any of the crew into the galley. Except when the diminished crew gathered to eat in the mess, Ghost, his silent guards, Sabine, and Jack were now the only people on board allowed in the stern cabins. It was safer that way.

The *Larsen* had become a stew of hatred and homicidal intent. Of the crew, only Louis and Tree did not look at Jack with murder in their eyes. Yet despite the animosity, he could feel that he was merely an afterthought for the sea wolves. They understood the usefulness of Sabine's gifts, but they could not comprehend Ghost placing an ordinary man in a position of authority over members of the pack. Even if Ghost intended to make Jack one of them, the pirates did not want him; in their eyes he was a symptom of whatever madness had come over their captain. Ghost had formed this pack, turning them into monsters and using fear, intimidation, and brutality to teach them the laws by which the pack would operate. Now he had thrown those laws in their faces. His pride had turned him into a tyrant who made decisions in order to remind them that he stood above and apart from them, not with them. The *Larsen* had become a powder keg of resentment and anger, ready to explode at the slightest further provocation.

More and more, as Jack heard the crew's angry rumblings and saw the way they watched their captain, he thought of the Roman senate drawing their long knives and turning on Julius Caesar. In the case of Ghost, at least one of the knives would have to be silver, and Jack wondered how many other such blades there were hidden on board. Ghost had thrown Finn's silver knife into the sea and kept his own, but would other members of the crew risk the captain's ire by secreting such a dangerous weapon among their own things? He suspected not. Only Finn had been that stupid. But there was no way to know for sure.

Those two nights he slept only fitfully, thinking of the softness of Sabine's lips and the depth of her eyes. But love was not the only thing that kept him from surrendering to sleep's embrace. The silent hostility and the promise of death that suffused every waking moment aboard the *Larsen* kept him wondering, not only about the outcome of a mutiny, but also about what might become of him should it succeed. He had no intention of still being on board when the mutiny concluded, yet he could not help but wonder if Louis and Tree were fond enough of him to prevent the rest of the pack from killing him after Ghost was dead.

He tried to shake the thought. He and Sabine would be gone from the *Larsen* by then, or they would already be dead. He did not really care who came out victorious when the men finally mutinied—as he felt sure they would do before long—except that if Ghost survived, he would pursue Jack and Sabine, reluctant to let her strange powers escape. Those who would rise against Ghost were less likely to give chase.

The hate simmered, like a volcano fit to blow. But the surreal quality of each hour that passed sprang from love just as much as it did from hate. He would walk the deck and issue orders to trim the sails, or for one man to spell another at the wheel or in the crow's nest. Then he would go below and begin to gather together the ingredients for a meal to feed those same men, and while he cooked, Sabine would slip into the galley to visit him. As Ghost could be relied upon to remain in his cabin for long hours, she even helped him choose spices and prepare certain dishes, and while they cooked, she would touch his hand or his shoulder or kiss his neck. Jack felt a wild bliss growing unrestrained within him, and that went some way to keeping him focused on their survival instead of the festering malignance of the crew.

Ghost had ordered that meals be delivered to his cabin. Sabine always obliged. In those moments, with the crew in the mess and Sabine distracting Ghost, Jack made preparations of another sort. He squirreled away food in various places throughout the galley so that they could be gathered quickly. There were old wine and whiskey jugs in a cabinet, and now some of them, hidden behind empties, had been filled from the store of fresh water below.

When Jack visited the food stores, the pirates' treasure was beneath the boards underfoot, and yet Ghost never sent anyone to oversee his work there. Either he truly believed Jack would not be stupid enough to steal from him, or he wanted to leave such concerns and suspicions to the crew. But the crew left him alone, perhaps reckoning that Ghost would decide his fate in time, or maybe they were more interested in their own plans for the captain.

Jack concentrated on his preparations, determined that he and Sabine would be ready when tensions finally erupted on the *Larsen*. There would be mutiny, or there would be an attack from Death Nilsson. Either way, that would be the moment of their escape.

"We'll want the long pork for lunch today, Mr. London," Ghost rasped, standing in the shadows beyond the galley entrance.

Jack could not hide the look of revulsion that swept across his face. "Long pork."

"You know the term, I take it?" Ghost asked.

"I know it. It's what the cannibals of the East Indies called human flesh."

Ghost did not smile. It was clear he no longer took pleasure from his rapport with Jack. Instead, he sneered.

"We are not cannibals, Mr. London. Cannibals eat their own kind for sustenance, and as you'd be the first to observe, we aren't human."

Jack felt sick. It had been challenge enough for him to cure and salt the remains of the prisoners taken from the *Umatilla*, but now to cook that meat and serve it to Ghost and his crew . . . it stained his soul to even contemplate such a horror.

"Surely you don't need it cooked for you," Jack said, glaring at him in the shadows as the ship creaked around them. "I remember well enough the screams and the blood,

Captain. You prefer your long pork raw."

Now Ghost did smile, but it was a warning. "When it's fresh, Jack. Only when it's fresh. Otherwise, I'm as much a gourmand as the fattest, wealthiest man in San Francisco. Spice it well. Make a nice sauce to accompany it. And serve it yourself, this time."

Jack held his tongue, knowing that he had pushed Ghost too far.

"What you and Sabine have for your own lunch is up to you," Ghost added.

A shadow approached from the mess. It was Maurilio, Huginn looming behind the rangy man, ready as ever to protect the captain.

"Kelly's in the crow's nest, Captain," Maurilio reported. "Says there's a thick fog forming due west. We're headed right for it, a few hours out."

"Keep on course. Our sea witch will let us know if we've anything to fear in the fog."

Maurilio darted off to relay orders to Vukovich, who was presently at the wheel. Ghost turned and looked at Jack.

"Go on, then. Your galley awaits."

Jack nodded. "Yes, sir."

The captain retreated into his cabin and closed the door. He hadn't even bothered to go on deck to survey the crew's efforts or check on their heading himself. Jack knew it wasn't fear of mutiny that kept Ghost in his quarters, because he feared nothing. The captain had been consulting with Sabine about the location of several merchant ships, but also of the nearest land, and Jack suspected that Ghost might be considering what to do about the venomous atmosphere on board. How much trouble would it be to kill most of his pack and begin again?

Jack would have to go into the hold to retrieve the long pork—he could not think of that meat by any other name, for his own sake—for the wolves' lunch, but first he wanted to see what else he might need. Standing in the galley, the ship swaying beneath him, he thought of what he was about to do and was nearly sick. Nothing frightened him. Jack London had confronted the wildness of human nature and the human heart, and had found himself undaunted. But this . . .

"Jack."

Her voice eased his spirit effortlessly, and he turned to Sabine, standing just inside the galley behind him. Silhouetted in the sunlight that filtered down into the cabin, she seemed for a moment like an angel come to save him from the hell of the *Larsen*.

Then he saw the fear in her eyes.

"He's coming, Jack," Sabine said. "Death is here. They'll

see the smoke from his ship any moment now."

Jack took her in his arms. He kissed her gently, then fiercely.

"For luck," he said.

They heard shouts and running footsteps, and then Maurilio was calling for the captain.

Jack pulled away, clasped her hand in his a moment longer, and then nodded.

"Be ready."

## CHAPTER TEN

# THE FOG OF WAR

Ghost slammed from his cabin so violently that the door cracked from its hinges, splintering against the bulkhead and scattering along the gangway. Jack pulled back into the shadowed corner of the galley, Sabine close beside him, and held his breath. *This is when everything begins to change,* he thought, and it was a strange idea. Change had been evident day to day, hour to hour, since Ghost had thrown him from the deck of the *Umatilla.* But this moment felt like the line between life and death, however thin or ambiguous that line might be.

On the deck above them, footsteps pounded and voices shouted for the captain—the crew calling for the man they had started to hate.

Ghost walked past the galley doorway, kicking the remains of his cabin door ahead of him, his breath a constant, rumbling growl, and he looked larger than he ever had before. He was a force of nature, channeled by these wooden walls and floors and ceiling but never contained, never tamed. His shadow passed through the galley and it seemed to abrade every surface it touched. Then he stopped, turned, and stared in at Jack and Sabine.

Jack thought he would comment on them hiding away in there, huddled against the wall like frightened rats. He thought the captain would pour scorn upon such fear and tell them both that they were less than people, and barely equal to animals. But Ghost only glared at them, reserving his longest, coldest stare for Sabine. And Jack knew what was to come. *She didn't tell him about Death*, he thought, and Ghost's expression held a promise of something more than mere retribution. She had challenged his intellect and betrayed his trust.

Ghost backed into the mess and did not turn away until he was out of sight. Jack heard him climbing to the deck, and then the level of panic up there seemed to lessen, Ghost's voice transmitted down through the floor as wordless growl.

The air seemed lighter with Ghost gone. Sabine slumped against Jack and sighed.

"They'll head for the fogbank," Jack said, because that was what he would do.

Sabine seemed surprised, and then annoyed.

"What is it?" Jack asked.

"Nothing." She waved away his concern. "It's just that . . ." She trailed off, then pushed past Jack and crossed to the galley door. She stood there with her back to him, secrets in her strained stance.

"Mr. London!" Ghost's voice roared. It shook the ship's boards and loosened the fill between them, and for an instant Jack believed that Ghost was scared. But that was not fear in the captain's voice; it was rage.

"I should go," Jack said to Sabine. "Remember the food. When our time comes, it will be brief, and we won't have long. Mere moments. But if we take that chance, then we can be away from here." He waved a hand at the skillet in which he'd been considering cooking dead people's flesh to feed this ship's monsters. "Away from *them.*"

"I dream of nothing more," she said. Her voice was soft, and Jack grabbed her shoulder and turned her to face him. There was not an ounce of confidence in her eyes.

"What is it?"

"What you said. He will race for the fogbank. And if he loses Death in there . . ."

"Then he will have time for you." Voicing his fear made it worse.

"I betrayed him," Sabine said.

"We're not destined to die here," Jack said, pulling her close. But Sabine laughed, a short, bitter sound that scared him.

"Destiny?" Her laughter faded, and a tear appeared. "It's my fault you're here."

"No, Sabine," Jack said. "With you is the only place I want to be."

"Mr. *London!*" Ghost called again, and Jack kissed Sabine on the cheek and rushed through the mess, leaving too many things unsaid, knowing he had no time to say them. There would be time, he was certain. He would make sure of that.

As he hurried on deck, tension hung heavy in the air. To the west, directly ahead of them, the fogbank seemed no closer, yet their sails were full, booms swung to catch the last breath. Ghost barked orders and the crew obeyed, trimming by inches, enslaving the wind. When they had done all they could, the pirates looked to the north at the vessel revealed there. It rode the horizon and left a smear of smoke in the air, and from this distance Jack could make out little. But it was a steamer; that would make it faster and more maneuverable than the *Larsen* in these conditions.

"There stands my brother," Ghost said quietly, staring at the distant steamer as if into the eyes of his brother, who stared back across miles of churning sea—the murdered and the murderer, one seeking revenge, the other completion.

"Death comes," Maurilio said from where he stood at the railing.

"Five miles out," Vukovich said from his station at the wheel.

"Four," Ghost said. He glanced ahead, at the wall of fog laid across the sea like a blanket. "And two to the fog. It'll be a close race."

Jack looked at the small skiffs fixed to the *Larsen*'s deck. He had already inspected the fixtures of the frontmost portside boat's fixtures, and had loosened one enough to be able to kick the bolt away with his toe. It would take a minute to hunker down and release the other bolt, and another thirty seconds to winch the craft up a few inches and swing it over the side. He'd have to drop it then. There would be no time to lower it properly—if it capsized and floated hull up, he and Sabine would have to jump in and attempt to right it without swamping it and sending it to the bottom. If it splashed down as he wished, they would still have to jump.

As an escape plan, it left a lot to be desired. But right now it was all he had. It was an escape that relied on chaos. Looking north, sensing the subdued panic exuding from the *Larsen's* crew right now, it seemed that chaos might descend within the hour.

"Mr. London!" Ghost roared. Jack blinked, coming to his senses just as the big hand clamped his jacket and he was lifted from his feet. Ghost slammed him against the bulkhead, leaned in close so they were almost nose to nose. The animal stink of him had never been stronger. "Don't you think that the first mate should be making himself useful in such a situation?"

"Wh . . . what's the situation?"

Ghost grinned. "Family's coming to visit," he said. "Yonder steamer is the *Charon*, Death's ship. Sad to say, my brother doesn't share my sweet and gentle disposition."

Ghost dropped Jack and strode forward, standing at the bow as if to reach out and haul them into the fog. But he kept glancing north at the ship rapidly closing on them. The *Larsen* ran straight for the fogbank, and now Death's ship had angled toward it on an intercept course. As the moments ticked by, Jack realized what a dreadful risk Sabine had taken. When these two ships met, the savagery would be more than either of them had ever seen.

"Er . . . ," Jack said, glancing back at Vukovich. "All speed for the fog."

"Of course," Vukovich said.

"Let's drag every breath of wind from the air!" Jack

called, voice loud but unsure. Nobody moved, because the crew was already doing everything that needed doing. He heard a snigger but was not sure of its source. He looked around, caught Louis's eye across the deck. He raised an eyebrow at Jack, offered a slight shrug.

The pursuit was not about orders but time. If the wind held and the fog did not shift, they might just reach the fogbank before the *Charon* bore down upon them.

Just.

At the bow, Ghost seemed to shake with anger and the promise of violence, sending vibrations rattling through the ship. Either that, or their speed caused the timbers of the hull to shiver.

Jack walked the deck, knowing that he had nothing to say to these half-men, because they all knew what was required of them. But he did discover something during that endless hour: Werewolves could feel fear. It was never overt, and never revealed in anything they said, but he could sense it in them—the way they glanced toward Death's ship as it closed on them, the uncomfortable silences where two men worked together, their determination to win the race, tweaking every ounce of speed from the sails, ensuring that the rigging held taut and flowed smoothly.

If Death caught them, they would know pain.

*Now's the time*, Jack thought. He moved for the skiff,

trying to place each member of the crew to see who might spot him, who might interfere. He would prepare to move, then dash below to fetch Sabine and their stashed supplies. And then—

If the *Larsen* reached the fog first, and Ghost managed to escape his brother, he would come looking for any alternative target.

"Mr. London!"

*Damn it*, Jack thought. *Damn it!* What little plan he had was barely a plan at all.

"Mr. London, as soon as we enter the fog, heave to."

"What?" someone said. Jack didn't see who. His eyes were on Ghost, the monstrous man standing there like some deformed figurehead. The captain's eyes did not even flicker from Jack's as he answered the dissent.

"Heave to."

"Yes, sir," Jack said, and he ran the length of the ship, relaying the orders as he went. Two men scrambled aloft, ready to drop sail the moment the call came, and Vukovich nodded even before Jack reached him. He had heard. He did not need the human telling him what to do.

"His own cleverness might be his undoing," Louis said.

"I don't understand," Jack said, pleased to hear, if not a friendly voice, then at least one willing to converse with him.

"He's trying to second-guess his brother. Any ordinary pursuit would continue into the fog, so Ghost won't do that. If we reach the fog in time, what then? Turn north, right across the *Charon*'s bow? It might work, but there's a chance Death will see us, or that we'll collide. We could run south, skimming the edges of the fogbank, try to put so much distance between the two ships that there's no hope of them regaining our trail. But perhaps Death would anticipate such a step, and if he guesses correctly and quickly, they could overtake us."

"So stop altogether?" Jack asked.

"Why not?" Louis asked. "At least it's not running anymore."

"But if Death guesses that as well?"

"Maybe he will, maybe not." Louis's smile was empty, almost distant, as he stared across the gently rolling sea at the approaching vessel.

Jack could see a lot more of the *Charon* now, and at last he could understand the *Larsen* crew's barely veiled concern. The *Charon* was at least twice as large as the *Larsen*, a black behemoth with five boats to each side, a single busy funnel, and what looked like a small deck gun mounted close to its bow. There was lots of activity around the gun, and Jack guessed that they would be in range in moments.

Ghost looked from the *Charon* to the fogbank, then

along the ship to Jack. He nodded. They were going to make it. . . .

The deck gun on the *Charon* puffed smoke, and the thunder of its report came just as a hole was punched in one of the *Larsen's* sails. An awful stillness descended upon Jack. The *Charon* had a working turret gun, firing projectiles that had to weigh over a hundred pounds each. It would be muzzle-loading, which meant a lag after each shot, but if they managed to get one or two right on target, the *Larsen* might be done for.

"Now, that's not fair," Louis said.

Tree and Demetrius crouched at the railing and started firing rifles, but the enemy was far out of range, and Jack shouted at them to hold fire. The sea wolves glared at him with undisguised hostility. Ghost nodded at him once again and then left his position at the bow and walked the length of the ship.

On the *Charon*, Jack saw, was a shape doing the same. The silhouette was of a big man, walking at the same pace as Ghost, bearing the same air of power and dominance, even though from this distance it was impossible to make out his features. It was something about the way he walked that echoed Ghost's disregard for anyone but himself—confidence and arrogance and a sense of complete entitlement; each believed he alone owned the ocean.

In Ghost's eyes as he passed, Jack saw an acknowledgment of his brother's presence.

"As soon as we're sheltered by the fog," Ghost said. "But make the order a quiet one. They're already in earshot."

*And then our time will come,* Jack thought.

Ghost reached the steps leading down and paused before descending. His men looked at him in disbelief. He stared around at them, then across at the *Charon*, closing on them. The gun coughed again, and Jack heard the shot before the round impacted close to the bow, shattering a length of railing and splintering a swath of deck where Ghost had been standing seconds before.

"You have your orders, Mr. London," Ghost said. "I'm not to be disturbed unless the plan goes awry. I have a sea witch to put on trial." His grin as he turned and descended into the shadows made Jack sick to his stomach.

*Sabine!* Jack thought, and his already precarious plan was in tatters.

From the rigging, Kelly called down, "First whiff of fog."

Moments later they entered the fogbank and, without Jack even opening his mouth to issue the order, the *Larsen* proceeded to heave to. Death's deck gun barked again, and the shot whistled thorough the rigging, flapping Kelly's loose trouser leg where he worked on the crosstrees. He paused, surprised, and then proceeded with his tasks.

The ship acted as if it wanted to sail on—straining against the wind, creaking heavily as it pitched against a swell, sails billowing in complaint as they were lowered and the booms swung and tied. *Cut the noise!* Jack wanted to shout, but his voice would have been more noise for their enemy to hear, and—

The *Charon* passed ahead of them, visible as little more than a shadow against the rolling fog. Jack might have taken it as an apparition if he hadn't known for sure the ship was there. Ghost's crew grew still and silent as they watched the shadow powering past, driven by humming engines, its passage marked by the angry swirl of water against its metal hull. Jack could almost feel everyone's held breath in his own lungs, and as the fog swallowed the *Charon*, they all began to breathe again.

"Orders, sir?" someone said, and Jack glanced around for Ghost. But Vukovich had been addressing him. His animal voice found sarcasm an easy tone to carry.

"We drift until I say otherwise," Jack said, brain working frantically. What could he salvage from this? How could he make the plan work, when Ghost always seemed to be there to haunt any chance they had at escape?

"And then?" Vukovich asked.

"And then . . . I'll tell you." Jack and the pirate stared at

*The* Charon *passed ahead of them,*
*visible as little more than a shadow against the rolling fog.*

each other, but he could never intimidate such a creature. He paced the deck instead, grabbing hold of something as each swell knocked against the drifting ship's hull and rocked the boat as if it rode a great storm. He paused by the skiff he had chosen, conscious of its slight movements each time the *Larsen* rolled—it ought to have been strapped down tightly, but he had loosened its restraints. With the ship drifting, it would be even easier to launch, and the temptation to do so then was great. The fog was so thick that from the *Larsen*'s stern, the bow would be a nebulous place.

But what of Sabine?

Jack wanted nothing more than to venture belowdecks to see what was happening. There had been no sound since Ghost's descent—no cries or screams, which was good. But Ghost had deemed going below more important than remaining on deck to oversee their flight from his predatory brother. Sabine was the only reason. *I have a sea witch to put on trial*, he'd said. Jack could not believe that any trial conducted by Ghost would be fair, and Sabine's guilt was already without doubt. Death had almost rammed them into the depths, and she had not whispered a word of warning about his arrival.

"I'm not sure I've ever seen him this furious," Louis said. He had come to stand beside Jack without making a sound, and now they both held on to the skiff's gunwale as the Larsen drifted side-on to the waves.

"He didn't look furious," Jack said.

"That's what I mean. He's holding it all in, like a hurricane contained. And Ghost is not a man to hold back his rage."

"That's no concern of mine."

"Really?" Louis asked. "Sabine is a concern, *non*? Because it's she who will be suffering. She had to know the *Charon* was nearby. We might have given Death Nilsson the slip for now, but there's blame to lay, and where there's blame there will be consequences."

"What consequences?" Jack asked, blood flowing cold. But Louis moved away, fading like a wraith into the thickening fog.

He had to go below. Prepared or not—and he knew that he would *never* be ready to face Ghost one-on-one— he could not remain on deck while Ghost was below with Sabine. It was not only the information she had withheld; there was that look in the captain's eyes when he had seen her and Jack on the same cot. Whether he loved her or merely lusted for her, the result was the same. He coveted her body and soul, and now he would punish her for the yearning she inspired within him just as much as for her sins against him.

Jack made for the covered stairwell, but just as he reached it, he heard the thump of booted feet from below. Ghost emerged, an enraged man being born from darkness into a world he could only hate. His teeth were gritted, eyes watering, hands fisted, and he brought with him a miasma of fury that seemed to scar the air around him.

Jack stepped back as Ghost lashed out, but he could not avoid the blow. The captain's huge fist caught him across the shoulder as he retreated, and he spun and fell, crawling quickly across the deck in a vain attempt to avoid the next attack. A dreadful realization hit Jack then, and filled him with a terrible hopelessness: *He'll kill me now, because he's mad at Sabine but cannot afford to kill her.*

But as Jack scurried away, he realized that Ghost had not followed him. Instead the captain strode the length of the ship, each footfall an impact as shattering as a giant wave, each gasped breath the whip of a hurricane. Tree stood before him, the mountainous man's black skin stark against the canvas of fog around the ship. Ghost batted him aside. Tree flew across the deck and struck the mainmast, the grunt as he hit not masking the sound of wood cracking.

The captain reached the bow and kicked at Maurilio, who was already making repairs to the railing shattered by the *Charon*'s cannon. The dark-eyed man jumped back, but Ghost's next kick caught him across the thighs. He bounced from the railing and tumbled to the deck, motionless, subservient beneath the glare of his attacker. But Ghost had no particular target for his rage. He was angry at the world, and his world was this ship and those who sailed it.

*Now, we go now!* Jack thought. He had to fetch Sabine first. He eyed the doorway leading down, thinking quickly through what he had to do and how long it would take. A fool's errand, he knew, and as he took in a deep breath in preparation, Louis spoke from across the deck.

"Be still, Jack." It was whispered but sounded loud against the silence on the ship. Ghost's rage had driven all noise down, and even the sea appeared calmer than before, as if afraid of this great beast's fury.

The captain stormed back along the ship, punching a hole in the forecastle bulkhead, glancing left and right as he came. He had caught Tree and Maurilio on the way to the bow, but returning he found no one in his way.

Pausing by the doorway, gripping the frame so hard that the wood was crushed to splinters in his fist, he turned and looked directly at Jack.

*He sees right into me*, Jack thought, and he had never felt so exposed.

"Make sail," Ghost grunted. "South, at all speed. We're

going after him. It's time."

He disappeared below, and a breeze whipped a skein of fog across the deck as the ship sighed with relief.

Jack prowled the deck above the rear cabins, circling Vukovich at the wheel, watching the other men work, seeing Tree's massive shadow as he helped Maurilio repair the damage at the bow, and his frustration and desperation were close to destroying him. Sabine was below with Ghost, and there was nothing he could do. He possessed both brawn and brains, but knew that it was only the latter that would save him and Sabine from a terrible fate. His frustration was in not being able to conceive of a plan that would result in anything other than their deaths.

Kelly was close by, and Jack had already caught that sly one looking his way more than once. With Ghost engaged below—and the thought of what he might be doing down there was terrible to Jack, abhorrent, because though he knew the monster would not kill Sabine while he still needed her, Ghost was not averse to torture—Jack felt the crew's antagonism toward him coming to the fore. He had never felt himself truly under Ghost's protection until that protection was absent. Vukovich sneered when Jack tried giving him an order, and Kelly's glances were becoming more and more threatening. Jack was sure he detected a slight lengthening of Kelly's teeth, and a prominence in his nose absent before now.

When he heard Sabine's scream, he was almost grateful it gave him reason to rush below. Whatever would happen, would happen now—no more pretense.

He went for the steps, but Kelly grabbed him from behind and threw him across the deck. Jack protected his face with his hands, but when he struck the railing, his shoulder exploded in pain, and he only hoped the *crack!* he heard was wood, not bone. This was the attack he'd been expecting, and it had come at the worst possible moment.

Jack rolled onto his back, drawing the knife he'd taken from the kitchen and bringing it around in a useless attempt to defend himself. Kelly was already airborne, midleap, fur bristling around his neck and across his cheeks, fingers merging into paws, and claws solidifying from his nails, and Jack hated the monster with all his heart. It was the unfairness of things that stung the most—he vowed in that instant that he would fight until he could fight no more, and that pain would fuel his fury.

But Kelly did not land. Louis struck him in the side, and the two of them rolled back against the wheelhouse. Hope leaped in Jack's heart—he would not fight alone after all. But Vukovich was already stalking around toward Jack, and he stepped over the snarling, brutal knot of violence that Louis and Kelly had become.

*They're not changing*, Jack thought, but then he saw that Vukovich had begun to change after all, the evolution subtle. He possessed the eyes of a wolf.

Jack stood, watching Vukovich, wondering how he could kill the monster, and then a massive shape appeared in front of him. Tree. But he was facing *away* from Jack.

"Not now," Tree rasped.

The big man's intervention had brought the scuffle between Louis and Kelly to an end. The two pirates rose to their feet, bristling with hatred and bloodlust. But the moment when they might have killed each other had passed, for now. The ship swayed beneath them all, waiting for the bones of those who did not survive the day.

"You're a fool, Kelly," Louis whispered. "This isn't the time."

"What better time for food?" Kelly growled.

"You think eating Ghost's human pet will nourish you?" Tree said. His voice rumbled like far-off thunder. No one replied.

"Whose side do you think you're on?" Vukovich said, and a light began to burn brightly in Jack's mind, a spark of hope and the seed of an idea.

*Sides.* Until now it had been Ghost and the rest, but with the crew fragmenting—over him, or Sabine, or whatever else might be the cause—they were becoming weaker than ever before. They had been growing angrier and more frustrated with Ghost with every passing hour, but none of them save Finn had confronted him. The way of the pack would be to challenge Ghost to single combat, with the victor leading the pack forward. None dared to do so, knowing they could never defeat him alone. But there had been rumblings and whispers, a shared anger, and now Jack had to take advantage of that.

It was his only chance at saving Sabine. Whether Ghost loved or desired her, and no matter how much he might need her, this time she had pushed him too far. If he could not trust her, he might well go beyond torture and just kill her. Either way, the time had come to act.

"Don't you see why he's told us to go south?" Jack said.

"Shut up, meat!" Kelly said. He was standing along the railing away from Jack, no longer wolfish but still with hunger in his eyes.

"Let him speak," Louis said.

"Why?" Vukovich sneered.

"Because Ghost intends him to be as much a part of this crew as you."

There was silence at that, broken only by a haunting, hooting sound from deep within the fog. *Whales singing*, Jack thought, but it could have been errant spirits in mourning.

"We're going south because he's not running," Jack said. "You saw the *Charon*. How many men does it take to man a ship like that?"

"None," Kelly said. "Death's pack is older than ours. He's not like Ghost; he'd welcome no mere *man* aboard."

Maurilio had appeared from the bow, listening, watching. Demetrius and Ogre were out of sight, but so were Huginn and Muninn, likely down in the cabin guarding Ghost's door while he—

But Jack could not think about what the captain might be doing to the woman he loved, and what that scream had meant. That would inspire fear and rage, and there lay madness. He needed all his wits about him right now if he hoped to save them both.

"He plans to swing around and attack the *Charon*," Jack said. "He fled into the fog to give himself time to plan, and project the impression that he was running scared. But within the hour Ghost will emerge from his cabin to give the order to sail west. Death will be searching for us. He won't be difficult to find. And when we meet the *Charon*, there will be a battle, and all of you will die."

"Don't be so sure," Kelly said, a growl behind his words.

"He wouldn't do it," Vukovich said. "It's suicide against that ship, and that pack. And if Ghost could kill his brother, he'd have done it years ago."

Jack shook his head, glancing from one crewman to another. "You don't get it—*any* of you. He's used you. Ghost isn't a pirate. Not really. He cares nothing for gold and treasure, and he hunts only to feed himself and to make the lot of you better killers. All this time, he's been working to best his brother, to make himself a better pirate and a more vicious wolf than Death Nilsson. He put this pack together to help him do that. You're his little army, and you never knew it. And every one of you is expendable."

"That's ridiculous," Vukovich sniffed. "There's never been a pirate like Ghost."

"You're just not listening," Jack said, voice low, drawing them in with his intensity. "Ghost ordered Sabine to keep track of the *Charon*—"

"To keep us away from Death, Jack," Louis said.

"Yes," Jack agreed. "But only until he was ready. That's why he's so furious with her. Not because she didn't warn him Death was near, but because she let him sail into this fight before he decided he was ready. Now he's decided— Sabine brought them face-to-face, and Ghost's going to try to finish his brother once and for all."

"He wouldn't do that," Kelly said. "He'll be killing us all. Ghost wouldn't sacrifice the pack for his own . . ."

Kelly's words trailed off as realization struck him.

"Of course he would," Tree said. "You know it, Kelly.

We all do. He's always expected us to be loyal to him, to follow the laws of the pack, but he's never had any loyalty to anyone but himself."

"Exactly," Jack said. "So you can fight over me, and my scrawny scrap of flesh and bone, or you can fight Ghost, take control of the ship, and steer your own destinies."

"He's our captain," Louis said, but his doubt and dread were clear.

"He's mad," Jack said, "and he's leading you into a fight that cannot be won. You knew this moment would come one day, Louis. You all did. Now it's here."

The wolves stood silent, violence hanging in the air as obvious as the cool touch of fog drifting across the deck.

"The pup speaks of mutiny," Kelly said at last. "That's word enough to kill him right here."

"He might speak mutiny, but haven't we all thought it?" Louis said.

"Ghost has considered himself dead since the day his brother tried to kill him," Jack went on. "As far as he's concerned, he's already a corpse. What does he care if he takes the rest of you to hell along with him? If you want to live, there's only one answer."

Tree grumbled what might have been agreement. Maurilio nodded. Even Vukovich seemed uncertain, his wolfish fury faded by doubt.

*They're almost there,* Jack thought. The idea of the violence he was striving to unleash was shocking, but events had reached a desperate point. Everything beyond here and now would be worse than anything that had gone before. His job was to ensure that it was worse for Ghost and the crew, not for himself and the woman who had stolen his affections.

"We'd need all of us," Louis said.

"We can't turn against the man who made us," Vukovich said.

"That's exactly what we *must* do," Louis replied.

"It would have to be a challenge," Kelly said. "That's the way of the pack."

Tree grunted. "Doesn't seem to me the captain's been too concerned with the law of the pack these days."

"The pack changes leadership by challenge," Louis said, nodding. "But we're at sea. And with a tyrant and a madman at the wheel, there's only one way for sailors to take a ship from its captain."

Jack stepped out from Tree's vast shadow, making himself an open part of the discussion. Kelly could come at him now, or Vukovich, and they'd split him from groin to gullet before Tree or Louis had a chance to pull them away. But such risk was necessary. Hiding behind Tree's bulk, he was a frightened victim cowering in the protection of a monster. Here in the open, he was almost one of them.

"I know you hate me for what I am," Jack said, "but you were all men once, before Ghost changed you. Our aims might be different now, but I've seen the man in all of you. The will to survive, the thrill of knowing the wild, and the desire to be something more. No one wants to be at the bottom. Finn was there, and now he's dead. And who's taken his place?"

No one replied, and Jack realized that Finn's death had caused an upset in the hierarchy that had yet to be settled. And he grasped this confusion and used it as his killing stroke.

"All of you," he said. "You're all bottom of the pack. Because Ghost is no longer your leader. He is your king."

A current of discontent swirled the wafting fog, and Louis seemed to grow in height and stature. He grinned, and the weak light glinted from his golden tooth.

"It'll be Huginn and Muninn first," he said. "So are you all in, lads?"

"Yes," Tree said.

"Yes," Maurilio whispered.

"Aye," someone said from behind Jack, and he turned to see Demetrius approaching them all. "I've spent years dreaming of revenge on that bastard. Never believed anyone other than me would seek it. Never dared to speak of it."

Ogre emerged from the forecastle and approached the milling sea wolves, his huge mass almost seeming to move the ship itself. He glanced from one to another, and his heavy gaze finally settled on Jack.

"Been a long time comin'," he said.

Kelly sniffed and nodded, then hooked a thumb toward Jack. "What about him?"

Louis frowned. "This is not his fight. When it's over, we'll decide what's to become of him."

Kelly and Vukovich seemed hesitant, but the rest behaved as if they had already forgotten Jack existed. They were following Louis's lead, especially Tree, and the anticipation of bloodshed had already carried them beyond this moment. Several of them had begun to growl deep in their chests, causing Tree to glare at them.

"Quiet," Tree grumbled. "There's only one way to do this. One of us draws him on deck with a challenge."

"No," Maurilio said. "Down below, he can't escape us."

Louis shook his head. "Where's he going to go? The water? No, Tree's right. We draw him out, and when he comes on deck, we take him together. He can't fight us all at once."

"He's not alone," Vukovich growled. "He's got the damned twins."

"I didn't say it would be easy," Louis said.

Demetrius shuffled up beside Jack and nudged him. "You should stay clear now."

Jack nodded, thoughts racing ahead. He'd been dismissed, and it felt like the opportunity he needed.

"So—who calls him out?" Demetrius asked.

Ogre laughed, an unsettling rumble. "Got to be Kelly. Won't surprise Ghost at all if he does it."

Kelly sneered. "It'll be a pleasure."

Now that they'd made their decision, all the humiliation and frustration they'd suffered at Ghost's hands seemed to be fueling a rage that grew with each passing second. They had existed in fear of him, each one believing that the rest of the crew would never join in an uprising but unwilling to challenge Ghost on his own. With shared intent, their hatred took free rein.

Jack edged backward, letting the fog close around him.

The wind had picked up, and a light rain began to fall. He looked up to see the clouds churning overhead. While they had been focused on Ghost, the fogbank had begun to transform into a storm. The *Larsen* rocked underfoot, but the pirates ignored the ship. It would withstand the storm at least long enough for them to murder their captain.

Jack retreated another few steps into the fog as the rain pattered the deck all around him. He backed toward the forecastle, thinking now only of Sabine and what Ghost might have done to her, what torture or indignity she might already have suffered at his hands. He wished he could kill the bastard himself, but if he tried and failed, then Sabine would never be free. Their only chance was coalescing around him with each passing moment.

His heart was thumping, blood pulsing, when he heard the growl. *Of course*, he thought, but the sight that met him as he peered through the fog was still enough to freeze the blood in his veins and cause his heart to stammer in shock.

A monster stared back, rushing toward him through the fog. Dark-brown fur, pointed ears, the glimmer of blood streaking from a dozen places across its hide, the werewolf crouched on all fours in front of Jack, the pained growl continuing in its throat. As it bared its teeth, he saw the glitter of gold in one fang.

*Louis.*

Beyond the monstrous wolf-thing that Louis had become, the others were also changing, or changed, figures shifting in the fog. Bones creaked and hides stretched, and the sounds he heard were the distillation of pain and pure wild hunger. He watched as Tree contorted, bones shifting, arms shortening. The sailor cried out in agony as the transformation twisted his limbs and stretched his flesh. Tree stripped off his clothes as fur sprouted from his dark skin, a thick coat that covered his body, rippling

*A monster stared back, rushing toward him through the fog.*

with the muscles underneath this new pelt. He opened his mouth in a howl, and his jaws thrust forward, teeth lengthening into fangs. Jack stared in horror and awe as Tree dropped to all fours, ears shifting, pushing up to twin points atop his wide, lupine skull, and his entire face thrust outward, becoming a snout. It took only seconds, and then the monster stood, this massive, murderous wolf, stamping and clawing at the deck of the *Larsen*, gnashing its jaws, glancing around with yellow, murderous eyes at its pack brothers.

In moments the crew had vanished and creatures of nightmare were in their place. All but Kelly, who was the only one of them who had remained human . . . for the moment.

Kelly headed aft toward the cabin, and the rest of the sea wolves followed.

"Ghost!" Kelly shouted. "Come out and face me! I challenge you! For the pack. For the *Larsen*. To the death."

Jack's mutiny was under way.

## CHAPTER ELEVEN

# MAELSTROM

J ack stood by the steps that led down into the fore-castle as the rain began to fall harder. The wind picked up and the sails swelled as if the whole ship was holding its breath, waiting for the violence to erupt. The wheel was secured, the ship blindly following its last heading, and Jack shuddered at the image of the *Larsen* sailing forever, everyone on board slain in the fight to come. A ghost ship in the Pacific.

Through the growing storm he could barely make out distant figures at the stern. The masts blocked much of his view, but even over the rising wind he could still hear Kelly shouting for Ghost to appear.

"It's time, Ghost! Show yourself or forfeit leadership! Or are you a coward?"

This last must have been the final straw, for the

timbers shook with the roar that followed, one that could only belong to Ghost. He ought to have sent Huginn and Muninn ahead, but Jack knew that his arrogance and fury would not allow it. Ghost treated his pack with a disdain that had only grown in the time since Jack had come aboard, and now his thoughts would be a maelstrom of hatred and vengeance toward his brother and confusion over Sabine's betrayal. He would see Kelly's timing as nothing more than a nuisance to be dispensed with as quickly as possible, but the suggestion of cowardice would enrage him. He could not ignore it. He would relish the opportunity to vent his rage on Kelly.

Jack knew him so well.

"You stupid son of a bitch!" Ghost said. "Now isn't the time—"

But the words were cut off. In the depths of the fog, the *Larsen* already looking like a ghost ship, Jack could not see the monster who had become his nemesis, but he heard the thudding of four-footed things pounding across the deck. Someone roared, and perhaps it was the first time he had heard Muninn or Huginn utter a sound as the mutineers attacked.

Jack clasped his knife, but it did not make him feel safer. His senses seemed sharpened by the thrill of fear.

Another scream . . . and then came the primal sound

of animalistic combat.

*Soon*, he thought, *soon, soon, when I hear—*

Ghost's rage-filled voice grew into an animal howl as he found his true form. And now the sea wolves were warring on their own ship, snarling and snapping in a bloody melee that Jack could barely picture in his mind's eye, its true savagery unfolding behind the mists of the quickening storm.

Jack bolted into the forecastle, sliding down the handrails without touching a step. In the dark, with the wind pushing rain in behind him, he turned to the door leading into the hold. There was one entrance fore and one aft, and that stinking, darkened artery in the ship's belly was the key to what little plan he had.

He yanked the door open and dropped into the gangway, entering the same way Finn had when he'd discovered Jack stealing the diamonds from the pirates' treasure cache. Then he dashed, trying to run silently as well as swiftly and praying that the mutiny would not be over too quickly. He raced past the room where the prisoners from the *Umatilla* had been kept before the night of the full-moon slaughter, then past the food stores and treasure cache, and finally the secure chamber where he and Sabine had been imprisoned for their own sakes, and where they had first shared secrets.

*More secrets to come,* he thought, but now was not the time for such musings.

As he passed beneath ceiling hatches, he heard the snarling and gnashing louder and louder. Claws scraped wood. Bodies thumped to the deck. Beneath one hatch, rain spitting down through the grille, a splash of hot liquid fell upon him, spattering his face and right shoulder. The scent of blood was overpowering. By now the deck would be awash with it.

The weight of dread for what Ghost might have done to Sabine nearly dragged him down. But Jack London had survived certain death in the Yukon winter, had tamed the wilderness of the frozen north and the wildness in his own heart, had fought an ancient, accursed evil and triumphed. He would not let love be his undoing.

At the aft end of the gangway he leaped up the steps and crashed in through the small door, heedless of what might await him there. He darted through the mess, glanced to the right where the galley awaited, then threw open the door of the chart room. It was empty. He rushed past the door to his own quarters and quickly picked the lock to the captain's cabin, then threw the door wide.

Jack froze in the open doorway, staring, his heart pounding in his ears.

"Thank God," he whispered.

Sabine sprang up from the chair, almost as if she had been waiting for him all along. She bumped the table, and a bottle of rum rolled off and struck the floor, spilling its contents into the thirsty wood. Jack glanced at the lamp in the corner, knowing there must be a match nearby. But he thought better of it. If they could not escape the ship, setting it ablaze would have been his last foolish act.

"Jack," Sabine cried, crushing him in her arms.

He kissed her hair, breathing in the lovely scent of her, feeling the press of her curves against his body and knowing that this—her voice and her touch, and the way his heart soared in her presence—was worth braving hell.

Jack pushed her back, studying her more closely. A large red welt colored her left cheek, her lip was swollen, and there was a streak of blood at the edge of her mouth. Otherwise, she seemed unharmed. He could hardly believe that Ghost had not done more to punish her.

"I don't understand," he said softly. "I've never felt such relief, but I was sure he would have tortured you. He must know that you deliberately hid Death's arrival from him."

Sabine nodded, squeezing his hands in her own. "I feared he might actually kill me, but he only struck me once." She touched her bruised cheek. "That was bad enough. But then he sat and stared at me, drinking rum and brooding."

"About his brother, no doubt," Jack said, thinking that perhaps Ghost did love Sabine after all. Forced to confront such feelings, the captain would be coming unhinged, all of his efforts to expunge human sentiment from his heart in peril. "But he's got more problems than Death Nilsson right now."

"What is it?" Sabine asked.

"Mutiny." He smiled grimly and led her from the room.

They hurried to the galley, moving in concert as they started gathering the supplies Jack had secreted away, packing them in small crates. It took only seconds, but Jack heard a clamor coming from the steps up to the deck and left the rest behind.

"Come on," he said, and they raced out of the galley and back through the mess, each carrying a crate, the ship rocking harder than ever in the growing storm.

"Where did this weather come from?" Jack muttered. "It was nothing but fog before."

Sabine said nothing, only clutched at the wooden crate in her arms. As they passed the stairs up to the deck, a tumbling series of thuds made them turn, crouch against the hold gangway door, and watch in horror as a shaggy, blood-and-rain-sodden body bounced from the treads and struck the floor. The werewolf had fur so golden it was nearly white, and Jack thought perhaps it was one of the twins. The monster twitched once and lay still, chest torn open to expose a gruesome cavity where its heart had been.

Silver, it seemed, was not the only way to kill a werewolf.

"Hurry," Sabine said.

They maneuvered the crates down into the hold and ran, carrying them, Jack warning her not to slip in the blood that had dripped down and pooled on the planks underfoot. With the mutiny unfolding on the deck above them, their only hope was to pass unnoticed beneath the fight and emerge on the other end of the ship, where Jack's plan could be enacted. At the end of the gangway, Jack paused at the steps up to the forecastle, sending his senses outward in an attempt to feel the presence of any wolves.

"Don't stop, Jack. Truly." Sabine was almost pleading.

"You know something I don't," he said, muscling his small crate up the steps.

Sabine passed him by, starting up the steps from the forecastle to the deck. He spoke her name, too softly even for the werewolves to hear over the howling of the storm.

She looked down at him. "We're closing on Death."

"Damn!" Jack said. "How long?"

"Not long enough."

And then she was out onto the deck. Jack followed her, the crate suddenly lighter in his arms, and heard the werewolves still at it. A handful of minutes had passed, but their frenzied fighting had not abated. Roars turned to shrieks of primal pain. Wood cracked. Part of the mainsail had somehow been torn, and a swath of it hung downward, billowing in the storm. Beyond, close to the stern, Jack could see forms slamming into one another, claws rising and falling, tearing flesh, blood flying.

*Freedom or death*, he thought. From the moment he had come on board, those had been the only possible outcomes for him. And it had all come down to this moment.

Sabine had already crept along to the closest portside boat, whose securing bolts Jack had loosened, and he followed. They settled their crates into the skiff. Most of the supplies would be fine if the boat did not capsize when it hit the water, but he worried about the water jugs. He had packed them in cloth, but if they cracked, he and Sabine would be without freshwater. But it could not be helped. They were quickly running out of time.

Jack kicked one bolt free, then got to work on the final bolt holding the craft in place. He nodded to Sabine, who cranked the winch, hoisting the boat off its wooden mounting. A howl of pain rose from the savage combat nearby. A shadow flew through the air toward them, a body thumped to the deck and rolled, slamming into the railing only ten feet away. The werewolf, chest heaving, jaws dripping with furious lather, rose on its hind legs, turning to growl at them. A great swath of hide had been ripped from its chest, and its left ear and a portion of its scalp were missing.

"Don't move," Jack whispered.

The wolf bared its fangs, and Jack saw the glint of gold.

"Louis."

The Louis-wolf reached them in one bound but did not attack. It shoved the skiff, and the small boat swung out over the water on its boom. The werewolf dropped to all fours again and took a step back, staring at Jack.

"Thank you," Jack said.

Louis bounded away, claws scrabbling on the deck, tearing up wood as the monster hurled itself back into the battle with Ghost.

Sabine waited by the railing, but Jack saw no fear in her now. She gazed at him with boldness and determination, her hair flailing her face as the *Larsen* surged across the sea. The rain soaked her clothes and they clung to her, making her look like some siren out of Greek mythology, risen from the sea to tempt him.

Jack threw the lever that released the winch. The ropes rattled through the pulleys on the boom overhead, and the boat dropped into the water. They had only seconds now if they hoped to keep the skiff from being swamped in the rough waters.

"You realize we're in big trouble if this storm goes on very long?" Jack asked, giving her one last chance to change her mind. But they both knew it was a false choice. If they stayed, they would die. At least in the boat they had a chance, however slim.

"We'll be all right," Sabine said, speaking up to be heard over the wind.

She stepped close, kissed him, and took his hand, and together they turned toward the railing. Jack drew in a deep breath—

—and the sky thundered with the boom of the *Charon*'s deck gun. Death Nilsson's steamship emerged wraithlike from the storm at the *Larsen*'s starboard side, powering through the water toward them.

"It's going to—," Jack began, and the *Charon*'s bow smashed into the *Larsen*'s stern at a sharp angle. The impact was massive, the sound shattering. Deck boards splintered and flew, metal ground against wood, and the larger vessel's gun boomed once more. The *Larsen*'s mizzenmast cracked, tipped, and tore rigging and sails down as it fell toward the stern.

Jack and Sabine were knocked from their feet, but she quickly grabbed his hand and hauled him to the port rail. "Come on!" she said, and their boat—their salvation— bobbed on the sea below. The schooner was shoved sideways

against the waves by the larger vessel's momentum, creaking and groaning, and the skiff was being pounded against
the *Larsen*'s hull by the surging water.

"I'll keep you safe," Jack vowed. "I swear it."

She smiled and nodded, but he felt sure there was
another component to that smile, and the secrets she had
not yet shared with him were deeper than he could know,
and perhaps darker.

Jack glanced back one last time, and he knew that the
end was close. The *Charon*'s bow was embedded in the
*Larsen*'s stern, and a dozen men, hardened and scarred,
partially transformed into the wolves hidden beneath their
human skins, began to leap from the deck of Death's ship.

Jack laughed as a strange elation flushed through him,
and he remembered a truth he had learned in the Yukon:
that he was most alive when death was close enough to
whisper in his ear.

Jack and Sabine jumped together, hands still clasped as
they plummeted toward the churning sea. For a moment
as they fell, Jack felt weightless and timeless, and anything was possible. Then the cold water enveloped them,
the violent sea tore them apart, and he kicked to the surface. Tossed on the waves, he reached for the skiff but was
bashed against the *Larsen*'s hull. He gasped in pain as his
cracked rib was battered, took in a mouthful of water, and

struggled upward again, scrabbling against the small boat. One large kick, and he rose high enough to grab the gunwale, and the first thing he did was look up.

The *Larsen*'s railing was above them, and as yet no one, or nothing, looked down.

Screams of hatred and rage swirled in the wind. Wood cracked, and Jack turned to see one of Death's wolves smash through the railing and flail wildly as he fell into the ocean thirty feet away. Jack prayed that Sabine and he would not be seen, that the werewolf could not swim, that the sea would drag the monster under.

Jack hauled himself into the boat to find Sabine already there. She smiled at him with relief, then they hurriedly untied the ropes binding them to the doomed *Larsen*. Jack raised the small sail, then grabbed one of the long oars and pushed them away from the hull. He had to push hard because the sea still drove the tiny boat against the *Larsen*, but inch by inch he shifted them along until the skiff slipped past the bow, and the sail caught the wind.

He fell back and clutched the rudder, watching the sail to sense which way the wind wanted to take them. Right now, that was the direction he would aim. The faster they could flee these two warring ships, the better.

"Jack!" Sabine called, and she was staring past him at what they were leaving behind. Keeping his weight on the rudder, he turned to see what had startled her so.

On the *Larsen*, the conflict had spread across the deck. There was a riot of activity at the bow—a pile of slashing, slavering bodies, tearing and gouging and biting—and in their midst, a battling shape that they both recognized. Ghost. He raged and roared, threw a wolf overboard, and picked up another by its legs, swinging it around and using it to batter others aside. Ghost was revealed at the heart of the onslaught, and he was a statue of blood and violence. For a moment Jack was afraid that the captain was more than man, more than beast, and more than anything he had ever imagined. But then he fell, and other monstrous shapes fell upon him, murder their intent.

Jack turned and met Sabine's eyes. He tweaked the rudder, and the wind filled their sails.

"We're away," he said, and she nodded.

The skiff carried them into the heart of the storm, and the battle vanished behind them. Savage, bestial cries and the scrape of the ships' hulls flitted like ghosts around the small boat, dancing on the wind and then blocked by rolling waves. As they sailed away, Jack's fear of the wolves also began to vanish, replaced by a total focus on the task at hand—not dying at sea. He gripped the tiller so hard his knuckles ached, and given the strength of the storm, it was all he could do to hold the sail in place. The skiff leaped over the waves, and Jack and Sabine did their best to hang on.

In minutes they were alone on the sea. Yet Jack could feel Ghost's rage following them, a bitter resentment that lingered long after the last wolf's cry had been swallowed by the wind.

Sabine shouted something to him from where she sat in the bow.

"What?" Jack called over the wind.

She rose up on her knees, dress plastered to her body, damp hair across her face, looking very much the sea witch that Ghost had called her. Sabine pointed off to starboard and turned to him, shouting to be heard.

"To the northwest!" she cried. "The nearest land is there, less than a day's sail!"

Jack nodded, struggling to keep control of the boat as he adjusted their course. A huge wave rolled beneath them, and for half a heartbeat he thought they would capsize, but then the wave tossed them back down and they were on their new heading. The rain pounded at them, gusts of wind battered the sail, and the small mast creaked ominously.

His muscles burned with effort, and he clenched his teeth and blinked away the rain. Whatever happened, he would not release his hold. His mind went back to the White Horse Rapids in the Yukon. He had maneuvered to safety then and he would do the same now, conquering the raging sea, triumphing over the vast, wild ocean. If that meant navigating through stormy waters all day and night, he would do it. Jack refused to allow himself to accept any other possibility.

The laugh began soft at first, then grew louder, and then Jack turned his face to the rain and let it come.

"You've gone mad!" Sabine called, though she herself was grinning.

"We've escaped him!" Jack said. "Damn Ghost and his pack. Damn all of them! We set them against each other, outsmarted them."

"You think a lot of yourself!"

Jack laughed at that as well. "It's true. And I think a lot of you! But we've survived because we're human. In our hearts and souls, we're *human*. Not the mere animals that Ghost insisted we all were."

Jack had to fight a sudden gust, tearing his gaze away from Sabine's beauty. He had been on the verge of speaking his heart and was glad of the forced interruption. In all his life he had never met a girl or a woman who had made him feel so breathless, who had enchanted him and made him feel such true devotion. Though the storm threatened to swamp them at any moment, he felt only glee at their rush to freedom and this adventure they now shared, away from the constant threat of murder.

He wondered, though, about the mutiny that had become a massacre. It felt to him like a story with no ending, and the questions would linger with him. Who had survived that terrible, bloody battle? Did Ghost still live, and if not, had he been killed by his own crew or by his lunatic brother?

Salt spray stung Jack's eyes, but he blinked it away and looked at Sabine again, realizing that these questions would not have to haunt him. His beauty, his sea witch, could stop him from wondering. She would know the answers, if he truly desired them.

Right then, Jack decided he did not want to know.

"I love you," he said quietly, expecting the words to be taken by the storm and swirled away.

But in that same moment, something changed around them. The sea grew calmer, the rain reduced to a sprinkle, and the wind became gentler, yet still firmly behind the skiff. It happened so suddenly that he had not even time to notice before the words were out of his mouth, and the breeze carried them to Sabine.

Yet her eyes were closed. As raindrops slid down her face, she breathed deeply and evenly. Jack studied her, nervous; she must have heard him.

A smile played at the edges of her lips.

"There," she said softly. "That should be a bit easier on us. Keep on with the wind, and it will deliver us to the island."

Jack stared. Island? Easier on them?

"Wait a second," he said, looking around to see the storm still raging behind them. Even off to either side of the boat, the sea remained a churning froth. But directly ahead the ocean had calmed, the clouds parted to reveal blue, and the breeze breathed true.

Sabine arched an eyebrow, her smile turning flirtatious.

"Is this you?" he asked. "You're doing this?"

She pushed wet strands of hair from her face and nodded.

Jack laughed in amazement. "But how?"

"I'm not really sure." Sabine shrugged. "I told you that I had other powers . . . gifts that I feared Ghost would inherit if he were to kill me. This shaping of the weather is one of them."

"The fog?" Jack asked.

"No, I didn't create the fogbank. But I called the storm to blind Ghost and Death and make it more difficult for anyone who might pursue us. All the better to hide our escape."

Jack guided the little boat, settling down into an easy rhythm as the Pacific seemed to welcome them now and to help guide them on their way.

"Are you really a witch, then?"

"I need to rest, Jack." Sabine curled in the bow, and he could hear the weariness in her voice. Much as he wanted to quiz her, he knew what she had been through.

Soon, Sabine slept, and Jack steered them across the ocean.

She woke after several hours, stretching stiffness from her limbs. She smiled at Jack. And in those hours, his need to know many things had grown greater.

"Not far now," she said after a moment's contemplation.

"What are you, Sabine?" he asked.

She stared at him, and he could see that she accepted his need to know. Perhaps she had dreamed of them together, or maybe she had dreamed of things he could never understand. Either way, he left the question standing, and her answering began.

"I honestly don't know. I'm not sure what a witch is. I only know that these gifts are mine, and that sometimes they frighten me, and if I could make a single wish, it would be to understand better what they are, and what I am."

A profound sadness filled her as she spoke, and Jack

wanted to reach out to comfort her, but he dared not move from his place for fear that the current would twist them around. Even if Sabine could influence the weather, she could not master every wave.

"I've been thinking on this while you slept, and I know what you are."

Hope lit her eyes.

"You are a woman, no matter what magic lies in your hands. And you are lovely."

She smiled, but her sadness remained. "I feared that if you knew the truth about what I can do, you would think me no less a monster than Ghost."

Jack scoffed. "You are hardly a monster."

Her gaze hardened as if she was challenging him. "I have more magic than I've told you, Jack. It isn't just the weather, or sensing the location of a ship upon the water. I sought out Death Nilsson, you see? It isn't only that I knew he was coming. I sought him and felt him, and guided him to us so that he would kill his brother. Or even better, they would kill each other."

"And I'm grateful for it," Jack assured her, listening to the slap of waves on the side of the skiff as they sailed beneath increasingly clear skies. The storm raged behind them, closing in once they'd passed, as if erasing their trail so that they could not be followed.

"I can disorient a man or hex him with bad luck," Sabine went on. "A talent I was sorely tempted to use on the *Larsen*, but which I kept to myself. Displaying my true talents . . . well, Ghost is a covetous man. I can touch the dreaming minds of those I have used my gifts to find, as I did with Ghost. Every time I helped guide Ghost to another ship, I tried to warn the ships' captains by whispering in their dreams, but it never seemed to matter how prepared they were for an attack. The wolves were too ferocious. Too swift."

"You tried," Jack assured her, wanting more than ever to take her into his arms again.

Sabine composed herself and gazed at him. "There is one other thing. One *last* thing."

"Go on."

"Ghost could have murdered me, I am sure. But I do not think I will ever die as an ordinary woman would, of age."

Jack stared. "You're . . . immortal?"

"There's no such thing as immortal. But I have lived a very long time, Jack. I'm afraid to tell you what I recall of my history, for fear it would frighten you to know what an old woman I truly am. Even *I* do not know exactly how old. I don't remember being a small girl. Those recollections are lost to me. But I believe I am . . . ancient."

Jack held his breath a moment, searching inside himself for some reaction, trying to understand what he felt. And then he realized that what he felt was not numbness; he simply did not care.

"You're not the first woman I have met with gifts that some might have called witchcraft."

Sabine leaned forward, eyes fixed on him.

"And not the first to show me magic," he continued. "But the other—her name was Lesya, the daughter of a forest spirit, an elemental—she was cruel, a madwoman. You are kind and gentle and loving. You are far from a monster, Sabine. I said I loved you. I know that you heard me."

She turned away.

"I love you still," he said.

Her smile returned, tentative at first, but blossoming.

"How can you?"

"How could I not?"

Sabine shook her head, took a moment to consider his words; and then her eyes narrowed in contemplation. "Jack . . . if you knew."

"Knew what?"

"Knew . . . nothing. Nothing, Jack. So, this Lesya. You must tell me about her."

Jack thought back to his time in the Yukon, the hardships and brutality of that journey and the beauty and madness of Lesya's forest. He tried to figure out where best to start relating his story. Even as he did, he realized that though he had professed his love, Sabine had not spoken the words in return. And he wondered if a woman who might be immortal and had lived many lifetimes *could* love an ordinary man.

Jack turned away from her, staring out at the ocean, lost in thought. When he finally began to speak, he was unsure if the words that burst forth would be the tale of Lesya or an inquiry about the nature and disposition of her heart. But as he turned back to Sabine, words failed him.

In the distance, beneath a clear blue sky, the island beckoned.

## CHAPTER TWELVE

# DEEP CURRENTS

Sabine might have been able to influence and steer the weather, but the ocean was its own beast. As the wind drove them toward the island, Jack dropped sail and let the waves carry them. He steered as well as he could, aiming for an inlet where the waves might not dash their boat to pieces at the foot of low cliffs or smash them against the rocks protruding from the sea. Sabine helped, using an oar to urge them aside when it looked as if they were heading for a violent clash of waves. They finally positioned themselves well and rode the waves in, and it was only when Jack allowed himself to relax and believe that they had made it that the splintering, rending sound came from below.

The boat drifted to shore and grounded on the sand.

"Is it bad?" Sabine asked. She sat at the bow, exhausted

and soaked. Jack still saw her as a gorgeous woman, not the old thing she claimed to be. What that displayed about his state of mind he was not sure, but his feelings were true. Perhaps the mystery she presented made him love her even more.

"Let's pull it onto the beach so we can take a look."

They jumped from the boat and landed on the coarse sand, where Jack had a fleeting thought: *Our island.* Escape had been his prime concern, and then reaching shore safely, but now he could consider the future beyond the hour or day ahead. This might well be their island, because they were as good as stranded here. In a small boat like theirs, an ocean journey of any length would be treacherous beyond belief, however much food and water they might be able to store on board. And if the damage the hull had just sustained by scraping over unseen rocks was as bad as he feared . . .

Jack and Sabine hauled the skiff onto the beach, each breaking wave aiding their efforts, until they were sure it would not be dragged back out to sea. Jack knelt and examined the hull, and the damage was even worse than he'd expected. There were three ragged holes, and several other boards were badly fractured. He could perform a repair job, he was sure, but it would not be quick. And without the correct tools, it would be ten times the challenge.

"It's not good," he said, but when he turned around, Sabine was facing away from him, looking across the beach and inland. She was so still that he thought she might have seen something dangerous or startling. But the scene was peaceful, and he took the moment to survey where they had landed.

Approaching the island, he'd been able to judge its width as perhaps half a mile. One end was mainly beach and low-lying land, the other rose steadily to a ridged hill perhaps two hundred feet high. It was crowned with a spine of sharp bare rock, but much of the rest of the island was green, cover broken here and there with protruding shoulders of stone. Birds called, insects buzzed, and somewhere to their left he heard the musical whisper of a stream finding the ocean.

There was no sign of habitation. The sandy beach was untrodden, and the jungle that grew to within twenty feet of the sea appeared untouched by human hands. The whole island exuded a wildness that was familiar to Jack, and that did little to unsettle him. At the same time it seemed to him that they were in the middle of a pause, as if the island was aware of their presence and was waiting to see what happened next. He had been subjected to such dispassionate scrutiny before. He wondered what the island saw.

"There are no people here," Sabine said. "But there

were once. Two men lived here for several years. Bad men, alone and lost. The shelter they built is beyond the spit of land to the north, close to the beach."

"A shelter would be good," Jack said. "So, you *know* all this?"

"I know it all. Each breath is history."

"And you read it."

"Well . . ." Sabine turned back to him, and he saw the remnants of a sad expression smiled away. "I live it, though only in brief flashes." She looked pained, as if talking about her talents was revealing her darkest secrets.

"Come here," Jack said, holding out his hand. "Help me with the food and water. We'll walk and find this shelter. And if you feel like talking as we walk, I'd love to know more of your life. I want to know *all* of you."

"Ghost," she said. She looked past Jack and out to sea, and over the horizon storm clouds still hung like bruises on the sky. Lightning flashed there, so far away that the thunder never arrived.

"We beat him," Jack said. "We won."

He felt a rush of unalloyed joy at their escape, and he swept Sabine into his arms and hugged her tight. Dry land felt good beneath his feet, a mark of their survival, an acknowledgment of success. But when he released her and Sabine pulled slightly away so she could look into his eyes, her delight was less intense.

"But Ghost is not yet dead," she said softly.

"That doesn't matter. He might not be dead, but he's many miles away."

"And we are trapped on an island with a holed boat."

Jack looked around again. There were fruit trees growing close to the stream running down the beach. Birds flitted from tree to tree. There would be fish, and farther inland perhaps small mammals inhabited some of the nooks and shadowy areas of the island's topography. Even with violence still playing across the horizon, this place might well be paradise.

"Let's find that shelter," he said.

As they started walking, Sabine told him why she was a mystery to herself.

"I remember the Great Boston Fire of seventy-two. I watched downtown burn, and even though I brought rain, it was only a light autumn mist. It had little effect against such flames. I saw a man I cared about die that day—he was not the first, and will not be the last."

They were walking along the gently curving beach, aiming for where a shoulder of land thrust out into the sea. Jack hoped they could climb this without needing to go too far inland, but he was not troubled. He enjoyed hearing

*As they started walking, Sabine told him why*
*she was a mystery to herself.*

Sabine's voice, unconcerned at being overheard and unworried about whether Ghost would like what she was saying. Her voice sounded different, and perhaps the difference was that she was finally free.

"I was in Quebec during the Lower Canada Rebellion. I was looking for a man who might have had knowledge of my history, but I never found him, there or anywhere else. That was 1838. I remember watching the Colonials burning down three buildings where they thought rebels were hiding, only to find that they had fled the night before. They'd left their families behind, believing them to be safe. The screams that day . . . horrible."

*That was decades ago,* Jack thought, but he did not speak. She had already told him that she was old—*ancient,* she had said—and he wondered how much further back she might go. He glanced sidelong at her; beautiful hair, radiant skin. Somehow she remained young, and he had the feeling that despite her age and sad wisdom, her heart remained youthful as well.

They left the beach and headed into the jungle, seeking a safe route over the ridge of land. Giant fronds hung from palm trees, creepers trailed across the ground, and blazing orchids spotted trunks and grew from rocks tumbled from higher inland.

"In the mid-seventeen hundreds I spent a lot of time

in Europe. I worked for some time with Jean-Étienne Guettard as he created the first geological map of France. Time and the ages fascinated me back then, when I thought perhaps they could answer some of my own questions about myself. But nothing like me can exist in layers of rock or the formation of gems. My history is a vaguer thing.

"I had returned to America during 1608, through the Jamestown settlement."

"Returned?" Jack asked. He tried blinking away the shock, heart thumping as he weighed the significance of what she claimed. And yet he believed her without a shadow of doubt. She had no reason to lie, and he felt the pain that excavating these memories inspired in her.

Sabine paused, and sunlight passing between heavy, moving leaves dappled her skin. "I have much more to tell," she said. "Earlier memories are not so clear, and it's difficult for me to recall the years." She leaned against a tree, closing her eyes, and Jack went to her, fearing her ill.

"Sabine?" He held her arms and she was cool, and when she opened her eyes again, she was in control, calm and unconcerned at her surroundings. She stared only at Jack.

"How can you claim to love a creature such as me?" she asked, and Jack felt his stomach sink in despair and sympathy. Was she really so consumed by her own strangeness? Lesya had been aware of her abilities, but mad at the same time. Sabine was not mad . . . but did that mean the weight of her years must crush her down?

"I claim nothing," Jack said. "My love for you is a fact. And if you truly believe yourself a *creature*, then I am a . . ." He scraped a shred of bark from the tree she leaned against, and an ant ran across his finger. "An ant. I am an ant." He dug deeper, and a glistening grub was exposed. "Or a grub, born, living, and dying in the dark. Because you are a fine, proud creature compared to me."

"No, Jack," she said, smiling. "Proud once, perhaps. But I'm too old for that now."

"You're not old at all." He thought of what he'd felt when he had first set eyes upon her, and all that he had seen of her since. "In my heart you're Sabine, in her twenties. A weight of experience in her eyes, perhaps, but still my young Sabine."

"Oh, Jack. It's *you* who are so young." With that, Sabine turned and started up the slope, heading for the low ridge from where they would stare down into the next small bay. And each step seemed to take her further back into the past.

"I met Leonardo da Vinci in 1502. An incredible man, he saw the enigma in me. I scared and fascinated him. He had such a beautiful mind, and for a short time I thought I had found someone similar to me." Sabine brushed a heavy, hanging leaf aside, and water dropped down her back. She shivered.

"I watched the Mongols rampaging through China. Lived through a dozen outbreaks of what is now known as the Black Death. Witnessed the dreadful results of the Crusades."

"Which Crusade?" Jack asked softly, because though it was impossible, he found it difficult not to believe Sabine. She was so convinced, and convincing.

"All of them." She glanced over her shoulder, perspiration speckling her nose and forehead. She was beautiful. Jack looked away and squeezed his eyes closed, fisting his hands, making sure he was possessed of all his faculties. He had let Lesya enchant him for a time, and his obsession with her strange splendor had blinded him to the truth of her barely hidden madness. But that was not the case here, at all, and it never had been. Sabine was a delicate creature, and she and Jack had helped each other through the most dreadful of times.

She waited until he looked back at her before speaking again.

"I remember things from so long ago. Plagues and wars. A family that took me in to help with their farming, and who I helped in ways they could not understand." She breathed a soft laugh. "They tried to burn me as a witch."

"You have no scars," Jack said. "*Any*where."

"The memory of pain fades over time," she said. "In this body, the memory of scars also disappears. And sometimes memories themselves . . ." She frowned, looked back up the slope. "I don't think it's far to the ridge." When she started walking again, Jack reached out for her hand.

"You wanted to tell me this," he said. "So finish it."

She needed no prompting.

"There was a man in France who said he could help me discover the truth of what I am, but he was killed in a Viking raid. Once, in Jerusalem, I saw a demon in the streets and thought it had eyes like my own. I felt sand between my toes in Egypt, I almost drowned in Russia, and in Spain I was tortured for so, so long that . . ." She frowned. "I think I was their plaything. Village after village, year after year. Their eternally bloodied offering to the gods."

"That's awful," Jack whispered.

"And that's why it's good I don't really remember." They walked on, and Jack looked at Sabine's back when she took the lead. The climb became steeper, but she seemed unconcerned at the fall beneath them.

"You said if Ghost killed you, he would take your powers," he said. "And yet you tell me you've lived for many centuries."

"Nothing is truly immortal," she said. "Ghost knows

that, and he understands killing better than anyone I have ever met." She paused, and the tension seemed to relax from her body. "Here we are." They were standing on a narrow ridge perhaps fifty feet above both beaches, looking down at the beach beyond. It was a smaller bay than where they had landed, and more sheltered from the breaking waves, its waters gentle and clear.

"We might be here for a long time," Jack said. Sabine did not reply. She looked unsettled.

"Come on," she said. "Their shelter is on the beach, I think. Battered now, and in need of repair, but it will be somewhere we can remain for a while."

"I'll paddle the boat around," Jack said. "Later, when we've rested enough that I can bail water at the same time. And then I'll go hunting. I've hunted before. We'll make a fire on the beach, cook some meat, and there'll be plenty of fruit out there."

As they walked, he thought of the time that lay ahead of them, and of his family, awaiting his return in San Francisco. Then there was his friend Merritt Sloper, who must surely now believe that Jack was dead, one of many victims of the pirate attack upon the *Umatilla*. He had responsibilities beyond the here and now that he should never let go. Lesya had *persuaded* him to forget; here, he had to remember.

The slope on this side was gentler, and Sabine confidently led the way until they were halfway down. She paused, head cocked, her right hand held out from her thigh and fingers spread. They caressed the air as if playing a piano, and then her shoulders slumped.

"This is where they died," she said, pointing off between the low trees to their right. Farther out toward the sea, the land had fallen away from the ridge long ago to form a sheer cliff, softened now with plant growth but still ragged and sharp.

"Both of them?" Jack asked.

"Together."

"Why?"

"I can put a hex on a living man, but I can't read the thoughts of the dead." Sabine started forward again, his beautiful mystery.

*What else can you do?* he wondered, and perhaps soon— when they had a fire lit and he'd brought the rest of their supplies from the boat—he would ask. But there was no rush.

They reached the beach and found the remains of the shelter built by the two doomed men. There was very little left—some cut branches, heavier logs buried in the sand, and the remains of a woven roof. But it was a start, and Jack relished the idea of some manual labor.

"Your turn to talk to me, Jack," Sabine said. She lowered herself onto a log that might once have formed part of a wall, staring uncertainly out to sea.

"What is it?" Jack asked.

"Nothing." She waved her hand. "Tell me about Lesya."

"You really want me to . . ." Even the thought of that mad forest spirit chilled his blood beneath the sinking sun.

"Jack! I feel like a . . . *freak*. I'm blessed with this"—she touched her face and body—"perpetual youth. But cursed at the same time with the *knowledge* of age and the staggering passage of time. You can have no idea what it's like living so long without knowing why, existing outside everyone and everything else without understanding what you really are. I've considered many explanations over the years—I'm a freak of nature, a demon. God, or the devil. But one thing I've *always* been is the only one of my kind.

"For a time, knowing his fascination with me, I wondered if Ghost might be able to understand the lonely yearning that comes of being unique. There are many other wolves, but none quite like him. And he sees the layers of the world in a fashion ordinary men simply cannot. But he has spent a lifetime killing all the empathy inside him, and I learned quickly that he could never truly know me. I believed no one ever would, until I found you."

"Even though I'm an ordinary man?" Jack asked.

Sabine smiled. "There's nothing ordinary about you, Mr. London. And that's enough fishing for compliments."

Jack laughed softly. "Well, you're right that there's no one like you."

"I've never met anyone even *remotely* like me, though there have been pretenders." She trailed off, looking out to sea once more.

"What happened to the pretenders?" Jack asked, not sure he really wanted to know.

"Time carried them away. So tell me about Lesya and why you think she might be like me." She turned to stare at him. "And then tell me where she lives."

On that hot beach where palm fronds touched the sand and azure waters washed lazily against the island, Jack London recounted his time in the frozen, haunted north. He told Sabine details that he had not yet found the courage to tell anyone else, even his good friend Merritt Sloper—about his time with Lesya in her cursed forest; his encounter with her mysterious father, Leshii, the tree spirit who had eventually saved Jack's life; Lesya's past victims preserved in the living wood of unnatural trees; and his final confrontation with the legendary Wendigo, the creature he had overcome to find and conquer the wildness within himself. Telling the tale was a catharsis, and by the time he had finished, it was dusk.

Sabine stared at him with an expression he had never seen in her eyes before. There was amazement and respect, but also a sense of longing that had nothing to do with Jack the man and everything to do with what he had lived through.

"You sound a little like me," Sabine said, and Jack knew the source of the longing.

"No," he replied. "I'm only a man."

"There can be no 'only' about you, Jack," she replied. "Your story is unbelievable, and yet I believe every word."

"You're only the second person I've told," he said. "Probably the last. Anyone else would think me mad."

"Perhaps," Sabine said.

"She's not like you, you know." Even mentioning Lesya had given Jack the heat of longing, and a chill of fear.

Sabine only glanced at him, a strange smile softening her face.

"I mean it," Jack insisted. "She might have had"—he paused, searching for the word—"*talents* that most people could never understand. But she was insane. She told me that her father had mated with a human woman, so she was part human, part spirit. An unnatural thing. To say you're like her is like saying I am similar to—"

"At least she knew of her parents," Sabine said. "I have

no concept of ever being born."

Her words hung in the air, floating like sparks. A silence fell between them, and Jack filled the time building a fire. When the flames took and he blew on the flickering kindling, Sabine's face caught the light, and he saw that she was watching him.

"Thank you," she said.

"For what?"

"For not fearing me."

Her words had such sadness that he studied her more closely, and so he saw the moment when something gave way within her. Sabine sagged just a little, and she wiped tears from her eyes.

"Sabine?" Jack said, his heart aching for her.

"I'm so sorry," she whispered, the words barely audible.

Jack felt a chill pass through him. "What are you talking about?"

A quiet sob racked her body, and then she inhaled sharply, getting control of herself. She glanced at him but could not hold the gaze. The corners of her mouth turned upward in a pained smile whose anguish it tortured him to see.

"It's my fault . . . ," she said, her voice breaking. "My fault you're here."

"Of course it's not," Jack said. "Yes, I wanted to get you

off the *Larsen*. But even without my fear for your safety, I had to escape or Ghost would have killed me."

"You misunderstand," Sabine replied, wiping away tears as she glanced at him quickly and once more lowered her gaze. "It's my fault you were on the *Larsen* to begin with. My fault that Ghost attacked your ship."

Jack exhaled, understanding at last. "It's all right. You were doing what you had to do to stay alive. You guided him to the *Umatilla* just as you had to so many other—"

Sabine threw up her hands, sorrow and truth spilling out of her. "I didn't guide him to your ship, Jack! I guided him to *you!*"

"What?" He could only stare. "You mean Ghost chose me somehow? Why?"

"Not Ghost," she whispered. She shook her head, the weight of guilt heavy. At last she said, "*I* chose you, Jack. Searching for a target for the pirates' hunger and greed, I found your ship, but it was no better prey than half a dozen others. Except that I sensed something else on board . . . something familiar. Your time with Lesya, the natural talent she unlocked within you, I recognized it as the closest thing to the magic within me that I have ever encountered. I had to meet you. To observe you. And the only way to do that was to tell Ghost the *Umatilla* was ripe for the picking."

Jack's mind spun with the implications. The hell he had endured as a part of Ghost's crew, the horrific slaughter of the prisoners that the sea wolves had taken from the *Umatilla* . . . none of it would have happened if not for Sabine.

*Yes, it would have,* he thought. *But to someone else.*

"You must understand," she said. "After so long alone, any chance to learn more, even the slimmest hope of an encounter with someone like me . . . I had to try."

Jack shook his head. "No. You can't have known that I would fight. That I would survive the attack and end up on board the *Larsen.*"

"I could hope. And I could work subtle magic as well. The pelican on the deck of your ship, the bird that drew your attention and alerted you to the pirates' presence . . . I guided it there. A hex on the crew should they encounter you, just a small suggestion that they hold back the tiniest bit in attacking you, make you a prisoner instead of a victim. And then I could only hope that Ghost would sense something within you worth keeping alive. He may not even have known what he saw in you, not fully, but—"

"And if he had just torn out my throat or put me with the other prisoners for the full-moon slaughter?" Jack demanded, anger flaring within him despite the pain he felt at seeing her remorse.

Sabine looked up at him defiantly. "I would have fought him. No matter that it would have revealed my true talents, and risked him killing me and gaining my magic. I would have tried to protect you."

It was Jack's turn to glance away. "Because you sense echoes of Lesya in me, and would have done anything to preserve your only connection to something that might be your kin."

"At first," Sabine admitted, her voice soft and ashamed. "But later, because I had fallen in love with you. The night we were locked together in the safe room—the night of the hunt—I saw the courage in you when you tried to get out of the room, to save them. And I saw your anguish when you knew you could not. You broke my heart that night, and at the same time, you filled it as it has never been filled in all my long memory."

Jack had nothing more to say, and Sabine seemed to have finished her confession. They sat like that for a while, neither of them speaking, the silence broken only by the crash of surf and the wind in the trees. Sabine hugged herself against the breeze, her tears dry and her expression grim.

Eventually, without a word, Jack moved across to Sabine and took her in his arms. Sunset splashed across the island behind them and spread shadows onto the sea, and as stars began to appear, they saw a shooting star flaming overhead, casting a brief, stark wound across the night sky. Neither of them commented. All the words that had needed to be spoken had been said.

Sabine had said she loved him, and he believed her. And how could he blame her for what she had done, no matter what it had cost him? Loving her as he did, he would gladly endure it all over again so that she could have the answers she had sought for so long.

As the fire started to burn down, Jack realized that Sabine had fallen asleep on his shoulder. He remained awake, pondering what she had told him—those incredible histories she had seen, everything she had done, and the uncertainty that such long life had instilled within her— and by the time the island's night noises started to intrude, he had silently vowed to aid her in any way he could.

He lowered Sabine gently, placing his jacket across her shoulders against the night's chill, and went about feeding the fire. After his time in the north, he would always welcome such heat.

Then he sat back against the log Sabine lay propped against, and the flames made the night that much darker.

Jack started awake. In those brief moments between sleeping and waking, when a soul's wealth of memory floods in to fill the blanks, his surroundings startled him. He felt more adrift than he ever had at sea, and the sense of something missing was profound. And though between blinks he became whole again, the loss remained.

"Sabine," he whispered. She had vanished. His jacket still lay across the fallen tree, settled as though she had disappeared from beneath it without actually moving. Did she have such abilities? He could not know. She had told him much, but such a long life could not possibly be revealed in one short day.

He stood and stretched stiffness from his limbs, looking both ways along the curving beach. There was no sign of Sabine, but fresh footprints led away from where they had camped for the night, trailing along the beach a short way before turning in to the trees. As he watched, a wave broke and washed over a stretch of footprints, removing more of their detail from the world. A few more waves and they would be erased. Sabine had not been gone for long.

A rush of enthusiasm filled Jack, flooding him with one of those moments of utter contentment that never seem to last long enough. All that was wrong left him for a while—Sabine's fears, his family's and friends' concern, Sabine's confessions and her determination to meet Lesya—and everything was right. He passed by the dead men's shelter, and behind it saw evidence that perhaps they had also been pirates. Rusted, dulled weapons were half hidden by undergrowth, and a collection of small barrels was stacked against the shelter's remaining wall.

When Jack used an old, broken sword to crack open one of the barrels, he immediately recognized what it contained.

"Oh," he said. He stared for a few heartbeats, then replaced the lid as best he could and set the barrel atop the others. As he continued in search of food, he wondered what use the gunpowder might be.

He moved farther into the trees, and as he started gathering fruit for breakfast, he was warmed by a background buzz of happiness.

"Mango," he said, picking three of the fruits. He worked his way deeper, up the slope heading inland. "Papaya. Guava. A regular cocktail!" He gathered the fruits in his shirtfront, then returned to the beach to peel and prepare them.

Sabine had still not returned. He thought of calling out for her but decided against it.

As he settled next to the remains of the night's fire, she emerged from the trees at the far end of the beach at a run, and he could tell from her gait that it was a run driven by fear. He dropped the fruit and grabbed his knife, looking past Sabine, readying himself for whatever might emerge from the undergrowth in pursuit. The beach was short, curved around the small bay, and the pursuer would be on them in moments.

But nothing followed her. Sabine's face was slack with panic, but in her eyes Jack saw a desire to reach him, not a need to escape something.

"What is it?" he asked, and she ran into his embrace.

"Death," she said, panting. "I was in the trees, sitting, exploring the island, and I felt Death closing in on me. On us. He's coming, Jack."

"Death Nilsson," Jack said, because for a moment he'd thought she had meant true death. Perhaps this was worse. "But how does he know of us? Did he torture the truth from Ghost? And even if he did, he can't know we came here."

"No," Sabine said, waving away everything he had said. She took deep breaths, calming herself. "He doesn't know of us, at least not yet. But I probed out as far as I could and touched on a mind I did not expect—Ghost's. He's still alive, along with some of his crew."

"Death did not kill his brother," Jack said.

"Not yet. But after he captured and sank the *Larsen*, he took Ghost and his crew prisoner. His own ship was badly damaged in the battle. They're sailing here for repairs, but Death has another intention. When they land, he means to finish Ghost here, on this island. Torture and kill him."

"How long do we have?"

"They're perhaps eight miles out."

Jack's mind was spinning, the good cheer he'd felt upon waking being rapidly abraded by old fears. But he and Sabine had already bested Ghost and his crew and escaped. And this time they were at an advantage—Death did not yet know of their presence, and they had time to plan. But escape wouldn't be enough; he knew that now. They would never have true peace unless they rid the world of the sea wolves forever.

"They'll sense us as soon as they arrive," Sabine said. "Hear, smell. And Death's crew is larger. They will track and capture us, and then kill us."

"You fear death?" Jack asked, instantly regretting the question.

"No," Sabine said. "But I fear yours."

Jack grinned. The fear slipped from Sabine's face, and her beautiful smile suddenly gave him hope.

"Neither of us is going to die," he said. "I already have a plan."

He sat down and started peeling fruit.

"Jack?"

"Breakfast," he said. "We have time. And we *need* them to know we're here, and to think we're unaware of their approach. So we'll leave as much evidence of our presence as we can."

Sabine sat beside Jack and ate, and for a while silence hung around them. Jack could smell Sabine's body, sense the heat of her where she almost, but not quite, touched his bare arm with hers, and her trust was comforting. As they ate, he thought through their situation. And as they finished their last piece of fruit, he knew what they had to do.

"We need to rescue Ghost. He's the only chance we have of surviving an encounter with his brother."

"Yes," Sabine said, and Jack was not surprised at her agreement.

"Prevent Death from murdering him, and free whatever might be left of the *Larsen's* crew."

"Ghost will fight for me," Sabine said softly. "Even after all this, I'm sure of that."

"Precisely," Jack said. "And we'll have to help him and his wolves defeat Death and his crew."

Sabine frowned. *So beautiful, so old, so innocent,* Jack thought, and his heart swelled once again with the love he felt for this woman. The thought of losing her was so terrible, and the challenges facing them were almost insurmountable. But his concept of the future did not allow defeat. He was not afraid.

"But how can the two of us possibly do that?" she asked.

"That's where the previous tenants of this island can help," he said. "Follow me. I have something to show you."

It took them two hours to prepare. Two hours of hard, backbreaking work, during which time neither of them even entertained the possibility of failure. There could *be* no failure. Everything Jack now lived for, and everything he had found, depended on their plan succeeding.

When they had prepared as much as they could, they climbed the shoulder of land between the two beaches and looked out to sea. The *Charon* was clearly visible, perhaps three miles out and drifting toward them. Sabine tasted the air and told Jack that the engines were flooded, and that the big steamer was being driven by wind and wave power alone. Ghost and his crew were locked away belowdecks—she could not place them accurately—and Death himself rode the bow, watching as the island grew larger before them.

"He might see us up here," Jack said.

"All the better if he does," Sabine said.

They watched the ship together. It was close enough to see but too far away to make out any real detail. Jack stared at the vessel's bow. Death might be there, but from here he was a speck, a blur. If their plan held together, so he would remain forevermore.

"It'll work," Jack said.

"I know," Sabine replied. They were comforting each other and striving to convince themselves.

There were eventualities that could not be planned for in such a short time, but their scheme had enough fluidity to allow for these. Partly with subtlety and the element of surprise, but mostly with something that the monsters sailing toward them would understand only too well.

Brute force.

## CHAPTER THIRTEEN

# CLOSE ENEMIES

*Couldn't they have made landfall in the dark?* Jack thought, grumbling to himself as he picked his way through a copse of prickly trees. He paused to test the breeze to make certain he remained downwind of the slightly listing steamship and its crew as they disembarked from the rowboats. As quietly as possible, he slid the last of the wooden barrels off from his shoulder and set it down with the four others that had remained intact enough to move. He could feel his pulse from his temples to the tips of his fingers. His throat had gone dry. He and Sabine were going to get only one opportunity at this, and failure would mean death.

*For me,* he thought. She might survive. And it was true, he wasn't completely certain of the extent of Sabine's powers. She could influence the weather, but could she lift herself up on the wind? It seemed impossible, but that word had become flexible of late.

Still, Jack knew that she would have told him about any abilities that would aid them against the sea wolves.

He took a deep breath and closed his eyes, picturing the camp where he had left her. Even now she would be stoking the flames of the fire they had built outside the ruin of that old encampment. The smoke had to continue to rise in order to lead Death's crew away from their ship. Sabine had made herself bait.

*Can you really do this, Sabine?* Jack had asked her. *Even with the ability to hex their minds and senses, can you elude them long enough to stay alive?*

She had insisted that she could do it. She had once beguiled Ghost and his crew on board the *Larsen*, but Ghost had kept such close guard of her when they were at anchor that she had not been able to escape. Jack could only hope that her abilities were as subtle and effective as she claimed.

Hidden among those prickly trees, Jack watched the werewolves come ashore. He did not recognize any of them, but in the lead boat was a huge, muscular man with a thick beard and grizzled features. With his obvious pride, and his air of command and utter ruthlessness, there could be no mistaking him—this was Death Nilsson.

Jack took a long breath and let it out, feeling the breeze

and listening to the trees rustling around him. If Sabine lost her concentration and the wind reversed itself, carrying Jack's scent to the wolves, their plan would end in blood and death.

Dragging their boats onto the rocky beach, Death Nilsson and eleven members of his crew came ashore. The captain would have left some of his pack on board to guard Ghost and his remaining crew, no doubt, but though it was a steamship, the crew wouldn't be much larger than twenty. At most there were eight of Death's men on board.

*Eight is too many,* Jack thought. *I can't* . . .

But he refused to let the thought go any further. There was no room for hesitation in their plan. Hesitation would kill them just as surely as claws or fangs.

With gestures, nods, and quietly growled commands, Death spread his pack out along the beach. Two of them dropped to their knees and snuffled along the rocks and sand until they reached the first of the jungle plants. The others simply waited. Death laid his head back and sniffed at the air, searching for a scent. They could all see the smoke rising from the fire beyond the rocks and on the next beach, and they would have picked up the scents that Jack and Sabine had left since their arrival . . . and perhaps the scent of Sabine herself, waiting for them right now, an easy target.

*Come on,* he thought, *what are you waiting for? You know*

*you have to at least go have a look. Might be someone good to eat.*

The thought, so full of cynical levity, horrified him, but his frustration had an edge he could not control. Fully half a minute went by as Death considered the island. Several of his wolves walked toward the shoulder of rock jutting out between the beaches, and they climbed with a grace and agility that made Jack gasp, pulling themselves up using trees, rocks, and undergrowth. Once at the top, they peered down at the beach beyond, but still did not hurry in the direction of the campfire.

Then, at last, Death glanced out at his steamship—its entire hull was painted black, save where it had rammed the *Larsen*. When he turned back toward the beach, he wore a smile that chilled the blood in Jack's veins. He uttered a command that seemed more bark than words, and the remaining werewolves ran toward the spit of land and the beach. They climbed as quickly as their companions, then disappeared beyond, Death among them.

Jack swallowed. They would be on the beach by now, and in the camp where Sabine had kept the fire burning. Jack's deception had begun, and the clock was ticking.

He took a deep breath, looking at the rowboats on the beach and the steamship listing slightly just offshore—a great black behemoth—and then ran, hoisting one of the wooden barrels up onto his shoulder again.

As quietly as possible, relying on the crash of the surf to mask his steps from any wolf that might have remained out of sight nearby, he made it to the rowboats. He set the barrel down in one of them and pushed it off the beach, shoving it a short way out into the waves before he climbed in and began rowing.

The *Charon* loomed large and dark as the gates of Hades as he approached, throwing its cold shadow over him. His life might end at any moment with discovery by the wolves who must have remained on board, but all he could think about was Sabine. Would she be hiding in the trees? No, she was not Lesya. That was not where the strength of her magic lay. Though she had given him precious few details, Jack knew she would have slid into the ocean to evade the wolves. She would let them have her scent, and lead them on a chase across and around the island, keeping them occupied as long as she was able. Though she did not sing like the sirens of myth, she claimed that she could muddle the minds of men and wolves alike, and blind them to her presence. But until he saw her again—until he held her in his arms and felt her kiss upon his lips—he would fear for her, and grieve the life he dreamed they might have together.

*Be safe*, he thought, sending it out to her as if in prayer.

When he was close enough to hear the clank of wood and metal on board the steamship, he rowed even harder, maneuvering the rowboat beside the netting that dangled down the starboard side and tying on. From around his waist, where he had knotted it like a belt, he took the section of sail he had cut away from the small boat that had brought him and Sabine to the island. Swaddling the barrel in that cloth, he tied the ends of the cloth around his waist, the weight like a heavy anchor.

Jack snagged the thick rope netting, took a deep breath, and began to climb. Veins popped out on his forearms and biceps. Gravity fought hard, and with the effort it took to carry the barrel beneath him, it was all he could do to remain silent. As he climbed over the *Charon*'s railing—carefully lifting the barrel onto the deck and unwrapping it—he knew that the true peril had only just begun.

Crouched by the railing, Jack steadied his breathing. He reached out with his senses, feeling for the savage spirits of the sea wolves. Some were in the hold, and he knew it must be Ghost and the other survivors from the *Larsen*. One wolf was on deck, but at the other end of the ship. None were near enough to come upon Jack suddenly. He only had to choose his moment and he would be committed to this final gambit. And the moment was now. He rushed from his crouch, and there was no turning back.

Sabine had begun to influence the weather, and clouds were slowly gathering. The overcast sky diffused the day's light to a dull gray, but even without much sunshine, he was exposed and vulnerable out in the open. The clock continued to tick.

The *Charon* was a double-masted steamer, but with its sails furled and its stacks silenced, it seemed like the moldering corpse of some ancient leviathan, floating upon the surface and drifting toward shore. Only the steamship's anchor saved it from that fate, but from the way it listed slightly to starboard, it was clear that it had serious hull damage.

Jack climbed the short set of steps to the wheelhouse and risked a quick glance through the window. There was no sign of anyone within. The ship creaked and rocked gently beneath him as he hurried along the deck in a crouch, using the long above-deck cabin to shield him from view and then taking cover behind one of the smokestacks. The steamer was almost twice the length of the *Larsen*, with much more hold room—how could he hope to search the entire vessel for Ghost and his men without being discovered by Death's guards? A moment of panic hit him, and then he heard the guttural laughter.

He cursed silently. If they came out onto the deck now, it would be almost impossible to avoid capture or death. But though he held his breath for long moments, awaiting discovery, no one emerged.

A patter of light rain began to fall: Sabine mustering her strength to bring down a new storm. Jack tried to push away thoughts of his love—if he started worrying about the cat-and-mouse game she was playing with Death, he would never finish the task he had come out to the *Charon* to accomplish.

He skulked along to the cabin and peered in a window, then ducked down quickly. He had sensed two of Death's wolves inside, and there they were—playing cards and drinking rum or gin in what looked like the ship's mess. That they had not yet caught his scent was either a miracle or the blessing of the alcohol they had consumed, and he knew that if he didn't hurry, his luck could run out.

Jack moved away quickly and quietly. Those two weren't the only wolves left on board, not with Ghost imprisoned here. But the last thing Death and his crew would be expecting was an assault on their ship from the island. Jack's senses were not so acute that he could pinpoint the exact presence of each beast, so he hurried from hatch to hatch, listening for activity in the cargo holds below. He moved aft until he ran out of boat and realized that the prisoners must be in the only hold he had not checked— the forward hold, right at the bow.

If he went to the hatch on the foredeck, he would be in full view of anyone stepping into the wheelhouse. The two card-playing pirates did not look as if they would trouble themselves to take a wander around the ship anytime soon, so with luck he would not be seen. His focus was slipping, and it was impossible for him to touch so many animal spirits at once. But there would be guards posted below, in the gangway outside the hold door, or in the upper cabin where the stairs from the hold levels emerged. Getting past them would be difficult and time-consuming, and time was in short supply.

He would have to use the other way into the forward hold.

Crouched down, he hustled alongside the cabin until he reached the spot just before the wheelhouse where he had clambered aboard. Had anyone walked the deck in the minute since he had climbed over the railing, they would have to have been blind or drunk to miss the wooden barrel. Now Jack knelt by it, his trousers dampened by the sheen of drizzle that filmed the deck.

Sabine could have mustered a larger storm by now, but she would hold off on the hard rain for as long as she could. Jack's plan might be undone by a true downpour.

From within his shirt he withdrew a small canvas pouch, and from the pouch a length of fuse. He pried up the edge of the barrel's lid with his knife, then slid the fuse down inside, making sure it was firmly in place. He wondered if the matches in his pocket would be dry enough, but this was no time for hesitation or doubt. He hoisted the barrel and—with one final glance around—ran lightly out across the foredeck. The wheelhouse loomed behind him, but there were no shouts or sounds of alarm.

*Of course not,* he thought. *There will be no shout.* All he would hear would be the *click click* of claws on metal, and the hungry breath, and—

He shook the thought away.

Jack took a closer look at the forward cargo hatch. It was iron, the heavy frame bolted to the deck, intended to prevent any hope of escape by prisoners the *Charon* might take, human or otherwise. Beside it was a smaller, open grating, too small for a man to slip through even with the bars cut away. Despite the thickness of the hatch and its heavy bolts, the savage strength of the wolves was so great that they might well have been able to break out if they could have put any pressure on it from below. But the hold was at least twenty feet deep, so it would be impossible for them to get any leverage.

"Young Jack!" a familiar voice said from down in the hold. Ghost knew his scent, and Jack was pleased at the captain's evident surprise.

"Hush," Jack whispered, wondering if the guards had heard Ghost speak. Not that it mattered. In moments, there would be noise enough to wake the dead.

He laid the barrel atop the hinges on one side of the hatch, then dug into his pocket for the tin box of lucifers he'd stolen from the *Larsen*. The match lit on first strike, and he held it to the fuse. It caught with a hiss.

Jack looked down through the grate and saw Louis staring upward. Hope flickered within him. Louis might be a beast, a member of the pack, but he had been the closest thing Jack had to a friend in Ghost's crew.

Vukovich, Tree, and Maurilio were down there as well, bloody and bedraggled but alive. Strangely, he felt a pang of regret that Demetrius had not survived. The fat sailor had seemed fairly even-keeled.

"What are you up to, Jack?" Louis whispered.

"Stand back and cover your ears," Jack replied, and he took his own advice, racing toward the bow and throwing himself facedown upon the deck. He clapped his hands over his ears.

The explosion shook the entire ship, roaring at the sky as if the sea had replied with thunder of its own, and thumping at the ship like a massive drum. Metal fragments ricocheted, and something wailed like a creature in pain. *Metal rupturing*, Jack thought, and he wondered whether the gunpowder load had been too much. When he looked into the hatch, would he see Ghost and the others pulverized down there? Crushed, spattered, taken apart by the blast?

The cargo hatch was now a smoking hole in the deck. Shouts rose from within, and Jack smiled with relief. But then a door banged open farther aft, and the two drunken pirates stumbled out.

Jack scrambled across to the ruined hatch. Ghost and his men were holding their heads and staggering to their feet as they recovered from the explosion, shaken but otherwise unharmed. With a clank and a screech, the hold door swung open and two guards rushed in, halfway through their agonized lupine transformations. Ghost howled as he changed, bones popping and skin stretching as fur sprouted all across his flesh. He leaped at the guards, and he tore out the nearest beast's throat even before the rest of his sea wolves had finished their metamorphosis.

Jack turned away then, loath to witness any more of the slaughter.

"How the hell did you get out?" one of the drunken sailors barked, pointing at him. He looked at his companion. "Wait. Have we seen this one before?"

Jack hesitated. They thought he was a werewolf! He wondered how he could use this.

Bleary-eyed, arrogant, and exuding cruelty, the sailors approached him carefully, taking his measure. One of them sniffed the air. "Kurt," he said, narrowing his eyes, "this little bastard is human."

Kurt grinned, teeth elongating and sharpening to points as fur sprouted from his skin. "Beautiful."

Jack drew his knife, wishing it were silver. He bent slightly, taking slow breaths, using the magic that Lesya had taught him—instilled within him—during his time in the Yukon. He could not only sense the presence of animals but channel their essence within himself and join it with his own innate wildness. There were fish nearby, of course, and if he extended his spirit far enough, he might find a seabird or two. But the true beasts were those standing before him—men who could turn themselves inside out, wearing their primitive rage and hunger on the outside.

The rainstorm suddenly strengthened, and Jack silently thanked Sabine.

The drunken werewolves closed in, going around the ragged hole blown in the deck. They ignored the sounds of slaughter from below. Fur matted to their huge, lupine bodies by the rain, they growled in hunger as they flanked him on either side.

Jack growled in return, baring his teeth. Knife in hand, he tapped directly into the essence of the werewolves, matching his savagery to theirs so completely that for a moment he almost lost himself in it, reveling in the sense of power and freedom. He was stronger than ever before, and if only he could harness this power and take control, release himself to the animal and become unhindered, unconfined . . .

But the bright, burning ember of his humanity remained within. And it always would. "Come on, you worthless dogs," Jack snarled.

The giant wolf that had been Kurt lunged toward him, but even on four legs it swayed drunkenly. Jack dodged aside and kicked the werewolf's leg with such force that it snapped, spilling the monster to the deck. As it thrashed and tried to stand, he stomped on its forelegs and slammed the knife into its chest, penetrating flesh and slipping past bone to impale the tough muscle of its heart. Blood pulsed from the wound, and the giant wolf screamed and writhed, slipping back to a form that was part beast, part man. The wound would not kill him, but Kurt would stay down for a while.

The other werewolf howled in rage and launched itself at Jack, who leaped over Kurt's bloody form, mind racing. He had no real options—his only avenues of escape were over the side into the ocean or a twenty-foot drop into the cargo hold with Ghost and his ravenous crew.

In a moment of indecision, Jack caught a glimpse of movement behind the werewolf. A dark streak of fur erupted from the open hatch and barreled into the drunken beast, jaws gnashing and claws dragging furrows in flesh.

Blood mingled with rain as the two werewolves clashed on the deck, tumbling over and over. They slammed into the railing, and it cracked but did not give way.

The dark-furred wolf clawed the other's face, flaying its jaw open to the bone and taking out an eye. The booze-soaked werewolf whined and staggered back; its remaining golden eye glinted with bleary fear. Jack longed for his knife but dared not try to retrieve it from Kurt's chest—Kurt had already transformed enough to tug the blade out of his heart.

The deck came alive with wolves as Ghost and his crew—spattered with their guards' blood—leaped out of the hold. The werewolves steamed, growled, stalking the deck with a hunger for flesh and vengeance. Counting the dark-furred one who had just half blinded the enemy, there were five of them against two drunken, injured beasts. Death's wolves had no chance. Ghost and what remained of his pack tore them apart.

Jack turned away from the slaughter and crossed to the starboard railing. If Ghost decided to kill him now, there would be nothing he could do to stop it, and he preferred not to watch the sea wolves taking their grisly meal.

The scrape of claws on the deck forced him to turn. He expected the hulking gray wolf that Ghost became when he revealed his true self, but instead the monster that approached was the dark-furred werewolf that had aided him. It panted and growled, but the noise seemed more greeting that threat. The werewolf began to change, its bones shifting and popping as it stood up, now half man and half beast. It threw back its head and howled, and bared its fangs in a monstrous grin.

The wolf-man had a single golden tooth.

"Hello, Louis," Jack said.

It brayed like a hyena and then transformed further, grunting as it resumed the illusion of humanity. Louis stood naked on the *Charon*'s deck.

"Jack," he said, "you are one crazy fool, but I'm happy to see you alive."

"Happy to *be* alive."

Louis started to laugh, but then his eyes narrowed and he spun to defend himself. Too late, as the huge gray were-wolf, soaked in blood and rain, plowed into him. The two crashed to the deck, and for a moment Jack thought Ghost would tear out Louis's throat. But the captain snarled and snapped, shoved Louis to one side almost dismissively, and turned his heavy head to glare at Jack.

With a cry that began as an animal's howl and built into a human roar, Ghost transformed. Breathing hard, teeth bared, he looked more bestial and barbaric as a man than he ever had as a wolf.

"I had plans for you, Mr. London," Ghost rasped.

"And I have plans for you. That's why I set you free. But I make my own destiny, Ghost. Always have."

One corner of Ghost's mouth lifted in a knife-edge smile. "Not today you don't."

As the other sea wolves transformed into the familiar figures of Tree, Vukovich, and Maurilio, Ghost began to move toward Jack. Any other time, the sailors' brash nakedness might have seemed awkward, but painted with their enemies' blood and with rain slashing down at the deck, they only appeared more savage. Somehow they managed to be both wild and unnatural at the same time, neither man nor animal. They were things that nature would never permit, no matter what Ghost might say.

"You betrayed me," Ghost said, moving closer, his fingers hooked into claws. "You took the witch off my ship before I could make her pay for turning on me. You could have been so much more than you are, Jack. So much more than a weak bit of bone and gristle."

"Cruelty and an appetite don't make you strong," Jack said, unflinching.

Louis and the other sea wolves—no longer a crew but still part of Ghost's pack—circled warily.

Ghost moved swiftly, wrapping one huge hand around Jack's throat and slamming him against the railing. He shoved, bending him backward so that Jack's upper body hung over the storm-tossed sea, the ship rolling on the strengthening waves.

"*Murder* makes me strong!" Ghost roared, spittle striking Jack's face. "Taking lives, eating flesh, drinking blood! I will destroy you with my bare hands as I should have done the first moment I saw you, before I suffered the disappointment of knowing you. *That* makes me strong, Jack. I am your master, and I'll hear you say it before I end your life."

"That's never going to happen," Jack croaked, barely able to draw breath. "I am my own . . . and only . . . master."

"You little bastard!" Ghost screamed. He began to change again, but only enough for his jaws to open wider and his fangs to grow longer. Then he bent forward, jaws gaping to sink his teeth into Jack's face.

Tree's massive fist struck Ghost so hard in the face that two of his fangs snapped off and were lost on the rain-swirled deck. With Ghost surprised by the attack and stunned from the impact, Louis and Maurilio were able to haul him back for Tree to hit him again. Vukovich grabbed a fistful of his former captain's hair and yanked back, exposing his throat, and the four sea wolves had Ghost at their mercy.

"That'd just be bad form, Captain," Louis said. "You can't kill Mr. London after he came out here to free us."

"Murder *makes me strong!*" Ghost roared.

Jack exhaled. He'd been prepared to die, and recovering from that required a moment to collect himself. He watched as Ghost struggled against them and then paused, nodded once, and was released.

"I'll have you," Ghost snarled at Jack, quieter now.

"Maybe," Jack agreed. "But your brother will have heard the explosion. There are a dozen of them and only five of you, and they'll be on their way back to the beach by now. I'm not afraid of you or of dying, but I'd rather avoid both if possible. And for all your talk, I suspect you'd rather not die either, Ghost. I've gambled on you being the lesser of two evils, on there still being a shred of honor and humanity in you, despite all your efforts to expunge them. If you want to live, we have to work together."

"Why bother, Jack?" Vukovich said. "We've got the ship now. We'll leave Death Nilsson and his crew behind. It's a big ship, but the six of us can get it under way, I'm sure."

"Haven't you noticed how it's listing?" Jack said.

"The ship's damaged," Louis said. "Death's gone ashore to see if there's anything he can use for repairs."

"And he saw my campfire and went to investigate," Jack replied.

"There's no avoiding this fight," Tree said in his deep, rumbling voice.

"The odds are not in your favor," Jack said. "But you

don't have to face them alone."

Ghost laughed. "You're one man, Jack. Clever, I'll grant you, but still near enough to being a boy that I'm sure you remember childhood all too well. What can you do to help even the odds against Death and his curs?"

Jack took a breath and let it out. Of all the risks he had taken since waking this morning, this was the one that most terrified him.

"It's not just me. Sabine—"

"Of course the sea witch is with you," Ghost snarled. "You fell in love. The two of you escaped together into some romantic dream. But she isn't here, which means you left her on the island. Death will have feasted on her heart by now, you fool. And even if he hasn't, what good is she? We know where my brother and his bootlicks are."

He jabbed a finger toward the island. Through the waving veils of rain, Jack could see the rowboats making their way out from the beach.

"There they are!" Ghost said. "No witchery required, Jack!"

Jack smiled, hating him more fiercely than ever.

"For all the books you've read and all the philosophy you've butchered in your monster's brain, you're not as bright as you think you are, Ghost. Or whatever your real name is." Jack raised his voice to be heard over the wind.

He wiped rain from his eyes. "You never felt her testing you. Never wondered about sudden changes in the weather, or questioned decisions that might have surprised you. Sabine made this storm! She summoned it, because she has power you have not even begun to imagine!"

The look of confusion, and then hatred, on Ghost's face was like a gift.

"If you all want to survive, you're going to need our help," Jack said. "And to get it, Sabine and I require promises. A truce, and a bargain. You won't kill us. You won't lay another hand on either of us, for any reason. And Ghost, you will not attempt to punish the rest of your pack for their mutiny. We all live together or we all die together. But you'll die alone unless you agree to our terms."

Louis and Tree both nodded in approval. Jack saw Vukovich and Maurilio regarding him with new respect and interest. He had linked them all into this bargain, made their forgiveness one of the terms of the deal. They could not help but see how all their fates were intertwined, and that Jack and Sabine were more concerned with their welfare than Ghost had ever been.

Jack offered his hand. "Do you accept the terms, Captain?"

Ghost looked revolted, his eyes full of loathing.

But he shook Jack's hand.

## CHAPTER FOURTEEN

# THUNDER AND LIGHTNING

**T**hunder rolled across the Pacific sky. Lightning danced in the clouds as if the gods of war were crafting their weapons . . . and it was weapons that Jack and the sea wolves required. The odds were against them, and even with Sabine's help they would need luck and ferocity to survive to see the sun again, or bay at the moon. Three rowboats were crossing the rain-lashed sea, and they brought a terrible storm with them.

Ghost led the way below, checking the *Charon* for guns and knives, and Jack knew that they were all hoping to find something silver. As Maurilio and Vukovich ransacked the crew's quarters, Louis headed down to the stores in the hold while Ghost and Tree searched the rest of the ship for some kind of armory.

Jack volunteered to check the galley for blades that

might be useful. A butcher knife would not kill a werewolf, but the right wound—or a great many of them—might slow one of Death's crew enough for Jack to get the upper hand. But as he moved through the aft cabin, he passed an ornate door, from which wafted an animal musk so powerful that it could only belong to the captain.

With a quick glance over his shoulder, Jack pushed open the door, twisting his face away as if that would protect him from the stench. It was horrific, reaching inside to scorch his nostrils and rake claws across the back of his throat. But what he saw in that cabin was even worse. Death Nilsson was a more vicious pirate than his brother, and far more of an animal.

In the corner of the chamber was a large, carved wooden furnishing that might have been an infant's cradle if not for its size. The woman folded half-eaten into the cradle had been dead for perhaps three days, but Jack had seen no sign of other prisoners on board the *Charon*. *She must have been the last*, he thought. *The captain's private stock.*

Bile burned at the back of his throat, and he concentrated to keep himself from vomiting. He breathed through his mouth so that the stink of death and Death would not push him over the edge. Ghost might appear in the doorway at any moment, and Jack wanted to search Death's cabin without that hateful bastard looking over his shoulder. So he forced himself into action, moving swiftly, searching the cabinets and beneath the small dining table and behind the bunk. A bookless shelf against one wall was laden instead with charts and maps, a leather-and-brass telescope, and an antique sextant that Jack imagined Death had retained as a souvenir from some great captain. On the top shelf was a sword in its scabbard, and Jack plucked it down and drew out the blade—a Spanish naval officer's sword, engraved with a message.

Es mejor morir con honor que vivir sin ella.

Jack sneered with derision. *It's better to die with honor than to live without it.* What would Death Nilsson know of honor?

He sheathed the sword but had no intention of using it himself. His skills at swordplay were amateur at best, and it might be more of a hindrance than an aid in fighting werewolves. He glanced once more at the top shelf and had already begun to turn away when he realized there was something else there. He reached into the shadowy space and retrieved a carved cherrywood box. It felt heavy and almost warm in his hands, and he stared at the lock on it for a moment or two before dashing it against the corner of the shelf. Once, twice, and with the third impact the hasp tore away from the wood and the box flipped open.

The revolver thunked to the floor, and bullets rained down around it. Silver! They gleamed even in the wan light filtering through the salt-grimed window, a chance at salvation.

With a furtive glance at the door, Jack dropped and began picking up bullets, shoving them into his pockets. A quick tally gave him a count of nearly twenty, and his heart swelled with the meaning of that number. More bullets than sea wolves. That didn't mean each one would find its target, especially if he was shooting while trying to avoid attack, but it gave him a way to fight them. It gave him a chance.

Hurriedly, he loaded the gun, and had just thumbed a bullet into the last chamber when he heard the floor creak behind him. Jack turned to see Louis standing on the threshold, one eyebrow raised.

Louis flashed his gold tooth. "Looks like Death left you a little present."

Jack hesitated, wondering if Louis would try to take the gun from him. They had been allies thus far, and he thought the werewolf liked him well enough. But would Louis let him keep possession of a gun full of silver? For half a second Jack thought about aiming the pistol at him, just to be safe, but Louis had helped keep him alive more than once. If he didn't trust Jack with the silver, then Jack would give him the gun.

"If anyone should have it, you should," Louis said, as if reading his mind.

Jack exhaled, relaxing. He picked up the scabbarded sword with his free hand and tossed it to Louis.

"I thought you might like this," Jack said.

Louis caught the sword, his smile turning to a playful grin. "I've always had a fondness for sharp things."

Jack closed the box and replaced it on the top shelf, hoping Ghost would not notice it.

"I want to thank you for speaking up for me," Jack said. "That's not the first time you've prevented me from having my throat ripped out."

Louis's grin faltered and his gaze dimmed. "That's not the worst thing that could happen to you."

"I know," Jack said. "I owe you."

"Maybe," Louis replied. "Though it must be said, I do not think he would find it so easy to kill you."

"I'm just human," Jack said. "Just me. I wouldn't stand a chance."

"You're clever, Jack," Louis said, eyes darkening further. "Your life is precious to you, as well as the life of another. There's great power in that. You will kill to live, but Ghost lives to kill. He is a hollow man."

The laughter from the gangway froze them both where they stood.

Ghost stepped into his brother's quarters and studied Jack and Louis as if they were misbehaving children.

"You're mistaken, Louis," Ghost rasped. "Hollow I may be. But I am not a man."

Jack felt the weight of the gun in his hand, the poisonous reassurance of the silver, but he had formed an alliance with Ghost and would not break it. Despite the monstrous brutality of the creature, some part of Jack could not help but admire his survival after his brother's betrayal, and wish for Ghost to have his vengeance. And with Death Nilsson and his men on the way, Jack's fate was intertwined with Ghost's.

"Did you find anything?" Jack asked.

"Maurilio and Vukovich found plenty of weapons in the crew's quarters," Ghost said. "Nothing truly useful. Blades, but no silver." He nodded toward the weapons Louis and Jack now wielded. "I see neither of you is empty-handed."

"We'll have to make do with what we have," Louis said, undoing his belt and threading it through the slit on the scabbard. "If that means I become a swashbuckler, so be it."

Ghost laughed, but the humor did not reach his eyes. He set his gaze upon Jack.

"Louis likes you, Mr. London," Ghost said. "For some reason he ascribes to you extraordinary abilities. Don't let his faith in you make you do something stupid that might jeopardize our pact."

"You don't have to worry about me," Jack replied.

"Of course not," Ghost said. "You won't kill unless your hand is forced, isn't that right?"

"That's right."

"I'd almost forgotten." Ghost's fingers crooked into claws, as though he wished for nothing more than to tear Jack apart. "But not to worry. You'll be forced soon enough. A baptism of blood for you today."

Jack didn't like the sound of that. Ghost had wanted to infect Jack with his curse—turn him into a werewolf and part of the pack—and perhaps that was still his plan.

"I have no interest in being anointed," Jack said. "Only in being alive when the storm clears, whole and human. And if my hands are stained with wolf blood when it's done, it'll wash off easily enough."

"Because my kind are less than human?" Ghost asked, ready to debate the point.

They fell silent. With Louis looking on, one hand on the hilt of his newly acquired sword, Jack and Ghost stared at each other for long seconds. The tension was interrupted by heavy footfalls pounding along the gangway outside.

"I've lost interest in talking philosophy with monsters," Jack said.

Before Ghost could reply, Tree burst into the room, grim resignation etched upon his features.

"They're coming!"

The storm had worsened. The *Charon* swayed violently, the creak of wood and metal like the wail of the banshee, harbinger of death.

"There!" Maurilio shouted as Jack, Ghost, and Louis ran onto the deck. There were four wolves in each of the three boats, and Death Nilsson's pack was rowing hard for their ship. As expected, the gunpowder explosion had brought them in a hurry.

On board the *Charon*, the five beasts remaining from the *Larsen* prepared for a fight, bearing long knives and machetes, and a pair of rifles. Jack held on to his pistol, the secret of its silver ammunition acknowledged in silent exchanges between himself and Louis. Once the enemy started to board, there would be claw and fang, flashing blades and close-quarters murder, and they would earn either victory or death. But for now they wanted to harry Death and his pack as much as possible. To that end, Tree and Vukovich, the best marksmen, took aim with the rifles and began to take shots at the boats as they came within forty yards of the *Charon*. With the churning waves rocking them all, there seemed no chance of finding a target, but at least two of Death's pack caught bullets.

The wounds would be little more than an annoyance, though they might slow them down during the crucial first moments of the boarding. Jack held his pistol, waiting for the boats to draw nearer, knowing the limits of the weapon and his own aim. His bullets would do far more than slow the wolves down. But only if he made the shots count.

"Where is the witch?" Ghost asked, taking up position next to Jack at the railing.

Jack was relieved to see no sign of Sabine on Death's boats. Somewhere on the island, or in the waters offshore, she waited for him, and she would do whatever was within her power to help.

"They didn't find her," he replied.

Tree and Vukovich kept shooting as Death's crew rowed the three boats closer. The veil of rain confused Jack's view of the boats, but he flinched as a bullet punched through the skull of one of the men on the rearmost boat. The pirate tumbled over the side and into the churning water. The rest of Death's pack continued on with barely a glance toward the place where the pirate had just submerged. Jack wondered if the sea wolf would drown before he could heal, but a moment later he saw a monstrous head come up from the water, partially transformed, and a huge, clawed hand grabbed the back of the boat.

A flash of lightning seared the sky, so bright it drove him back from the railing. Arcs of fire splintered the air around the ship, and thunder crashed in the heavens, rolling away on the storm.

"This is her?" Ghost demanded. "This is Sabine's doing?"

Jack nodded, getting a tighter grip on his gun.

Louis shouted for him, beckoning urgently from a place along the railing. Jack ran to join him and looked down to see Sabine crawling up the netting on the side of the ship. The three small boats were thirty feet away, rising and falling upon the swells, and the wolf-men snarled and shouted the filthy things they intended to do to her.

"Sabine," Jack breathed.

Maurilio had joined them, and he grabbed one of Sabine's wrists and lifted her over the railing. Jack reached for her, the deck rolling underfoot, the rain soaking them all to the skin. He had feared that he might never see her again, and now, though Death's pack was moments from boarding, he needed to touch her, embrace her, just to assure himself that she was truly here and unharmed.

Sabine looked at him, but her gaze flickered past Jack's shoulder.

Ghost caught Jack from behind and hurled him aside. Jack dropped the gun and it slid across the deck in the rain.

He scrambled across to the gun, snatched it, and turned to see Ghost grab a fistful of Sabine's hair and hoist her off the deck. The captain held her up, screaming hideous abuse whose precise phrasing was lost to the wind. His features had begun to contort, fangs stretching his mouth wide, snout pushing forward, body distorting and fur sprouting. Sabine's feet dangled beneath her and she kicked, batted at his grip, clawed at his arm. Whatever hex she might use, Jack feared she would not have the time or focus to defend herself.

Jack leaped through the rain and jabbed the gun against Ghost's skull, hard.

"Silver!" Jack shouted against the storm. "Can you smell it, Ghost?"

"I trusted her, and she betrayed me." Ghost gnashed his teeth at Jack.

"You fools, they're coming!" Louis cried. Tree and Vukovich kept firing, and Louis waved his sword high. "Death is coming!"

"Let me go!" Sabine screamed.

"You kept her prisoner," Jack said. "You *tortured* her!"

Ghost stared at him with such hatred that Jack held his breath, finger twitching on the trigger. The captain started to speak. Jack saw a spark of something in his eyes—shame?—and knew precisely what those words would have been. Ghost was about to declare his love for Sabine. But it went against everything he believed, and after an endless moment of conflict that Jack had never before seen in him, the captain sneered, eyes narrowing.

"I'll eat her heart! I'll have her power!"

"You don't know that for sure," Jack said. "She doesn't even know what she is!"

"I have black curses in my heart," Sabine said, her voice quiet in the storm yet somehow audible, as if the wind carried it to both Jack and Ghost. "And I will put them all on you if you don't release me."

A barrage of lightning danced down from the sky. A single bolt struck the farthest of the rowboats and it split in two, one half on fire and both halves quickly sinking. Midtransformation, two of the werewolves on board burst into flame, their flesh charred and smoking as they disappeared into the waves. The third fell into the water, pawing at the sea in a frenzy, unable to swim. Only the fourth, who had fallen out when he'd been shot in the head, seemed likely to survive. He swam toward the other two boats, unwilling to drown and eager to kill.

Jack pressed the barrel harder against Ghost's temple. "Put her down."

Ghost dropped Sabine to the deck and turned to the railing, where the last of his pack awaited him. They mocked Death's pack with promises of pain and torment.

Jack took Sabine into his embrace at last, watching over her shoulder as the wounded werewolf dragged itself onto one of the two remaining boats.

"I love you," Jack whispered.

"And I you," she replied. "Dying would ruin everything."

Jack did not smile but kissed her once more.

There was a momentary lull in the storm. In that instant of calm, Jack stepped away from Sabine, took aim, pulled the trigger, and put a silver bullet into the wounded werewolf's chest. The creature screamed as it slid back into the raging sea, and for a moment all eyes—on deck, and at sea—turned to Jack. Death's crew marked him, and he knew he had just made himself a target. The temptation to fire wildly and try to kill them all almost overwhelmed him, but he had a limited supply of bullets. Every one had to count.

The two remaining boats were close enough now for Jack to see hatred in the eyes of the crew, and the cold fury carved into Death Nilsson's features. Ghost snapped orders to his surviving pack, but Jack barely heard him, able to focus only on the hatred bristling in the space that separated the two brothers.

Lightning struck the water around the two rowboats.

One of them was grazed and began to burn, but it no longer mattered. The *Charon*'s crew had returned. The boats bumped alongside, and the first of the sailors leaped for the netting, scrambling toward the deck at inhuman speed.

Jack fired as the werewolves flowed over the railing. They moved so swiftly that several of his bullets hit only open air, but two of them struck home in the shoulder and abdomen of the same creature. The wolf spilled onto the deck, twitching and dying as the poison raced through him, and then Death's pack had been reduced to eight.

Jack dropped to one knee, fishing bullets from his pocket and reloading. Sabine stood beside him, swaying as she mouthed the words to some silent song. The ship rocked beneath them and wind battered them, but her motion seemed not to be influenced by the world around her, guided instead by a storm within.

There was war on the *Charon*'s deck, and the bloody melee spread from starboard to port. Some of the sea wolves had completely transformed, but Ghost and his remaining crew fought in the median shape of the savage wolf-man so that they could use the weapons they had scavenged from Death's ship. Louis swung his sword, cleaving the arm from a werewolf and forcing the monster to shift to the median form as well. Blood sprayed the deck and was washed away in the rain, all of it—the death and gore around Jack and Sabine—bleached to the gray hue of the storm.

Ghost and his brother, Death, fought back and forth across the deck. If they rolled toward another melee, those pirates would scramble aside, fear and perhaps an element of respect giving the two captains room to indulge their grudge. Tooth bit, claw slashed, and wherever they rolled or fell, they left bloody imprints of their hatred.

Jack emptied his gun for the second time, but with even worse results. With the wolves' swiftness, and the curtain of punishing rain, only one of his bullets found its target, and this one he only managed to graze. The silver staggered the wolf, slowed it, but the poison was working slowly.

He knelt to reload again, gauging how many bullets he had left. He had to be much more precise this time. It might be his last chance.

Other gunshots cracked the air, but rifles were ineffective for hand-to-hand combat and were quickly cast aside or used as clubs. As Jack thumbed a bullet into its chamber, he glanced up to see two werewolves drag Tree down to the deck and begin to tear him apart, one ripping at his belly and the other at his throat. Tree fought hard, but then Death appeared from out of nowhere—Ghost no longer on the attack—and drove his hand straight into the big man's chest. When Death withdrew his fist, Tree fell hard.

Ghost leaped from atop the cabin. The fight must have taken him out of sight, and now he was back at his brother again. He did not even spare a glance for his fallen crewman.

The odds were lengthening, and Jack realized that if they hoped to live, he and Sabine would have to make the difference.

"What's wrong?" Jack asked, looking up at her. "Is your hex not working?"

Her hair was plastered to her face, clothes clinging to her curves, and she looked like the ancient sea goddess she might well be.

"It *is* working," she said. "But I can do only one or two of them at a time, or it would affect all of you."

Even as she spoke, Jack saw the hex take hold of one of Death's pack. The wolf staggered, turned toward Maurilio, and began to lunge at empty places, snapping at raindrops. Maurilio darted away from another enemy and leaped on the hexed wolf, drawing a huge, serrated blade across its throat. He drove the wolf down onto its back and stabbed again and again, gutting it in seconds.

The fight began to turn, as Sabine's hexes took hold and the ferocity of Ghost's pack continued unabated.

"Jack!" Sabine shouted.

He heard the growl even as he turned and looked up to see the slavering werewolf launch itself from the top of the wheelhouse, all fur and claws hurtling down upon him. He twisted to face it and brought the gun up, but the monster struck him before he could fire. They crashed to the deck together, Jack's skull impacting hard enough to darken his vision. In that instant he felt the gun pressed against his chest, heard the muffled bang as it fired directly into the werewolf's throat and up into its skull, and then felt the flesh of his left shoulder punctured. Bright, searing pain roared in.

*Bitten!* he thought. As his heart sank, he felt the stain of savagery infecting his soul, and from the first moment he vowed to fight. If he *had* to be both wolf and man, he would conquer the barbarism of that unnatural beast, just as he had triumphed over the natural wildness of the human spirit.

Sabine screamed his name, and he saw her tugging at the werewolf's corpse, even as the wolf began to return to its human self. Jack pushed as Sabine pulled, and together they toppled the dead werewolf to one side. She sank to her knees in the rain, so lovely, yet so fragile in spite of all her extraordinary magic. Naiad, sea witch, water sprite . . . whatever miraculous creature she might be, he was perilous company for her now. His heart shattered as he realized that he had changed forever and could never doom her by remaining with her. If he loved her, he had to forget all the wishes he had secretly made, all his fantasies of their future.

Sabine must have seen it in his eyes, for she began to shake her head. A smile touched her lips, and despite the rain, he saw that she was weeping. She laughed as if a great lightness had touched her heart.

"I see the wound," she said. "It didn't bite you, Jack. Those were its claws."

He forced himself to sit up, shaking off his disorientation, and looked down at his shoulder. He shifted his shredded shirt aside for a better look. A great, uncontrollable laugh bubbled up within him, and for several seconds he felt as though he had become some kind of hysterical madman.

A howl danced upon the wind, taken up and redoubled by the storm so that it seemed to echo across the ocean.

Unsteady but alive, energized by survival, Jack picked up his fallen gun and rose to his feet. He turned to see that the deck of the *Charon* had become a tableau of death. Vukovich and Louis were unharmed. They stood over their dead enemies as the rain washed blood and gore from their matted fur. Maurilio had been badly wounded, but even as Jack caught sight of him, the deep gashes in his flesh were knitting together, healing over. He crouched, grunting and snarling, in front of the last survivor of Death Nilsson's crew, a huge, copper-furred werewolf.

"Don't be a fool," Louis told the wolf. "Surrender."

Death's survivor glanced around and saw that he was beaten. He transformed, straightening up and resuming his human shape—a red-haired, thick-bearded pirate with huge, powerful hands and a strange wisdom in the cant of his head and the set of his eyes.

Which left only the brothers.

The other wolves knew better than to interfere. Ghost and Death were both in full wolf form, Ghost huge and silver-gray, his brother even larger, with fur as black as pitch. They faced each other on the foredeck, the bloody kings, the monstrous leaders. Hatred sizzled in the air around them like ball lightning.

They kept the ruined, charred hole of the cargo hatch between them, circling it, each looking for an opening in the other's defenses, waiting for the right moment. Waiting for the kill.

With a sound that was half growl and half laugh, Death Nilsson stood on his hind legs, transforming back into a wolf-man, his golden eyes gleaming in the gray storm. His claws were wicked things, long and curved and so coated with blood that even in the rain they were red as the devil's horns.

Ghost shifted as well, standing on two legs, half man and half monster, but he remained utterly silent. Once he had worshipped his brother, had given up his humanity to join the pack, and he had been cast aside and left for dead. Jack wondered whether Ghost still had love for his brother, and if that was what fueled his hatred. Or perhaps his heart truly was as cold and withered as he had always pretended.

"They feel us watching," Jack whispered.

"Yes," Sabine said. "And even now they bristle with pride."

Without a sound, Ghost leaped for his brother, lunging across the shattered cargo hatch.

Death met him in midair.

## CHAPTER FIFTEEN

# BLOOD BROTHERS

As Ghost and Death struck each other, lightning flashed across the island's craggy ridge, and thunder hammered so hard that the ship shook beneath their feet. Jack and Sabine had staggered back until they were pressed against the cabin, and before them the remaining wolves formed a rough half circle around the warring brothers.

A wide circle. None of them wanted to be involved in this fight. Whoever won would claim the bloody heart of the defeated, and whatever scrap of soul he might have left.

They fell, a fury of flailing limbs and hacking claws, and Jack heard the sickening sound of teeth clashing together. Landing across the hold's blasted hatch, they seemed to be shredding each other to pieces—fur flew, blood pattered down across the wet deck, and as lightning thrashed again, Jack was sure he saw the purplish gleam of exposed muscle.

Then Death rose up, batting Ghost's fist aside before stomping on his brother, cracking bones and forcing his victim against the ragged hole in the deck.

"They'll both end up dead," Sabine said.

Jack held her hand in his. "We can hope." Her grip was strong, as though she wished never to let go again. He knew how she felt.

Death stomped one more time and then fell, sprawling face-first onto the deck, as Ghost lost his grip, falling into the hold where his brother had kept him prisoner. The other wolves moved a step or two nearer to the ruined open hatch. Louis glanced back at Jack. He looked fully human now but would never be a man again.

Death stood with a foot on either side of the hatch, and he took a moment to look at his audience. Half man, half beast, there was nothing remotely human in his eyes, and when his mouth fell open, he only growled.

Jack clasped the gun in his hand, ready to take aim and fire should the need arise. He had three silver bullets left. It would take all three to put Death Nilsson down, and maybe not even then.

"If he comes, run back along the ship and—," Jack began, but he said no more. Death dropped down into the hold atop his battered brother.

The watching wolves glanced at one another—Vukovich, Maurilio, Louis, and the red-haired survivor from Death's crew. There was much in the balance here, and now the fight had moved below.

Amplified by the echoing hold, the sounds of conflict raised themselves above the increasingly stormy sea and the wind and rain that continued to batter the *Charon* and the island. Jack glanced sidelong at Sabine, and her eyes were wide. He had an idea that she could no longer stop this storm, even if she desired to.

With screams and thuds, growls and roars, the fight went on. Jack was sure he could feel impacts through his feet, and he dreaded to imagine what pure hatred could become in that confined space. Like the echoing howls, the hate the brothers had long harbored for each other would be concentrated down there, and the violence would stir it thicker.

Something changed. It took Jack a moment to realize what it was, and then he recognized only one voice, not two. Another growl, an impact heavier than any that had come before, and then a howl rose up that challenged the storm, sending the wolves back several paces.

All fell quiet. The storm seemed to settle a little—a pause, and Jack thought perhaps Sabine's own breath was held—and then Louis took several steps toward the hatch. A few feet from the opening he froze, crouched down; and the silhouette he threw changed shape, subtly but clearly. Fur bristled across his bare back.

"Jack!" Sabine said. But they could both see the hand that now clasped the edge of the torn hatch, its nails longer than a man's but shorter than a wolf's, and they could see how the fingers were tensed as they supported the weight of whoever hung below.

If it was Ghost and he had been victorious, Jack and Sabine would soon discover whether he would keep his word. Perhaps the monster had learned something and would honor their pact, but Jack thought not. He thought that Ghost's honor stopped where it began—close to his own heart.

If Death emerged, then they were all faced with a very different problem.

"Jack, the gun."

"Yes," Jack said, but he kept the gun down by his side. However much he doubted Ghost, he would give the captain a chance.

The shape that rose from the hold might have been either of the brothers. So soaked in blood that the color of its hair was difficult to discern, its build hidden by the hole, it looked down beneath itself as it strained to haul itself up.

It dragged itself onto the metal deck, panting hard and spitting blood. Then, with a growl that was so low Jack thought he could feel it vibrating the deck, the victor stood.

And Death Nilsson looked up.

"Reverend," Death said, and his one surviving crew member looked around at the others with terror in his eyes.

"Death . . . ," the man muttered.

"Reverend, if you do not continue the fight, then you become a victim of it." Death's voice was barely human, even though he now stood there as close to a man as he could be. He looked past Louis at Jack and Sabine, and grinned. "Two of us left, and I already see how we can double the size of our crew." Then he looked at Sabine again, and the smile dropped a little. "Or her . . . perhaps she will have another use."

Jack raised the gun and pointed it at Death's chest. *One in the chest, a second in the head, and the last in his heart, once he's down.* The inhumanity in the man's eyes reminded him so much of Ghost.

"What's this?" Death said.

"Silver," Jack said.

"My own stock," Death said. "Yes, silver. You'd best make sure you pump enough into me, boy."

"My name," Jack said, his shaking ceasing as quickly as it had come, "is Jack London."

*"My name," Jack said, his shaking ceasing
as quickly as it had come, "is Jack London."*

"Well, Jack, you and I are going to—"

Death's eyes went wide as he caught a scent, or a sound, and a shadow rose behind him. Arms flung around his waist, hands grasping him, and as the shadow fell back into the hole, it took Death with it.

He fought. Arms and legs stretched out, Death propped himself over the hole, using his left hand to beat back at the risen Ghost.

"Damn you, Brother, I'll have your heart!" Death shouted. But it was not to be.

The fist punched up through Death's chest, ribs cracking and catching the storm's final slash of lightning. In the fist—Ghost's fist, clenching tight—was Death Nilsson's beating heart.

Ghost squeezed, and as the muscle ruptured, so the light went from Death's eyes.

Louis dashed forward and hauled the corpse from above the hatch. Vukovich helped, and the man Death had called Reverend joined in as well, pulling on his dead captain's leg and then stepping back as Ghost climbed from the hold.

He was a mess, naked and torn, but resplendent in the blood that clothed him. He was grinning through broken teeth and slashed lips. He raised his arms at the sky, and the roar was so joyous that Jack felt a shout rising in his own throat.

Sabine squeezed Jack's left hand and held on tight.

"I've never seen him so wild," she said, "not even as a wolf."

Ghost kicked Death's body toward the railing, then lifted it up and flung it into the sea. He followed it with a gob of bloody spittle and turned around to face them all.

"Now then, Mr. London," Ghost said, breathing heavily. The rain did little to wash his brother's blood from across his face and chest, and Jack thought perhaps he would be stained forever.

Jack raised the gun again and pointed it at Ghost.

"Now then, Ghost," Jack echoed. "I hope you mean to—"

Ghost came at them, violence incarnate. Jack's breath froze and his finger squeezed, but too slowly, too *slowly*, and he had maybe a second until—

Louis tripped Ghost and fell on him as he sprawled on the deck. Vukovich held down one leg, Maurilio the other, and Reverend came to help them again, falling across Ghost's head and doing his best to avoid his teeth.

"Jack, kill him!" Louis said.

"No."

"You fool," Maurilio said, shifting as he struggled to keep Ghost's leg from kicking him away. "He's weakened from the fight, the change is slow. One bullet to the heart will finish him. Now!"

"No," Jack said again. Sabine touched his arm, and he knew he was making the right choice. It was the *only* choice. Kill or be killed was fine for those on the hunt, but if he shot Ghost like this, it would be murder.

"He means to do you in," Vukovich said. "He'll never honor the pact, and you know it."

"You don't understand. I *must* let him live," Jack said.

"But why?" Louis asked.

"It's the human thing to do."

Ghost had twisted around to stare at him, and Jack thought perhaps the old werewolf now hated him as much as he had his brother.

"There must be another hold to keep him in," Jack said. "We have much to discuss, and a ship to fix."

The sun shone and the sea was calm the day they prepared to leave the island, and Sabine promised Jack she had nothing to do with it.

"The weather is smiling on us," she said, and she continued pacing the deck of the *Charon*. It had been scrubbed down several times, the bodies of the dead werewolves buried in a mass grave on the beach. But the ship would always retain the mark of the fight. It was scratched and stained into the metal like a painful memory.

There was an air of nervousness on board. They all

knew what was to come. It had been only two days, but in that time Jack had seen such a change in Ghost's surviving crew that he could barely recognize them. Louis had displayed an intelligence Jack had never credited him with, revealing that he'd always held himself back around Ghost so that the captain would never view him as a threat.

"Weren't you?" Jack had asked.

"Of course," Louis had replied. "I was simply biding my time." Jack wasn't sure about that, and he had mixed feelings about Louis. It was because of him that Sabine had been brought to the *Larsen*. But if Louis had *not* brought her to Ghost, Jack would have never met her.

Vukovich and Maurilio held fewer surprises, but they became much more relaxed and were able to work hard at fixing the *Charon* with Reverend's help. Reverend—a huge man, grizzled and rough-looking—denied that he had ever been a man of the cloth. He claimed that Death had named him because of his gentle voice and his predilection for standing at the bow and praying each night before he turned in.

"A werewolf talking to God?" Jack had asked.

"Death never knew which god," Reverend had said. "And he never bothered to ask." Jack did not ask either. But Reverend fit in with the others reasonably well. He'd had no love for Death Nilsson, and had no argument with them taking the *Charon* for their own. He even showed them the three hidden holds containing the ship's spoils, and he and Vukovich quickly struck up a friendship.

As Jack stood at the railing and stared out at the island, Sabine joined him again.

"You're certain about this?" she said, and it was the third time she had asked.

"Of course. Do you see any other way for us to sail this boat?"

"No," Sabine said. She pressed close to Jack.

"I trust them," Jack said. "They've been through as much as we have, and they'll take us to San Francisco as they've promised."

"And after that?" she asked. "After we leave the ship and they sail away again, they will build another pack. Louis will be captain, perhaps, and Vukovich first mate. They'll recruit more men, turn them as they were all turned by Ghost. It might be months or even years, but sometime soon the *Charon* will be a hell ship again. They have their hunger. They have their needs."

"Maybe I have a solution to that," Jack said, and as Sabine raised her eyebrows at him, the cabin door clanged open.

"What do you mean?" she asked.

"Not now," he said.

Stress hardened his shoulders, and he drew the gun from his belt as Ghost emerged from the cabin doorway. He looked up at the sun and blinked against the light, his face marked by a network of claw and fang scars. Jack thought his body could have healed them away, if he desired it. But perhaps a creature who thought himself so wronged wished to display his history upon his skin. Anyone who looked at him from this day forward would know the violence he had seen.

"Ready to sail, Mr. London?"

"Ready," Jack said. "But you won't be coming with us."

Ghost snorted. "Of course not. And why would I? A ship like this, I'm afraid I'd soon turn into a coward like the rest of you."

He stumbled forward as Vukovich prodded him onto the deck, and the rest of the sea wolves followed. Ghost might well have been able to tear them all apart, but the silver bullets in Jack's gun kept him from trying. Though there were times when Jack wondered if it really was the silver that held Ghost at bay, or if perhaps the old wolf had simply decided that this chapter of his life had come to a close.

"You still believe your way is better," Jack said. "That morality and principle are nothing but weakness."

"Of course," Ghost said, as if it was a foolish question. He looked around at everyone there to see him on his way.

Sabine stood close to Jack, but as usual the others had spread out, each of them alone. To fight Ghost in case he fought back, Jack had thought initially. But he also realized that alone was all a monster could be.

"I'm sure you'll know this one," Ghost continued. "'We all live in the protection of certain cowardices which we call our principles.' You, Jack, are scared to see yourself for what you truly are."

Jack smiled. "Twain also said, 'Courage is resistance to fear, mastery of fear—not absence of fear.'"

"So you're saying you still fear me," Ghost said with almost childlike pleasure.

"Over the side, Ghost."

"No."

Jack raised the gun. The air on deck thickened with potential, and beside him Jack sensed Sabine stiffening. She'd told Jack that if it came to a fight, she would do her best to touch Ghost's mind and confuse him. But secretly, all Jack's faith was in gunpowder and silver.

"Over the side," Louis echoed.

Ghost looked at the wolves one last time, his expression not altering when he gazed at Reverend. Everyone was beneath him, his crew or another. He was the god of his own mind.

"Very well," Ghost said. He turned back to Jack and

Sabine. "But I will see you again."

Then he ran at the rail and threw himself overboard, the splash as he struck the water loud and final.

A tremor of surprise stirred those on deck, but then they rushed to their stations. The ship began to vibrate as Reverend increased the steam engine's power, and Vukovich and Maurilio raised anchor.

Jack and Sabine stood at the rail, looking down at Ghost treading water below them, only twenty feet away. He stared back up but said nothing more.

The banished wolf did not speak a word as the ship got under way, and he began to swim after them.

The *Charon* picked up speed as it left the island astern, and still Ghost continued following them, falling behind as they plowed through the water. He stared silently after Jack and Sabine, and though Sabine went and stood at the bow to look ahead, Jack would not entertain turning away.

At last Ghost stopped swimming, but he remained treading water until he was less than a dot on the ocean, and the island blurred across the horizon and then vanished over the curve of the earth.

It was only then that Sabine rejoined him.

"Your solution, Jack? Your idea to stop these cursed men from becoming monsters again?"

"Only an idea, for now," he said. "I have yet to ask them.

But once we've returned to San Francisco, and I've brought my small bag of gold to my mother and seen my friend Merritt, there's a place I promised to take you."

"The Yukon," she said. She gazed somewhere far away, back through the centuries. "Lesya."

"Yes," Jack said, the wood spirit's name causing a shiver even in the blazing sunlight. "And the way I see it, we'll need a ship like this to get us there. And a crew."